FENG ON A SHUI STRING

Shani Solomons

Also by the same author:

"All Things Bright and Beautiful"

"Last Graffiti Before Motorway"

Feng on a Shui String

Published in 2013 by FeedARead.com Publishing – Arts Council funded

Cover Drawing: Sheba Solomons

Cover Design: Naomi Stolow

www.shanisolomons.co.uk

CHAPTER 1

GLASTONBURY

The mists swirled round the top of Glastonbury Tor, making the wind and water look like an ocean beneath the green mound at the bottom of the steep hill. The "Isle of Avalon" certainly looked like an island now – cut off from the mainland by thick, grey cloud which Marion imagined you could only get through by slicing it with the sword of King Arthur himself.

This place was steeped in mystery and legend – Arthur and his knights, witches, fairies, magic; the atmosphere was as enchanting as it was ever so slightly eerie. Yet it was neither enchanted nor haunted that Marion felt. She felt depressed and beaten, like every step she took was being weighted down by leaden boots. With every intake of breath she felt she would cry and yet.....she had cried so much already.

The energies of Glastonbury seemed to bring suppressed emotions to the surface; what had happened seemed so traumatising and painful and so uncomfortable that Marion thought her whole body would crumble and self-destruct if she let her feelings out. She was twenty-four years old and her heart had just been broken. It had happened before, but this time it felt like the crack in the middle was tearing away the very tissue.

Marion had come to Glastonbury to heal. In this little town she could drink from the Chalice Well and meditate in the surrounding gardens, get a tarot reading, buy beautiful velvet and woven clothing and climb the Tor. There was a need to be well away of anything that reminded her of her time with.....him. It was August but a cool wind and light rain pricked her face, turning her cheeks rosy pink as she climbed.

Marion felt the fresh air doing her good as her heart pumped with the steepness of the climb and the wound felt like it slowly, gradually, might be beginning to close up. As she neared the dilapidated tower, Marion saw a beautiful older women sitting cross-legged and gazing down at the valley below. She had curly, auburn Pre-Raphaelite locks with flecks of grey that spilt down her shoulders and back, almost to her waist. She wore a purple velvet cloak and long turquoise dress with pointed, witchy sleeves.

Marion couldn't help but stare. The woman seemed so serene, so focussed. On the middle finger of her left hand was a large silver ring with a turquoise stone, but she wore no wedding band. Perhaps she was from the "Order of Isis", a group of women who based their teachings on ancient myth and druid knowledge. Marion had heard that they lived communally, independent of men. If anyone could teach her how to live without a man in her life, then they could.

Marion approached the woman slowly and asked if she'd mind if she sat beside her. The woman smiled and patted the ground. Marion sat. She felt guilty disturbing her, but she was longing to ask so much – yearning to soak up this sort of wisdom.

"Would...would you mind if I asked you a question?" Marion dared to venture forth. The woman smiled again and looked up at her in anticipation.

"It's just that – you have this wonderful, powerful vibration to you. You seem so independent and sort of, well, Goddess-like. Please, please could you tell me sister, how you manage to live free and yet fully-spirited and without the need for a man in your life?"

The woman turned to face Marion. Suddenly her soft, gentle face had etched on it a lifetime of world-weariness. She sighed deeply and then said, "If I knew the answer to that, do you think I'd bloody well be sitting here.....?"

****

Now Marion was sixty years old. Since that Glastonbury visit in her twenties, she'd met another man, married him and had a son. Then she'd divorced him and these days never spoke to her son. All her close relationships now seemed to be with an increasingly growing number of single women varying in age, profession and cultural background. They all seemed to be looking for *something* and the fact that no one ever seemed to find it was irrelevant.

All great lovers of Self-Development workshops, her friends had this year met up in Glastonbury where there was no such better place in which to partake of such things. Marion painstakingly felt obliged to explain to those not in the know that she wasn't attending the music festival, but heading to the town centre which at its heart, consisted of little more than a couple of streets.

Yet, what streets they were! Arriving by coach or car, Glastonbury merely looked like a little provincial place which you would pass through en route to a larger city like Bristol or Bath, but thousands flocked here in all year round pilgrimages to undertake courses and all manner of healing, druid workshops and esoteric studies or to be healed themselves.

Whenever Marion arrived in this town it always seemed to be bucketing with rain. She couldn't find any information anywhere that said Glastonbury was on a particularly wet "ley line", yet somehow didn't believe that the weather was entirely due to its West Country location. Putting up her umbrella and feeling glad she'd remembered her wellingtons, Marion thought about how excited she was just to be here – she was going to meet friends, but this was the kind of place you could come on your own and get chatting to all manner of strangers.

It was usually in the little tea shops like "Avachar", that she met the most interesting individuals. Some decades ago, still trying to get over her divorce, she had come back here for some healing and respite. Now she was trying to find somewhere to eat. Remembering that most eateries shut after 8pm, she opted for an early dinner in Avachar. Everything looked delicious, but on closer inspection, smelt a little strange.

A man sitting across the table from Marion winked at her. "If I were you, I'd have the Spelt and Spinach Ponderous Pie. Delicious. And the Giving Gravy is very good with that as well." All the dishes had such wonderful names – apparently you were supposed to take these very much to heart and chose your dinner based upon how you *felt*, not on what you felt like *eating.* Based on that, how did Marion feel exactly?

She looked up from her menu. If she had been at another time in history, then the man opposite her was most definitely Merlin, magician and advisor to the legendary King Arthur himself. But this was the twenty-first century and

Merlin had expired several centuries ago. Maybe he'd decided to re-incarnate for the millennium.

That was the beauty of Glastonbury. Mixed in with ordinary, urban small-town folk were wizards, witches and fairy queens. Behind Merlin sat a group of women in green leotards, focussed intently on a batch of papers on the table in front of them. Marion observed that they were also wearing pink, gossamer wings. Merlin had long white hair and a beard to match. He didn't wear a pointy hat, but he was clad in a royal blue velvet cloak over a long black tunic and Marion observed he was wearing boots that curled up at the ends. These had little bells on, which tinkled every time he shuffled from his sitting position.

Merlin moved forwards to introduce himself. "I'm Stephen" he said, somewhat surprisingly. Stephen the Wizard? It somehow didn't quite fit his image. Marion shook hands with his very firm hand shake, as he asked her if she'd visited the place before.

"Many times" replied Marion.

"Here for anything special?" asked Stephen the Wizard, aka Merlin. Special? Wasn't Glastonbury its very self special? Marion gazed into the distance wistfully.

"Do you know what?" she replied, "I think I'm just here to be." Then she cringed, realising just how New Agey and clichéd that sounded. Stephen stroked his long beard.

"Hmm. To be, eh? To be or not to be. Whether tis nobler to have Ponderous Pie or the Serendipity Shortbread...Indeed, life is a series of decisions...." Indeed it was, thought Marion, as she drank in his words. Stephen reached beneath the table to retrieve his walking stick – a long twisted piece of pale beech wood. "Do enjoy being," he said, "I'm off to create some magic". And no doubt he was.

****

August and Glastonbury was teaming with international tourists. In the Avachar, Marion met a group of Portuguese girls in their twenties, a family from Birmingham, a gay male couple from New York and a variety of elves, goblins and sprites who had just arrived by coach from Exeter for the "Elementals Festival". And all this before even one of her friends had arrived. Marion browsed the leaflet for the course she was doing, "Internal Feng Shui". She had to confess that she had never really been that much into Feng Shui and found the title off-putting, but she desperately wanted to come to the town, be with her friends, and any excuse would do – especially when she was so badly in need of a break. Things had been very full-on at The University of Sussex where she lectured in History of Art and her migraines had become more frequent.

She also desperately needed to get away from Professor David Pepper, her Head of Department. She couldn't face any more academic prattling – all his conversation was littered with references to "the earlier Matisses" or "the logistics of the better known works of Raphael" and he couldn't even say "please sign this" without making several comments about Picasso. Much as Marion loved her subject, there were times when she needed to talk to her girlfriends about reality television, the increasing price of food and whether Marks and Spencer's knickers were really better than Primark's.

All these things she could discuss to her heart's content when with her friends. This weekend however was going to be devoted to Internal Feng Shui. A little shiver ran down Marion's spine – what exactly had she let herself in for? Was she going to be told that the only path to true health was to shift your organs around? Did Internal Feng Shui mean that placing your kidneys right up by your heart meant your energies would flow better than if they remained in their "lowly" position? Would it be better for the body if the lungs were a little further over to the right? As for the bile duct, didn't it get rather lonely? Should it be around other organs a bit more? Should....

Marion stopped speculating as her friend Bea trotted into the cafe and threw her arms around her. "Marion! It's so brilliant you're here! I'm really excited about this weekend, aren't you?" Marion was, but probably not for the same reasons as Bea. Bea was in desperate need of a healing weekend as she had still not recovered from a relationship that had ended seven years ago. She was a witty woman with a real zest for life, but that had been drained somehow, in her depression. Bea had little round John Lennon style glasses at the end of her pinched nose and her very thin lips had their usual lick of pale pink gloss, even though they practically disappeared. A very thin smear could sometimes be found on her moustache line and would frequently get mixed in with her cappuccino, turning it a strange colour.

Today, however, Bea ordered a lime leaf and mulberry tea. When in Glastonbury, do as Glastonbury does. Marion watched Bea sip at the tea and make the same kind of face one does when sucking lemons. Extremely sour ones.

"You don't look much like you're enjoying that" said Marion, "Can I get you something else?"

"Christ, no" said Bea. "If it tastes this disgusting, then it must be doing me good."

Marion let out a long sigh. "Oh...do you really buy into all that? I've had some delicious organic foods and some equally as vile ones. I don't care if it cleanses my colon. I just want to eat it because it tastes nice." Marion hadn't realised quite how loudly she'd said that and got some very disapproving looks from the table of sprites. She lowered her voice. "Food is something that you *want* to eat, surely?"

Bea nodded. "Yes. Well – usually. But this is sort of medicinal, isn't it? I'm going to swallow it, even if it kills me." Bea held her nose and gulped down the liquid, receiving even more disapproving looks from the hippies at the next table. Marion tried to stop herself laughing. "Sometimes Bea, you really are a contradiction in terms." Bea wiped her mouth.

"Ugg, that was *seriously* horrible. Now please can we find somewhere to get some ice cream? *Please?*" Marion laughed and looked up to see Roberta blowing air kisses at both her and Bea. She pulled out one of the chairs from under their table.

"Hello ladies! Getting busy in here, isn't it? Better see if I can grab some more chairs."

"Well, better not ask them" said Marion pulling a face at the hippies. They pretended not to see her. Roberta however, went to seize her opportunity. She was a stunningly attractive young woman, even if at times she could be intensely annoying......She liked to preach about all things New Age and would never listen to or even acknowledge any opposition. As far as she was concerned, if Deepak Chopra had said it, then it was so.

Marion was normally quite mild mannered, but sometimes the red head in her would kick in. These days, she dyed her hair an attractive strawberry blonde and kept it cropped short. With her petite figure and lovely posture, people often remarked how similar she looked to the actress Shirley Maclaine. This was a reference Marion didn't mind at all. She'd read that the actress was a deeply spiritual woman and Marion had retraced many of her journeys and attended several similar seminars.

The hippies, who had so disapproved of two "truth seeking" middle aged ladies making fun of organic food, changed their composure when it came to their friend. Roberta glided over to their table and Marion observed how both the men and women reacted. The woman looked at her out of the corner of their eyes, trying hard not to show any signs of jealousy, but really making it quite obvious that they were envious of her youth and looks.

The men just stared. It was hard not to. Roberta was very tall and willowy, dressed in floating chiffon and dark navy velvet and ruffled up her raven-haired bob before pressing her long, elegant fingers down on the hippy table. "I was just wondering if you're going to be using these two chairs?" Her beautiful bee-stung lips smiled and pouted. One of the women in the group looked at her male companion and knew he had already lost his tongue. She sighed. "No. Take them" she said.

"Thank you sooo much" said Roberta. One of the male hippies went to put a spoonful of Sensual Saffron Pudding in his mouth and missed. A sticky mess fell onto the lap of the lady next to him. He didn't even notice, so fixated was he on Roberta. The woman said nothing, but took a napkin off the table and wiped her skirt, knowing that however "enlightened" were the men in her company, they could still be so easily distracted by a pert bosom...

Marion was determined not to get irritated with Roberta this weekend, but even before they'd had a conversation, she just couldn't help herself. How dare this woman be so effortlessly beautiful and not just walk, but glide across a room. She was tall, but not so tall that she would intimidate shorter men. She was so good-looking that men never seemed to mind how irritating she was – at least, not initially.

Roberta didn't even have to carry any of the chairs to the table, as other men in the cafe willingly did that for her. The minute she sat down and opened her mouth, Marion felt the need to be distracted by some horrible health drink. Roberta regaled Marion and Bea with the most "amaaayzing" book she was reading , even though as far as Marion was concerned the book was full of hypocritical twaddle and the author highly overrated.

Marion sidled over to the counter and asked for a very large ground coffee. She was going to need it to listen to Roberta and she knew that would take a while. When she returned, Roberta was waxing lyrical about the end of the world.

"Apparently, we've only got a couple of years to get it right."

"Get *what* right?" asked Marion. It was easy to see she wanted to pour her coffee right over Roberta's head. Bea kicked Marion under the table.

"Oh Marion, *you* know" said Roberta. Her patronising tones were always excruciatingly painful, but now Bea was actually twisting the heal of her shoe down on Marion's toe to keep her quiet. Roberta was her friend, and Marion had promised....

"Do carry on Roberta" said Marion, wearily. Thank goodness the course was starting tomorrow and she could listen to a proper lecturer. It seemed that a lifetime went by whilst Roberta explained that if they weren't careful they would all be disintegrated by aliens pretty shortly and unless everyone raised their spiritual awareness in order to be "saved" then that was pretty much it.

She added that she thought Bea stood a pretty good chance of making it through to the next "earth stage" but she wasn't so sure about Marion because Marion was stubborn and pig-headed and so much a "typical Taurean." Marion resisted the urge to say surely that made her "bull-headed", but she bit her tongue – so hard, that she felt little metallic tasting drops of blood in her mouth. Fortunately she was one of the "saved" – by the arrival of her friend Carolyn.

Carolyn was a little older than Marion, although nowhere near as glamorous. She always wore fleeces over long, baggy trousers and never wore make-up, giving her a kind of "archetypal lesbian" look. She was with a new friend called Helen, who she introduced. Helen was very attractive, but the hippies didn't pay any attention at all, assuming the two women were partners. As it happened, Carolyn was one of the biggest man-eaters going. Unlike Roberta who just liked talking about sex "in a spiritual way", Carolyn had a voracious appetite for the act of love. Subsequently, she always had a variety of lovers on the go and whilst she happily divulged their "skills" quite freely, she never actually boasted about her activities. To her, it was all simply earthy, organic and natural – the very qualities that Glastonbury embodied.

Marion liked Carolyn. She always told it like it was – always called a spade a spade. Right now however, she was calling something clearly displayed as a "Cyclical Crunch Bud", a chocolate chip cookie. The waitress turned from a mild-mannered dreadlocked student with an attractive flowery nose piercing into a fierce looking warthog, ready to fight.

"Madam....." you could see the girl was biting her tongue so hard, it was painful. "We spend a lot of time deliberating over the names of the dishes. Quite simply if you don't like it, you don't have to buy it." She was quite right of course, but Carolyn was having none of it.

"I understand about the crunch" she said, "Because that's what normally happens with biscuits. But as for it being a cyclical bud, I hardly think this thing is going to reincarnate as a flower, once I've eaten it. Besides, once something has found its way into my stomach, it will never want to reincarnate again."

Whilst Carolyn and the waitress argued, Helen spoke. She explained how embarrassed she was that they had only just arrived and Carolyn was having a row. Marion told Helen how well she knew Carolyn and that they always ate in this cafe. Carolyn liked to pick on the new staff, just to be controversial.

Roberta automatically switched into "patronising therapist's voice" mode. This was the voice she used when she felt awkward conflict around her. "Carolyn obviously has low self-esteem" she said "No one bullies people if they don't have low self-esteem". Marion was unimpressed.

"Oh for God's sake – she's not bullying....just having a bit of a laugh. It is a bit pretentious and up itself here, anyway. Bea and I are thinking ice cream is the way forward. Sometimes you just need to get away from wholesomeness, don't you?" Helen looked like she found that idea very appealing. She put down some foul-tasting tea that she desperately wanted to spit out, made a move towards the door and for once, Roberta fell silent.

****

Cherry Tree Cottage was a quaint little building with three guest bedrooms and had been turned into a bed and breakfast by its owner. Carolyn and Marion were going to share the largest room, Helen and Bea the other and Roberta, insisting on staying where she could be "quiet and contemplative" had booked the far more expensive Devonshire House Hotel, slightly up the road. She'd spent hours on the phone to the tourist board explaining her exact needs and was angry upon arrival when there appeared to be a mix-up with her room. Also, Roberta was expecting something more like a stately home with some marbled, ornate stairway than the modern, red brick family run place she was in.

Eventually, a woman with rosy red cheeks and a dinner lady perm came downstairs to apologise and sort a room for Roberta. As the door was opened, Roberta curled up her nose. The single room was functional and clean, but it was very basic. Roberta was used to staying in twee places with character and wind chimes and didn't want to accept that maybe this time she had messed up.

The "dinner lady" started to explain about breakfast and where everything was. At least Roberta would get the full English here – everywhere else had started to serve only muesli and various organic substances that were both literally and metaphorically hard to swallow. As she found out more about breakfast, Roberta's face dropped. "What do you mean no sausages?" she said, aghast.

"You can have the full English Madam, but it comes without sausages. People don't want them anymore. They always want to know what they're made from and it's so expensive to keep buying organic ones, that we no longer serve them."

"Well then, it's not a *full* English is it!" Roberta protested. The landlady calmly replied that they'd provide extra eggs or bacon to make up for it, but Roberta would not be pacified. "But that's outrageous. You advertise as offering the full English experience, and then you don't provide it. I'm not sure I want to stay here anymore."

"I'm sorry" said the dinner lady, "But I don't think you'll find any of the bed and breakfasts around here are serving sausages. Haven't done for a while now. If it's sausages you're after then you'll need to go out of town, but I daresay they're all fully booked, as well. Especially at this time of year." The woman said this so matter of factly that Roberta felt all she could do was feebly unpack her case. August was high season in the little town and people flocked from miles around to attend the festivals, rituals and workshops presiding in the vicinity.

Roberta pulled her nightdress out of her designer luggage bag, kicked off her shoes and lay back on her bed with a sigh. She needn't tell the others how disappointed she was...

****

Marion, Bea, Carolyn and Helen all sat down to a full English breakfast of eggs, bacon, toast and... sausages. In between mouthfuls of delicious food, Marion chatted to their landlady, whilst she continuously fried for the other guests. What she didn't know about Buddha, Buddha himself didn't know. Pulling back a curtain, you could see all manner of Buddha statues adorning the beautiful garden – stone, wood and jade statues perched on benches, tables, raised clumps of grass; they were all stunning. It was so wonderful to come to a place like this and talk to people who could not only discuss the esoteric, but fried eggs as well. Marion called them people with not so much non-conformist as "irregular lives." She felt honoured that she had met such a variety of rich and colourful characters in her lifetime. It seemed that people in "regular lives" missed out on this.

As a young woman, the world for Marion was full of art galleries and folk clubs and political protest groups – she was in no hurry to settle down. That was until she was twenty-two years old and *he* came along and stole her most precious asset – her heart. It was the first time Marion could say she had truly been in love and now she wanted it all – marriage, babies, the lot. On paper, it all looked so perfect.

This man had the charm, good looks and an Oxford degree – he'd even been a hit with her parents who seemed only too delighted at the prospect of him being their future son-in-law. It was only Marion's sister who didn't seem to like him, but Marion put that down to jealousy. She told Marion over coffee one day that she thought he had a bit of a roving eye, but Marion dismissed it.

Marion was absolutely certain that her boyfriend was just about to propose. Instead, she found him in bed with her flatmate. Marion never spoke to either of them again, moving back home with her parents. And that was how she first found herself in Glastonbury – all those years ago.

****

It turned out it wasn't only Roberta's hotel room that had been double-booked. When the women arrived at the venue where the "Internal Feng Shui" course was about to take place, they were told they were being moved elsewhere. People started organising lifts, whilst Roberta grumbled about the need for better organisation. Carolyn and Helen started to organise, and Marion and Bea hung around until everything *was* organised.

It appeared that all the lifts had been taken, and the other venue was about half an hour's walk. A lady started to phone a cab company. A tall man in his late forties and with an estuary accent asked Marion and Helen if they'd like a lift. They gratefully accepted. In Glastonbury you didn't stop to question whether the person offering you a lift was an axe murderer – chances were they'd be a harmless hippie much like everyone else.

It turned out the man driving was Peter, the Internal Feng Shui course leader. He had a gentle manner, subtle, warm sense of humour and was quite fascinating to talk to. Marion thought she actually might enjoy the course. Once they arrived at the Angel Haven Centre, it was everything you might expect a place with that name to be. Two stone angels guarded the entrance whilst at the same time appearing to be pointing out some very pretty hanging baskets to visitors.

As soon as you entered the front door, the smell of sandalwood and incense practically floored you, on account of its potency. If you could still see your feet through the smoky haze, then you needed to take off your shoes and place them on one of the ethically sourced shoe racks.

A very English-looking young woman with long blonde hair and pale skin, yet decked out in a sari and long beads, ushered the course participants into a large pale blue room adorned with cushions and dried flowers. Bea couldn't make herself comfortable. She suffered with an osteo-arthritic knee that flared up from time to time and a chair would have been better.

Marion tried not to laugh at her as she piled up cushions in different configurations, watching as everyone else effortlessly appeared to manoeuvre themselves into lotus positions. Eventually, Bea found a way of sitting like she was a little girl, with her bottom raised high and legs sticking out in front of her.

The sari-clad girl who had previously been smiling beatifically, scowled as she carried in a small tray of drinks and saw Bea's outstretched legs. She lowered herself to Bea's ear. "Please tuck them in" she said, "I'm going to be walking around a lot."

"I'm sorry, but I can't" said Bea "I have a bad knee."

"Oh, Oh," said the girl, very agitated. Marion asked what was wrong.

"Apparently" whispered Bea, "I am not conforming to the correct sitting procedures". Marion tried not to titter. The sari-girl next appeared to be having some kind of confab with Peter. He went to get a chair for Bea.

"Excuse me, perhaps you'd like to sit here?" Peter offered. Bea decided she liked him immediately. He seemed to have a warmth and compassion that was devoid in sari-girl. He returned to the front of the room, at which point tinkly New Age music which had been filling the air, promptly disappeared. With a sudden jerk it came back on again, until one of the Angel Haven staff realised they had turned up the volume on the CD player by mistake. The sari-girl gave an even more severe scowl than the one she'd reserved for Bea.

Peter clasped his hands in front of him and addressed the room. "So...." Then he said nothing more for several minutes. During the silence, some people looked around very bemused, whilst others joined in the clasped hands posture and appeared to stare adoringly at Peter. Peter proceeded to smile at each individual in the room with what seemed like a real aura of love. The sari-girl did the same, but it just didn't *feel* the same.

There was a particularly awkward exchange between sari-girl and Marion. Marion remained neutral in her expression as she felt uncomfortable, which in turn made sari-girl feel uncomfortable. Sari-girl tried smiling at Marion, but her mouth started twitching and she started blinking a lot before averting her gaze to the next person, who happened to be Roberta.

Roberta was far more open. The two young women felt an immediate sense of bonding. Marion observed this interaction, and "got" what the exchange was all about. Peter genuinely seemed to love everybody, whereas the girl hated everybody. Roberta couldn't tell the difference.

Helen pulled a beautiful embossed notebook out of a crushed purple velvet bag, afraid to miss anything important. Finally, Peter introduced sari-girl properly.

"This is my assistant, Priyanka. It means Beautiful Symbol in Sanksrit."

"Beautiful Symbol, my arse" whispered Carolyn to Marion. "She's probably really called Kylie, or something."

"If there's anything you need to ask during the course of the day, don't be afraid to ask Priyanka" Peter continued.

I'd be afraid, thought Marion. Priyanka wafted across the room and more twinkly music joined her. Peter led a guided meditation and after a couple of minutes, Marion found herself being lulled into another space and time and visualising all sorts of shapes and colours. When Peter told the group to visualise the colour green, Marion was at once transported to the beautiful Greek island of Ittica where she'd done a workshop holiday....

The place had seemed like paradise on earth, until....until....Priyanka abruptly switched the music off. Marion suddenly found herself shocked back into the room, her body and the real world and away from things she wanted to remember. But she was in Glastonbury and Peter was just about to reveal part one of the course and this was a new seminar and another learning.

A whiteboard was erected at the front of the room and Peter drew various shapes on it with a black marker pen. The first part of understanding Internal Feng Shui was to have a basic knowledge of how all the systems of human design, physical, emotional, spiritual and mental linked up. Peter had a soft and yet compelling teaching voice, which kind of sucked you into his lecture. He also had a way of describing things with clarity and humour, which made you remember what he said.

He then mentioned that during the next bit, people might like to take notes. At this conjecture, Carolyn let out a very long, loud yawn. Never a woman afraid to express exactly how she felt, she ignored the looks of shock and horror. Priyanka's delicate eyebrows formed into a "mono-brow of death" as she glared at Carolyn with all the pent up hatred of a Ninja about to leap on his victim.

Peter, however, just smiled and said nothing, simply casting his "all knowing" eye around the room. Eventually he asked, "Has anyone else noticed that today there seems to be a preponderance of purple in the room?" Bea looked at her bag. It was a large, cloth holdall made largely from purple and mauve patchwork squares with bamboo handles.

She'd bought it in Glastonbury last year thinking how beautiful and unique it was. This was the case in London, but when she glanced around the room, she saw several identical bags. Peter went on. "Purple is a very spiritual colour – obviously you are all very tuned in." Marion was about to write something down, but then thought, wasn't he stating the obvious?

The title of his workshop would have automatically attracted people who were "spiritual". She glanced over her shoulder at Roberta's notepad and noticed she was doodling. Roberta had drawn little love hearts and flowers and spirally patterns. They were more the doodling of a schoolgirl than a High Priestess.

As Roberta turned a page over, Peter stared to explain about chaotic and disorganised living spaces and how they affected the psyche. He then said that even though people cleared these spaces, they'd frequently become cluttered again very quickly and instead of keeping on top of their *physical* mess, they needed to take a good look at all the rubbish in their *minds*, first. This, he explained, was the first principal of Internal Feng Shui. And now it was time for a tea break.

****

Whilst the others chose selections of green tea mixed with a variety of flavours or "Gagging Tea" as Carolyn had christened the Camomile, Roberta collared Priyanka. The two young women appeared to be instant soul-mates as Priyanka was only too happy to chat to a bright young woman her own age rather than a plethora of middle-aged women, who usually attended these events.

Marion stared at Priyanka. She thought she would have looked far more comfortable in a starched white office shirt and very high court shoes, rather than the soft flowing lines of her sari. There was just something about Priyanka that all looked very wrong. Carolyn observed Priyanka's look as well. She'd travelled a lot in India and in Priyanka's trying to emulate their dress style, there seemed to be a "juxtaposition of souls".

Also Indian women smiled a lot whilst Priyanka frowned a lot and really didn't look like the sort of woman you could have a bit of a laugh with. She embodied everything that was hard and cold and so very far removed from what Carolyn knew as spirituality. Marion wondered how on earth Priyanka had become Peter's assistant.

"She doesn't look like she comes from the East, does she?" she whispered to Carolyn.

"Stepney, maybe" replied Carolyn "That's East, isn't it?" Marion quietly choked on some Green Tea. She surveyed the room to see if she recognised anyone apart from her immediate group of friends. Often people were drawn to similar workshops and it was nice to have some unexpected re-unions, although sometimes it wasn't...

People chatted quietly, moved out of the main room into the corridor and kitchen, and compared notes.

Marion really hoped there wasn't anybody there from her time in Ittica when it had all gone horribly wrong.....

****

CHAPTER 2

ITTICA

Three years ago Marion had been in Greece. Not a keen flyer, the first couple of hours of the flight had been extremely bumpy and Marion found herself glancing at the faces of the stewardesses to see if this kind of extreme turbulence was normal, or if she recognised any signs of terror. She had once seen someone turning white on a flight to Israel, but that was an elderly Jewish lady who'd realised the meal she'd been served wasn't kosher.

Suddenly the "fasten your seatbelts" sign flashed up. Marion hadn't unfastened hers yet. That meant they were really in for a roller coaster ride. She gripped the arms of her seat tightly, before she realised she was tightening her grip on the arm of the man sat next to her. This could have been the stuff of Hollywood movies.

Attractive, older divorced woman accidentally takes hand of dashing widower whilst on a flight to a new life in an exotic country with palm trees. Only Marion was at least thirty years too old to play someone her own age in the Hollywood movie of her life, and the man sitting next to her was more Danny De Vito than George Clooney. Nonetheless, the small, chubby, balding chap squashed into the seat next to her was determined to play his part.

He placed his other hand on top of Marion's so that she couldn't release her grip.

"Scared?" he asked "No need to be. I take it you don't fly much? Me, I'm a frequent traveller. I need to keep an eye on all my international businesses." He winked at Marion. She felt nauseous. "I'm in Combustibles" continued the man, now removing his glasses to indicate that he was very proud of himself. You look like you're about to combust yourself, thought Marion.

There was nowhere to go and another two hours of this to come. Marion was less a captive audience, and more of a captured one. After at least another half an hour of self-congratulatory prattling, the man finally asked Marion what she did. Without really thinking, Marion found herself replying, "I'm in Pyrotechnics" as she felt the grip on her hand loosening.

"That's to do with er....fire, right?" said the man. "That's right" said Marion. Then just for good measure she added, "As a little girl, I always found I enjoyed setting light to things...."

"Would you excuse me for just one moment?" asked the man, "I just need to go to the er..." After he got back from the toilet, he buried himself in the in-flight magazine and didn't speak again. Sometimes Pyrotechnics come in very handy, thought Marion.

The weather calmed down as the plane approached the Greek island. Dazzling sunshine shone down the runway and Marion inhaled deeply. It was always exciting to touch down in another country. Waiting at the luggage carousel, mild panic started to set in. Marion always panicked about whether or not her suitcase would arrive in the same country as her.

Once she'd purchased a tartan suitcase so that it stood out and could be grabbed quickly, but she hadn't accounted for what might occur, taking it on a flight to Edinburgh. Whilst Marion waited anxiously, she was unaware that the luggage handlers had held her case back to laugh at. They thought she must have been an American tourist who'd bought some "really cute" luggage for her visit. Another luggage handler joked that he'd have to detain it, because it belonged to his clan.

The case was placed back on the carousel, just in time for an anxious Marion to march off to the customer services desk, angrily plonking down her passport. "Oh...you're British...." said a surprised sounding receptionist. She looked at the boarding pass stub. "Everything should be off there by now..... Just bear with me....." She made a call and then pointed over to the carousel.

"I think it's coming round now...." said the receptionist, then, trying not to giggle added that she understood it had been held as a "suspect package". Marion looked at her quizzically, before being told her case had been released and that there weren't any problems. She was free to collect it. As she lifted the handle, she noticed a little note had been attached. It read; "The Loch Ness Monster doesn't really exist. Enjoy your trip."

****

Marion had a plain, navy blue suitcase for Greece. It ricocheted through the plastic flaps along with all the others – so good, so far. Wheeling her way over to an easily spotted "Holis Holidays" representative flashing her white card and teeth, a group of around twenty people were ushered onto a coach. As they rolled through the countryside from Cephalonia airport towards the seafront, Marion realised that not everyone was booked onto the same Holis course and were headed to other islands. She herself was soon on a little ferry to Ittica.

Driving past olive trees, harbours and white buildings all glistening in dazzling sunlight, this really was an idyllic holiday spot and Marion wasn't the first tourist to immediately go all dreamy and start wondering if she could make a Shirley Valentine style life out there....

Watching the waves go by once on board the ferry, Marion went to get a cup of tea. A boy of about ten covered a tea bag in a polystyrene cup past the brim with boiling water whilst his father, busy serving sandwiches didn't seem to notice or care. Subsequently, Marion didn't really look at the cup before grabbing it and before she knew it, scalding hot water was trickling all the way down her arm.

There was no immediate pain with such a deep burn, at first. Marion just muttered about being clumsy and went off to find the toilets and run some cold water on herself. When she sat down, she noticed something that looked like white tissue paper, stuck to her arm. Seeing as she didn't have a cardigan on and therefore didn't have any tissues stuffed up the sleeve as usual, then this wasn't tissue paper - it was her skin, peeling off in shards.

Trying to remain calm, Marion went to find someone who knew first aid but only got advice from someone who told her to plunge her arm in the sea for natural antiseptic and another woman who said she was a healer and started spraying Marion's arm with lavender oil. Marion was sure you shouldn't put such substances on an open wound. Eventually, it was the coach driver who covered her arm with dressing from the first aid box, whilst the Holis representative took one look at the wound and screamed. They were miles from anywhere and there was nothing for it now but to wait several hours until they got inland and to the nearest hospital.

It turned out the hospital was very far away, especially when everyone had to stop for lunch. Suddenly not feeling much like the calamari and feta cheese salad set in front of her, Marion felt her arm burning up, like a radiator switched on high. The tavern didn't seem to have any ice, so Marion had to be content with pressing a cold can of coke against her arm. After that, much to the amusement of her fellow passengers, she had to hold her arm up under the coach air conditioning for the rest of the journey.

****

The "hospital" on Ittica shut at 7pm, half an hour before they arrived. Emergencies had to be flown into the mainland. Meanwhile, one of the Holis representatives said she would take Marion to a friend of hers who was a jeweller. A jeweller? What was he going to do, brand her? Marion felt very nervous as she followed the rep up the hill to the house of a man named Pacos. "It's fine. Really. I'll leave you here. You know your way back to the centre, don't you?" said the rep. Thanks a lot, thought Marion. All that money she'd spent on her holiday – she would've thought she'd have been looked after a little better.

Tentatively, she knocked on the door of the little stone house and a tall man about her age with a white goatee beard opened the door. Marion was at first afraid he wouldn't speak any English, but she needn't have worried – not only did Pacos speak perfect English, but he was extremely adept at dressing burns, explaining that he was forever injuring himself on his soldering irons.

Marion thanked him profusely, but she'd already forgotten her way back to the Holis centre. Fortunately, an elderly Greek woman complete with donkey appeared outside Pacos' house as if by magic and beckoned Marion to follow her. The centre was probably only about a five minute walk, but in the dark, around many twists and bends, it seemed to take about twenty minutes. Once they reached the doorway of the centre, Marion could see two little teeth in the mouth of the Greek woman, glistening beneath the porch light as she smiled. These were the only teeth the woman had. The woman outstretched her hand, into which Marion clumsily placed a 20 Euro note. Then the woman curled up her gnarled hand and walked away.

Marion did not sleep well. She was in pain, for several reasons.

****

In October, the Greek islands weren't always that warm. No one had told Marion that there might be a particularly fierce wind this time of year which seemed to be determined to churn up the entire al fresco breakfast. Marion was hoping she'd be able to sit on the beach that afternoon, but at the moment it seemed like an unlikely option. She was also alarmed to discover that the first module of her workshop holiday course was going be taught outside on the patio.

After shivering over freshly ground coffee for at least ten minutes, the "Manifest Abundance" coaches eventually arrived. The beautiful young Greek Holis guide introduced herself, first. She had the sort of skin that looked liked she'd been dipped in honey and she had huge, clear brown eyes and long dark curls that spilled across the shoulders of her starched white blouse.

She spoke about how she'd been drawn to the island and the idyllic life she had with her husband. They'd been childhood sweethearts and now lived and worked in Ittica in a small stone-walled home at the top of the mainland where they grew olives, peppers and oranges in their garden.

Marion started to dream of escaping....she visualised a home of her own somewhere like here or maybe Tuscany where terracotta dishes would just appear alongside red wine from the grapes of her very own vineyards. Suddenly she became aware of searing pain in her arm. She'd been promised that someone would come and get her as soon as the hospital was open, but when was that?

Little beads of sweat started to trickle down Marion's brow – what if Pacos had done something horribly wrong? Suppose the worse-than-useless healer woman had damaged the epidermis? What if the wound got infected? What if the hospital never opened again and she got gangrene and.....the young Holis rep tapped on her shoulder. "Marion? My name's Elena. I'm going to take you the hospital. We can walk. It's only a short way." Marion felt relief until she realised what a short distance meant on Ittica. Thank goodness she hadn't burnt her leg.

****

The "hospital" was little more than a tiny out-house in a valley. Marion was glad Elena was with her in case no one spoke English. She had remembered quite clearly what Pacos had said the previous evening about the dressing that he'd put on and how it should be taken off very slowly. A man in an open white coat and brylcreamed hair beckoned Marion into a side room.

His flies were undone and he didn't look at Marion as he arranged various lotions, cotton wool and bandages. Marion looked at his crotch. The Dr didn't speak. As she sat on a trolley, Marion saw a man in bed next to her and a woman sat beside him holding his hand. He looked like he was dying. Maybe he was. The Dr pointed to Marion's arm. "Lift please."

With one swift, but shockingly painful movement, he ripped off the dressing. Marion was too shocked to even yell as the Dr then dipped some lineament in yellow ointment and pressed it hard against the burn. Marion felt like she was being branded. "Owww!" she yelled. The dying man lifted his head.

"Sting a bit, but you fixed now" said the Dr as he deftly wrapped a bandage around his handiwork. "Off you leave, bye bye. Come back two days." Marion hopped off the trolley and went to find Elena.

"OK now?" Elena smiled. Marion nodded. She couldn't speak.

****

Marion had missed a little bit of the first part of the course, but someone offered her their notes to copy up later. The group were on a break by the time she got back. "How's your arm?" one lady asked.

"I really have no idea" replied Marion, before bursting into tears. It was delayed shock. She was fortified with coffee and baklava and then participated in the rest of the morning's seminar. When she had originally received the Holis Holidays brochure Marion hadn't really stopped to consider what she was reading. They had a very good reputation and their number of centres was growing. Of course she would make sure she'd read things exceedingly carefully these days....

Holis had courses on several of the Greek islands, all in the "holistic" mould, hence their name. The Manifest Abundance course was the one that caught Marion's eye. At the time she'd run up some bad debts and things were difficult at work, as well. She also liked the sound of the blurb which stated that the course wasn't just about attracting material goods into your life, but also abundance in areas like health and relationships. At that time, it hadn't even occurred to Marion that there was something very wrong in the sentence in the brochure that read, "Manifest Abundance. Only £840."

These days, Marion would have realised that an awful lot of abundance would be going out before you were able to manifest any......However, she had £1k earmarked for a well-earned holiday and this seemed very reasonable, considering all the favourable reviews she had read. Besides, she was desperate for a break. She'd been thinking about her son Gabriel a lot and how the last time she had seen him he'd walked out the door with practically every part of his body tattooed, including some peculiar symbols on his neck.

When Marion said she found them gross, he snapped at her and said if she was so bloody esoteric, then she would understand what they meant and the importance of having them permanently etched onto your body. She didn't. With that, he'd chucked a few things in a rucksack and left. She hadn't seen him since. Maybe it was better that way – at least he'd be out of that stinking squat. Calling the angelic little baby who stared up from his hospital cot Gabriel, was Marion's ex-husband, Alan's idea.

And baby Gabriel did indeed look like a little cherub with a few strands of flaxen hair, huge blue eyes, rosy red cheeks and a cupid's bow of a mouth. He looked just like a Raphael painting – all he needed was the wings. It was Marion who began to doubt that the name suited him. Whilst Gabriel would gaze angelically at his father, whenever Marion peered into the cot she noticed that the baby's left eye narrowed and that he looked angry.

Marion was convinced Gabriel loved her husband and hated her, even though Alan told her not to be so stupid. "Babies can't even focus properly" he said. Their baby probably wouldn't even know which parent was which and when Marion saw the eye close up, all Gabriel was trying to do was discern who was Mummy and who was Daddy.

"But he doesn't do that with you" protested Marion.

"He's probably just trying to suss out which one of has the titties" said Alan. Marion wasn't convinced. Later on, little Gabriel didn't seem interested in breast milk at all and would only accept a bottle from Alan. Marion cried and cried despite the best efforts of the district nurse and Alan telling her that not everyone could breastfeed. Marion was diagnosed with post-natal depression, although she was adamant that she was not depressed, but that her baby hated her.

This seemed to be the case as he grew older. Little Gabriel would always crawl towards Alan and away from Marion. She didn't know what she'd done to deserve this, but no matter how hard she tried, and no matter for how long she'd wanted to be a mother, it didn't seem to be that she could be one to this child.

He'd give her the "evil eye" whenever she picked him up to cuddle him and on his first day at school, he happily let go of her hand and ran from her without looking back, unlike all the other children who bawled and clung tight to Mummy. The relationship was always tenuous and although she didn't like to admit it, cracks were also appearing in Marion's marriage.

Many years of child psychiatrists and doctors' assessments later, Marion and Alan decided to go their separate ways. Marion told friends they had simply fallen out of love – grown apart. It was true, but also true that Marion could never really deal with Gabriel never having been in love with her. Her marriage had become one long stint of stressful visits to "experts" and all other areas of life suffered badly.

Eventually Alan moved into a small flat and the family home was put on the market. Alan met a new partner only six months after the divorce came through. Marion remembered bemoaning this fact to Bea. "Men move on quicker" said Bea. "Just think of everyone we know who's gotten divorced. We know so many single women and so many second time married men. It just seems to go that way." Marion sighed deeply and held out her glass for a refill of red....

****

Ironically, it was from her ex-husband's new partner that Marion discovered Gabriel was living on a commune in the South of France. Marion thought that sounded very appealing – perhaps some of her influence had rubbed off on him. Alan hit the roof – he couldn't bear his son to turn out just like his mother..... She was over a barrel. She'd spent years trying to figure out why her only child hated her and more years trying to understand why it was so easy for Alan to fall back into a steady relationship when she had so much trouble meeting someone suitable herself. It was time to look after herself, put herself first. Take some personal development courses.....

****

Marion woke up after the meditation class and rubbed her arm. Elena came over and talked to her. "Arm hurting?" she asked. Marion nodded. She was assured that the hospital, albeit primitive, was a very good one and that she would definitely go home with two arms....As Marion gently came back into the room after reminiscing on times gone by, Elena handed her a leaflet. It was a course back in London for the meditation they had just been doing – half of which she'd missed.

"Isn't this just what we were doing this morning?" asked Marion.

"Yes" said Elena, "But there won't be time to go through it again here. This is a shorter introductory course back in London. It does contain what you missed, but also so much more...." Marion frowned. Elena continued, doing her best to explain that these courses were a lot more intensive, packing in a lot more information than the Greek seminars and as a Holis participant already, she would get a very good discount. As Marion tried to work this out in her head, Elena was already filling in the forms for her and before she knew it, Marion had already spent another £300 just trying to catch up on what she'd missed out on by not concentrating and falling asleep the first time round....

****

There could not have been more delicious food than roasted peppers, feta cheese, sesame bread and salads dripping with olive oil under the faint Mediterranean sun. It was simple food, but somehow everything tasted better when eaten at round, wooden tables alfresco, overlooking olive groves and steep, rocky hills. The buffet was a strictly help yourself until bursting affair, and when she finally felt she would actually burst, Marion moved to the other side of the porch to get a mint tea. She got chatting to a young man who was also from London and told her that this was his seventh Holis holiday. He told Marion that seven was a very magical and mystical number, and that if he managed to manifest as much after this visit as his previous ones then it would confirm everything he thought about the place.

Which was what, exactly, asked Marion. This seemed to throw him. He had "stock lines" about mysticism and symbols, but when someone asked him his own views, then.....Nonetheless he was an easy going young man, and good to talk to. It turned out he had taken courses in yoga, chanting, chakra alignment, creative writing....Marion asked him where he got the time and money. This also threw him.

Holis holidays didn't come cheap. Somewhat tentatively, Marion said she'd just signed up for a London weekend workshop. "But that's wonderful!"

exclaimed the young man. "They're brilliant. I've done those as well." Then he laughed, "You'll find they're kind of addictive – once you start, you can't stop." Marion smiled, but looked slightly nervous.

****

Part 2 of the meditation day, after lunch, was easier to concentrate on. For the sake of another £300, much easier, in fact. Marion opened a leather-bound notebook and wrote slowly in italic letters, "Manifesting Abundance" at the top of the page. The she remembered she didn't yet know how to do the first part of this, left a couple of pages, and wrote "Part 2" at the top of the next page. The lecturer started talking about "blocks" to getting what you want in your life. Blocks could be anything from an unsatisfying job to demands from other people or lack of money.

A chart of the "Seven Negative Nags" was drawn up on the whiteboard. These apparently, were "little voices" that told you couldn't do things. Oddly enough, not taking a holiday was listed at the top. Marion sat up. She'd debated going on a Holis break for years but had found all sorts of reasons not to go – the cost, mainly. Cheap package tours just didn't seem like proper holidays anymore and Holis seemed different. Marion had wanted something that appealed to all her senses – somewhere warm, quiet, somewhere she'd meet interesting people and learn new things.

As the lecture went on, Marion felt absolutely right that she deserved this holiday and sat up when she heard the lecturer say that it was no co-incidence who was here at this time. Holis participants were the sort of aware people already tuned into their "inner needs" and if anyone felt guilty about treating themselves, then they needed to "reframe" their way of thinking.

Marion glanced around the group. No one there looked like they were guilty or anxious – not about money, anyway. In fact, all Holis holidaymakers would have needed to be pretty well-healed in order to meet the costs of their courses. There was an eclectic mix of accountants, lawyers, managers and people who ran their own businesses. Judging by their clothes, they were all doing pretty well. Marion worried she hadn't packed enough nice dresses, assuming she wasn't going to need much in the way of dressing up on a Greek island. A couple of swimming costumes, a sarong, a cardigan, three vest tops and her passport were about all she'd brought. Alas, everyone seemed to be wearing "designer ponchos".

The women were all beautifully made-up and the men in nice chinos and expensive trainers. Marion wondered if she should wander into the town the next day, as she'd heard there were very nice clothes shops there. The lecturer, almost as if she'd read Marion's mind, continued on the theme of treating yourself and being deserving and the more she spoke, Marion thought she hadn't been shopping in a very long time...

****

The long steep hill into the tiny town area reminded Marion a bit of Glastonbury, only with sunshine. So did the shops. Everything Marion loved was in these shops; hand-made arts and crafts, woven shawls, clothes...oh. The clothes. Marion started to finger a cotton wrap longingly and dared not look at the price. The Greek islands were supposed to be cheap, but the ones Holis holidays ran their courses on were the exception to the rule.

The shop owner, a Greek woman with lots of red lipstick and perfect English, approached Marion with a beaming smile. "Beautiful, no?" Marion nodded. She desperately tried to crawl her fingers up towards the price tag. "But not your colour" continued the shopkeeper. Marion heaved a sigh of relief, until from under the counter, the woman pulled the most beautiful garment she had ever seen. *"This* one is your colour" said the woman.

The wrap was Olive green with a few deep purple tiny sequins along the top seams. Marion gasped. "Try" said the shopkeeper. This was dangerous territory, and Marion knew it. She looked at the woman, her face registering deep "shopping fear". The woman knew exactly how to handle this. "I know. You're thinking, I shouldn't buy this for myself. It's just a shawl. But it's also a unique and exquisite shawl. Handmade. And you're thinking, why *shouldn't* I buy myself something so beautiful? Yet, you are also thinking about spending money on yourself when you feel you should be getting gifts for your loved ones, back home."

It was remarkable. How did the woman know the exact thoughts going on in Marion's head? Marion let the shopkeeper drape the shawl over her shoulders. It felt so decadent. She knew the colour would suit her – green always offset her red hair. It was possibly the most perfect piece of clothing she had ever tried on. Marion eventually spoke. "H....h....how.....m......much?"

The woman left Marion standing in front of the mirror and said nothing for a while. After a somewhat uncomfortably long pause, the woman asked Marion, "Tell me...what do you think *you're* worth?" Oh. That was *so* unfair. Marion usually expected to haggle on holidays abroad, but only once she knew what the original asking price was. Part of her felt like throwing the shawl on the floor, but instead she just looked at the woman and shrugged. The woman gently lifted the shawl from Marion's shoulders and showed her the price tag. 350 Euros.

Marion found it difficult to react with the right amount of etiquette. On the one hand, she would never pay that sort of money for a shawl and on the other hand this was a stunningly original piece of craftwork that must have taken some old Greek peasant woman with no teeth, months and months to knit. Marion fingered the shawl lovingly, but the shopkeeper shockingly snatched it away from her and hung it back on the rail.

"You are welcome to think about it, but I warn you, think too long and it will be gone...." The information was delivered in some kind of terrible hell fire and brimstone kind of way. It felt like this woman was a tarot reader or psychic delivering some dark and terrible warning. The decision was agonising. Only British tourists did "polite haggling", the sort where you didn't try and knock the price down on something too much, even if it were excessive, lest you should cause offence.

As if by magic, the psychic shopkeeper started to read Marion's mind again, although Marion was sure she'd heard what she was saying somewhere before...." We all have these strange blocks inside of us. Something tells us that when we really want something, that we don't deserve it." That clinched it. Marion felt her hand uncontrollably reach into her purse and pull out her credit card. In a moment, the shawl was wrapped and handed over. No haggling had been done. "You won't regret it" said the shopkeeper, as Marion walked out the shop in a daze.

When Marion got back to the Holis centre only the housekeeper was there, preparing dinner. "All at beach" she told Marion. Beach? In this wind? Thank goodness she'd just bought a shawl. Marion carefully unwrapped it from the tissue paper and put it around her shoulders. The housekeeper gasped. "I know, I shouldn't" said Marion, "But..."

"No, no, you should!" said the housekeeper. "My friend, she make. Each one take three months. All this...." She delicately caressed the beaded area. "All this, she make like...she.....she...."

"Sew" offered Marion.

"Yes. Sew. All herself . She make." Marion's guilt began to subside. She had truly purchased something very precious and maybe even a good amount of the money would go to the designer herself. Marion really liked to think she was helping out a lady who sat and knitted and sewed for long hours as she made her way down to the beach. She didn't see the housekeeper laughing and shaking her head as she made her way out of the centre...

****

Elena passed the shop where Marion had bought her shawl. She peered in the window. The olive green shawl was gone. Elena smiled.

****

Marion found the main group of Holis participants in a small cafe, just off the main road to the beach. She ordered a cappuccino and eyed up some deserts. The young man she met earlier that morning started chatting to her again. A woman started eyeing up her shawl. "Oh my God, that's gorgeous." Marion smiled.

"Do you think so? Just got it about ten minutes ago."

"From here? You got it from here?" The woman could barely contain herself. Suddenly, Marion found herself giving directions to the shop, to a highly excitable group of women, who started to gather around her and her shawl. The young man suddenly became intrigued by Marion as well, if not by her shawl.

"Do you, do you really feel like you're getting something out of being here?" he asked. He had deep blue eyes. Marion found herself blushing. I've got a 350 Euro shawl out of it, she thought. The young man looked at her more, like he really wanted to know what she had to say. She studied his face. He had closely cropped medium brown hair, a bit of stubble and a chunky wooden bead necklace around his neck. If I was thirty years younger, thought Marion, but....she wasn't.

Marion had to admit she had never really got the whole "toy boy" thing. She knew if she'd told her friends back home then Bea would have told her to go for it and Carolyn would already be asking who his friends were. But younger men had never had that much appeal for Marion. Besides their lithe, taut bodies, clear smooth skin and lack of baggage, what did they *really* have to offer....? Marion felt herself reddening as she realised she must've been staring at this man for at least five whole minutes.

"You have a very interesting face" he said. She turned full-on beetroot. "May I?" he asked. It was all bit much. Gently the man pushed a strand of hair back off Marion's face with the most tender of touches and stared deeply into her eyes. "My gosh, yes. You are such a deep thinker. Even a bit clairvoyant, I wouldn't wonder. You're receptive, yet impulsive – generous of heart and soul." It was all bullshit, but bullshit that worked. Marion enjoyed being flattered.

As she decided to touch the young man's cheek in return, he recoiled. Marion looked bemused and apologised. "Um, maybe later" he said, placing his empty coffee cup back on the counter and checking his watch. "Yoga starts soon, I think."

"No. Not for ages" said Marion, deliberately pouting and pulling down the front of her top in order to try and reveal some non-existent cleavage. Then, she deliberately crossed and uncrossed her legs. The young man gulped. "Nice talking to you" he gulped before fleeing the tavern faster than a rat up a drainpipe.

****

Elena arrived for a little impromptu talk before the evening Yoga session. She flicked back her thick black hair, flashed her white teeth and tanned thighs and said she wanted to welcome everyone, not only to Ittica and Holis but to the Greek way of life – her life. She said how everything they ate was grown on the island and the Holis meals were made fresh off the trees. She spoke about the town and shops and the best places to eat before slowly and deliberately pointing out where the internet cafe was.

Then, with incredible passion and a little water in her eyes, she spoke about her husband. They had known each other since they were seven years old and married when she was eighteen. He was her soul-mate, her friend for life, and everything about the island, he loved as much as she did. Whilst she worked on Ittica, he was a tour guide, an island hop away. Every morning she would wave him off with a chunk of sesame bread and fresh mandarins and olives from their garden. All day long she would miss his company and then greet him at sunset. Her talk was emotional, romantic and so impassioned that several people found themselves weeping at the end. Oh, to have found true love like that.

****

Marion wasn't unfit, but she was a little bit rusty when it came to yoga. Her "Salutation to the Sun" only got about as far as Mercury and she had to relent, just crossing her legs on the mat and chanting "Om" for a while. It was only by the fifth "om" that she realised her stomach was rumbling like mad and dinner was still two hours away. She thought about Elena's talk and how the island was littered with olive trees and fruit....maybe she could sneak off and pick some?

Marion complained that her arm was aching and excused herself. She got a filthy look from a man wearing lilac linen trousers, with pockets. Marion headed down the hill in the direction of the shop where she'd bought her shawl, but then veered off into an alleyway where she thought she'd remembered seeing some olive groves. She wasn't wrong, a little way off were olives, lemons and nectarines all glistening in the afternoon sun. One nectarine in particular caught her eye. It was the most beautiful specimen of fruit she had ever seen.

Large, luscious, enjoying the sun's rays, this was begging to be picked and eaten, but it was over the other side of a high wall and clearly belonged to someone else. A moment of pure determination gripped Marion. All those words about how important it was to "treat yourself..." As she pushed her hand down on top of the wall to lever herself up, pain shot through her arm. She'd managed to forget about the burn for a while, but now that she was needing to use the full force of her muscles, her arm just wouldn't comply. Sitting down on the road with frustration, Marion started to form a plan B. If she couldn't physically get up on the wall then the only other option was to find a long stick and knock the fruit off the branch.

As luck would have it, a Y-shaped branch was just lying there on the ground – perfect for poaching. Marion carefully and deliberately prodded at the fruit. When she got frustrated that it wouldn't budge, she started to prod the stick around the stem. The owner of the house and orchard came outside. Seeing what Marion was doing he yelled, "Kleftis, Kleftis! Thief Thief!" Marion dropped the stick in horror and froze to the spot. The man looked her up and down.

Then, he clocked her beautiful shawl and started speaking in broken English. "Holis Centre?" he asked. Marion nodded. "I guessed so" said the man. Marion pulled her shawl tightly across her chest as the man noticed the bandage on her arm. "What wrong with arm?" he asked and then added, "You try climb my wall with hurt?"

"I...I'm sorry" stuttered Marion "I didn't think I might be stealing. It's just that – the fruit you grow here is so magnificent. It tastes wonderful. So much better than what we have in England, by the time it's imported."

"Hmmmm...." the man looked at her shawl again. "Don't tell me Holis Centre no feed you?" Then he let out a huge belly laugh. Marion felt terribly ashamed. All that money she'd spent on a shawl and now here she was, trying to steal a nectarine. "You here, wait" said the man. He placed the small ladder he kept in the orchard up against the tree, picked the nectarine and handed it to Marion.

"Oh no, I couldn't possibly...." said Marion.

"Take. *Please*. Brave lady, I like. You want fruit so much, you climb wall with hurt arm, you deserve." He smiled and Marion found that she didn't have the heart to argue. Besides, she liked being called brave. As she climbed the hill back up to the Centre, Marion stared at the golden orb in her hand, not wanting to take a bite out of something so precious.

****

Yoga morning class hurt Marion's arm. Instead, she left and went to find Elena to ask about a part of the island she thought she might like to visit. Elena wasn't in the office, but someone else said she thought she might be up in her room. Marion was told that if the door was open, to just walk in. Finding the right room, the door was slightly ajar, prompting Marion to ask herself whether or not the Greek regarded this as a shut or open door. There seemed to be a strange noise coming from the room. Being very British and not just wanting to barge in, Marion pushed the door slightly wider, just to check if Elena was there. Not only was she there, but she was in there with a naked man on top of her, in the full throes of love-making. Marion gasped and tip-toed away, although it was unlikely the couple would have heard anything but the sound of their moaning. As Marion heard voices, she crept down a couple of stairs, so as not to be seen and then peered over the top step.

A man was pulling on his t-shirt, whilst trying to kiss Elena who just had a sheet wrapped around her body. "Go. Please. Whilst no one can see you" said Elena, pushing him away. It was too late. Someone had already seen him. Marion recognised the man as the charming young chap who had flirted with her in the tavern. As he ran off down the opposite stairwell, Marion felt herself redden, but she wasn't sure if it was with anger or jealousy.

Beautiful Elena who was so in love with her husband, her soul-mate, her twin flame. So besotted, that she was having sex with someone else. What exactly was it she saw in this beautiful young man with his twinkly blue eyes, designer stubble, tight stomach muscles and as Marion had just observed – a real peach of a bottom?

Marion was shocked. Did Elena have many lovers? Did she pick and chose from the Holis visitors? Did her husband do the same? Marion headed to the lecture room and a lady came out of the office. "Did you find Elena?" she asked. If only you knew *how* I'd found her, thought Marion.

"Um no. Don't think she was there" said Marion.

"That's strange said the woman. I was sure she went upstairs. Would you like me to find her for you?"

"No" replied Marion. "It's not that urgent, anyway." It was a hell of an eye-opener though, she thought.

****

That morning in the lecture, Marion couldn't look at Elena's lover at all. She did her best to sit the opposite side of the room and felt very uneasy, especially as they'd had such nice chats. The lecture turned out to have the title "The Art of Giving in Order to Receive." As Marion listened to the notion of giving out and getting ten-fold back, she thought that obviously the lecturer had never had a husband or children.....a husband....Elena had a husband.

Marion felt her eyes welling up and drifted off somewhere in an altered state of mind as she tried to work out what was upsetting her so much. A certain emotional state was very much what the Holis Centre liked their participants to reach.....Elena came over in the break and handed Marion some papers. Not being able to bring herself to speak to her, Marion just signed them, blindly.

In the meanwhile, Elena's lover was ready to move on. He'd always wanted to go with an older woman and he liked Marion. He might have backed off from her initial advances, but if he was honest, that was because he liked her. *Really* liked her. Back home there were loads of beautiful young women and Elena was much like the rest. But a woman Marion's age – now that would be a *real* challenge. He'd heard that Holis holidays were full of older, single women who hadn't had sex for years and were "gagging for it".

If he was honest, Marion intrigued him. She was very attractive and he'd guessed her age a lot younger than her chronological one. She also seemed devoid of that look of "desperation." He decided to approach her that evening, but she seemed very keen to ignore him. He couldn't handle the rejection.

He'd been attentive, sensitive, interested – he knew he was good looking....what on earth could he possibly have done wrong? As he stared at her whilst she chatted to a group of women, he noticed they were all wearing the same shawl as Marion, only in different colours.

"We'd been admiring you enviously for days!" said one of the women. "I just had to go and see if there were any of those shawls left."

"There were *loads* left" piped up another woman.

"But don't you think it's strange" said the other, "That they were all in different colours? That you couldn't get one identical to another?"

"Perfect for us though, girls!" laughed yet another lady.

"....And didn't that shop lady seem to know exactly what was the right colour for all of us?" piped up another woman from the group. Marion recalled when she'd gone in and originally picked up a darker green shade than the olive colour she now wore. Without a doubt, that particular shade of green was perfect for her colouring. She thought it strange now, though...The women continued to giggle and drink coffee as Elena's lover shrunk back into a corner with a sad cup of herb tea going cold in his hands.

****

It was 9pm and the shops were still open, but there were no shawls left. Elena entered the shop and went up to her friend who was cashing up for the day. "All gone?" asked Elena.

"Yes. Fantastic" said her friend. "Thank you for giving me a description of all their looks and colouring - I knew who was coming and could keep track of them." She handed Elena a large wad of cash.

"Well" said Elena, "It worked last year, didn't it?" Then the two women laughed. Elena threw the cash up in the air before gathering it up again and locking arms with her friend as they headed back down into the village together.

****

The two weeks on Ittica started to draw to a close. Marion had made notes throughout, but she mentally tried to remember the ethos of the course – the notion of treating yourself, giving in order to receive, asking and trusting the Universe to give you all that you needed. She had two souvenirs from her holiday – a second degree burn that was forming into an interesting shape on her arm and a shawl that she'd practically had to take out a mortgage on.

As Marion relaxed into her seat on the plane back home she pondered on the promises of the brochure and wondered what she would really take home with her.....she certainly hadn't, as the brochure kept quoting alongside smiley sunshine photos, "Made friends for life" or even really anyone she just thought she might email and meet for coffee.

Arriving home, slightly jet-lagged, there was a bundle of envelopes by the front door. There couldn't be anything that urgent – Marion had been very diligent in paying everything off before she'd left. After an hour or two of watching evening soap operas, checking if there was anything in the store cupboard for dinner and then thumbing through some take-away leaflets, it was time to open the post.

Marion was surprised to see some of the letters were stamped with a large, red "Urgent and Overdue" sign. The temptation was to shove them in the "Later" file, but no...

"Give out what you want to get back", she remembered. The first letter showed she was badly overdrawn, even though she should have had a sizeable amount of money still in her account. Scrolling down, she saw that someone called Elena Stakovis had taken over £2000 out of her account.

Marion turned over the bank statement several times. She'd vaguely remembered signing something...opening another envelope from Holis Holidays, was a bill for "Extra Curricular Training." Reading on, Marion realised she had signed up to a set of DVD's, two copies of her lecturer's book, a wall chart and a ticket for a David Icke seminar.

Marion was horrified upon opening the next envelope to see an invoice for 80 Euros for the medical treatment to her arm. Well, that one clearly wasn't right. She was a European national with travel insurance and had a right to be treated for free. That one, she'd contend right away. Only upon further inspection, the invoice wasn't from Holis or even the Medical Centre. It had been sent directly from someone called Pacos – the jeweller who had first patched her up.

When Marion finally totted everything up, she realised she must've been nearly £5k in the red. Her face metamorphosed through several shades of green before arriving at a sickly white shade. It appeared that all the money had been taken out legitimately. Marion hadn't read the small print. And just as easily as it was to sign up for a course called "Manifest Abundance", so abundance just as easily disappeared.....

****

CHAPTER 3

MEANWHILE, BACK IN GLASTONBURY

Bea had thought of booking a Holis trip for quite some time, but was thoroughly put off by Marion's warning. They spoke in the break from the lecture on "Personal Joy", during which Priyanka snarled all the way through. "The crooks" said Bea. "Did you manage to get any of your money back? You know, like those P.P.I thingies where you were 'knowingly missold' something.....or other.....or something like that...."

Bea never did have a grasp on the world of credit. Marion sighed. "No...it was my fault entirely. These people get you when you're at your most vulnerable – that's how they make their money. I signed my life away, but I won't do that again in a hurry, I can tell you."

That afternoon really resonated with Marion. Apparently, if your "Internal Feng Shui" was displaced, it was very easy to be taken advantage of and she realised that's what must have happened in Ittica. She was worn out, jaded and desperate for a holiday when she went there and was caught very off-guard. Peter explained a little about Chinese medicine and the body's internal organs and how these related to his philosophy.

He said the feelings of vulnerability often related to "low spleen energy" and recommended various forms of massage and acupuncture. Bea leant across to Marion. "Have you ever done that?" she asked.

Marion shook her head. "I wouldn't mind trying it, though."

Bea stifled a gasp. "Really? Oh my gosh, I *couldn't*. I absolutely hate needles. Can't stand the sight of them." Peter then announced that he was a fully qualified acupuncturist and was shortly going to do a full demonstration. Suddenly Bea screamed. All faces turned in her direction, as Bea clasped her hand in front of her mouth.

"Is everything ok?" asked Peter.

"My friend is needle-phobic" explained Marion. "She doesn't have to watch, does she?"

"No, of course not" said Peter looking very concerned. Simply mentioning a demo had never got that kind of reaction before. The class turned their attention away from Bea, but Bea frantically signalled to Marion something happening outside the window, beside which they were sitting. Marion nearly screamed herself. Waving and smiling from outside on the lawn, was a naked man. He appeared to be waving at Marion, however and not at Bea. "Do you *know* him?" Bea whispered.

"How should I know? I can hardly cop a good look, can I?" said Marion.

"He's got long white hair and a beard and... I daren't mention anything else" said Bea. Marion looked over.

"Oh my God – it's Stephen the Wizard!"

"*Stephen* the Wizard?" asked Bea. Marion nodded.

"So you *do* know him.....what's he doing out there with no clothes on? Hedging his bets a bit, isn't he?" Marion stifled a giggle, but it came out as a loud snort. Peter asked again, "Are you two ladies sure you're ok?"

"I think we may just need to go and get a drink of water" said Marion, excusing them both. They tiptoed outside, relieved to see that Stephen had put his robe back on. "Hello there!" he shouted cheerily. "Wasn't sure if you recognised me!" Marion resisted the urge to say not like that, but luckily he explained his reasons for being there undressed. "I belong to a Druid order" said Stephen. "We often participate in rituals, out on this green."

"Completely stark bollock naked?" said Bea, not mixing her words.

Stephen frowned. "The correct term is *Skyclad*". Bea frowned back. Marion tried to diffuse the situation.

"No one minds if anyone gets naked in Glastonbury, Bea. It's practically traditional in these parts, I mean areas....." Stephen seemed to be getting quite angry. "I...I mean *really* traditional" said Marion, "As in the Druids and ancients, and um...the work *you're* doing, Stephen."

Stephen looked Marion and Bea up and down. "I was going to invite you ladies to our traditional sunset ceremony at the bottom of the Tor, but if you're going to be facetious...."

"No, no we're not at all" interjected Marion, poking Bea hard in the ribs. "It was just a little bit of a shock for us to see you like that, as we were deeply in meditation."

"Hmm. Well. Come if you like" said Stephen. "Skyclad is optional. We start at 6.30"

"We'd love to" said Marion, trying to stop Bea from emitting a loud, choking sound.

"What have you done?" said Bea, aghast.

"Don't worry, it'll be fun" said Marion.

"Fun?" said Bea, "I'd rather stick needles in my..." she stopped, realising the irony of her statement.

"Well, half a dozen of one" said Marion. "Either watch Peter sticking needles into someone, or watch naked Druids dancing. Which would make you less squeamish?"

"Can I think about it?" said Bea.

****

Whilst Bea wasn't all that sold on the naked Druids idea, Carolyn seemed overly keen. "I can't guarantee they'll *all* be naked" explained Marion, "And seeing as I think they only take their clothes off at sunset, I don't know how much you'll see."

"Oh, what the hell – it's a night out, isn't it?" chortled Carolyn.

"Literally" Marion laughed.

"Do you think there'll be anything to eat?" said Carolyn, "Maybe I should bring a picnic? Or a few burnt offerings..?"

"I'm sure a bottle of wine would be fine" said Marion.

"But what if Druids are teetotal?" asked Bea.

"What if they are? We're not" said Carolyn. "Might have a wander in a minute to see if I can find anything still open around here." The shops on the High Street had strange opening times. Most restaurants were shut by dinner time, so the chance of finding an off license open, was slim.

"Maybe that's why Druids don't drink" offered Bea. Suddenly Carolyn spied a man locking up the local co-op.

"Waaaaittt!" she shouted after him, "Don't lock up yet! Single women here! We *need* wine!"

"Wine, my love?" said the man in soft, Somerset accent. "Not sure we've got any left. Lots of festivals on this time of year, you see. Druid, mostly. They usually come in early and buy most of the wine."

"Bloody lush Druids" muttered Carolyn under her breath.

****

Roberta sat in the back of Peter's car, chatting away happily to Priyanka. They were driving into the town of Wells where good restaurants would be open. "Do you like Indian?" asked Peter, looking at Roberta in his rear view mirror. Roberta hesitated as she noticed Priyanka starting to tremble. Really, Peter should know better. All things Indian were sacred to Priyanka. Religion, clothing, food. She'd even changed her name whilst she was in an Ashram. The thought that her new-found friend might not like dhal, was galling.

Luckily Roberta said she loved Indian. Peter said "Bengal Nights" should still be open which surprised Roberta. She thought it sounded a bit cheap, like the sort of restaurant you'd find in a TV soap opera. Nonetheless, her company for the night would surely know good food. When they arrived, the decor at least clearly disappointed Roberta.

Lurid red and yellow tablecloths practically burnt out the back of your retinas and the waiter who bounced up to the table seemed too cheerful to be real. "Mr Peter! Miss Priyanka! Good to see you again! New friend? Good to see you, too!" Roberta suddenly felt terribly disconcerted by the Asian man's broad West Country accent.

Priyanka handed Roberta a menu. There was no disappointment with the food. After filling her belly much further than it would stretch with delicious breads, sweetmeats and dhal, Roberta could barely move. She went to reach in her handbag for her purse and let out an embarrassingly loud burp. Peter laughed. "Glad you enjoyed it!" he said.

Normally Roberta would have felt shameful, but Peter and Priyanka were so laid back that burping actually felt like the most natural and comfortable thing in the world to do. She reached out for the paper bill, but Peter snatched it away. "No way" he said. "You're our guest." Roberta tried to protest, but Peter had already handed the waiter his card.

"Our absolute pleasure" said Peter. "Do you have plans for tomorrow evening, by any chance?" Roberta had promised the girls she'd join them for a talk outside the Chalice Well and had already purchased a ticket, but thought she'd much rather spend time with this couple. "Dinner, chez us" said Priyanka. It sounded perfect.

****

Beautiful people danced at the foothill of Glastonbury Tor as the sun started to fade. Druids and visitors danced around food and drink and scarves and rattles and drums and ladies in purple chiffon with very long hair wafted around offering biscuits. Marion couldn't help noticing the shape of the biscuits. She took one off a plate and whispered to Carolyn. "Don't you think they look rather like..."

"Vaginas?" said Carolyn. One of the long-haired ladies smiled and said that was exactly what it was. A fertility dance was being performed. "Hmmm...." said Carolyn. "Got any penises?" Marion tried not to chortle, as the woman wafted away in a frown of disdain. "No harm in asking" said Carolyn. Much to her surprise, a lady came up with distinctly phallus-shaped biscuits. Carolyn took one off the plate and smiled. "See?" she said to Marion, "Don't ask and you don't get." She took a bite. "This is absolutely delicious" she told the biscuit-carrier. "What's in it?"

"Dried fruit, honey, flour, butter and a magic ingredient added in for alchemical purposes."

"Alchemical?" asked Carolyn.

"Yes. Fresh semen" said the woman as she danced away swirling the plate above her head as Carolyn choked.

****

Helen and Bea wanted to relax back at the bed and breakfast. Helen dived into the shower whilst Bea lay across their twin beds, reading. The book was controversial - it had led to many an argument with Marion.

It was part of a series which claimed that aliens walked amongst humans on earth and had done for centuries. The author suggested that these aliens were indistinguishable from humans, yet here to aid the human race in its spiritual development. Marion was always highly sceptical about such claims, whereas Bea had very strong beliefs that the author's viewpoint was correct. Helen leapt out of the shower, making Bea jump.

"Anna Lee Merchant!" she gasped, seeing the book cover "One of my favourite writers!" Bea sat up.

"You like her?"

"Love her" said Helen, drying her hair off with a towel. "I mean, she makes so much sense. In the first book, 'The Ships Are Behind Us', I know I really got how she felt. I've felt that way most of my life". Bea's eyes lit up.

"Gosh – I've never met anyone who, who feels like I do about this."

"Well then" Helen smiled "We were *meant* to meet each other." Unfortunately, Bea hated it when people said that. They were the same people that were always claiming, no matter how shit a hand life dealt you, that it was "meant to be." She'd been told that when she broke up with Michael, it was because her true soul-mate was "only just around the corner." Seven years later, it must have been a bloody big corner, thought Bea.

It may have been meant that just at that moment Helen's towel conveniently fell off as she fell on top of Bea and leant forward to kiss her. Bea most definitely meant to scream, but alas in the action of pushing Helen away, found both her hands on Helen's breasts, causing Helen to believe that this moment was for her at least, definitely meant to be.....

****

It was 2am. The Druid festival was still in full swing, but Marion and Carolyn were most definitely not. Tired, a little bit drunk and a little bit high, they waved goodbye to Stephen the Wizard and tottered unsteadily back down the high street. Carolyn stopped for a while to steady herself. "Blimey, it's been ages since I've stayed up this long and at least the same amount of time since I smoked weed, as well."

"You didn't smoke it" said Marion. "Those penis biscuits also had hash in them."

"Christ" said Carolyn "Semen and hash? That's quite hard to swallow....." then she let out the dirtiest laugh ever. Marion put her arm around Carolyn's waist and they staggered onwards, meeting all sorts of revellers on the way. "Come to the Goddess Festival!" waved some girls with angel wings.

They walked past wizards and witches, people with Venetian masks, flag waving people and dancing until finally they reached their destination. Marion was relieved to be flopping into bed, or so she thought. She found Bea in her and Carolyn's room with a packed bag, sobbing into a snotty tissue. Marion's head thumped so much - a crying Bea was not a welcome sight. It wasn't, however, all that unusual.

Bea would have "moments" that she allowed herself for mourning Michael and you knew when it was coming. She'd go very quiet and then her eyes would well up and then she'd talk about him. That was OK – Bea could talk as much as she liked, but at this hour, in this hotel room....

"So sorry" said Bea, "I thought you'd be back earlier – I told the landlady we were doing a swap, and she let me in. Do you mind if I crash out here tonight? I'm going to see if I can get a coach back in the morning." Despite being the worse for wear, Marion made Bea tell her and Carolyn "all about it." Eventually they managed to persuade her that it was all just one big misunderstanding. Marion let Bea have her bed, telling her she'd probably just snore away, not even feeling the floor through her alcohol-induced state. She tossed and turned all night as she felt the hardness digging into her, beneath her coat.

****

Helen didn't come down for breakfast. Marion was glad as she was exhausted, aching all over and not in the mood for confrontation. In contrast, Carolyn who had slept like a baby was raring with energy. "The Full English please!" she beamed. Marion started with cornflakes, but every crunch seemed to hurt her head so she gave up and got a bowel of tinned grapefruit segments.

"Mmm, yummy" teased Carolyn.

"It's ok for you" said Marion, "You had a bed last night. In case you hadn't noticed, I sacrificed mine for a friend who was in rather a state of shock. It was *your* friend, Helen, who came onto her. Bea is traumatised."

"Oh come on" said Carolyn "All she had to do was say she wasn't gay."

"And could you explain that to someone if they fell on top of you naked, fresh out the shower?" asked Marion.

"Look, what the hell. It was only a naked woman" said Carolyn "Everyone gets naked here. Surely Bea could have dealt with it."

"I don't think you're being very supportive" said Marion, pushing away her grapefruit segments. "Where is Helen, anyway? Come to think of it, where is Bea?" Marion and Carolyn spent a few minutes glaring at each other. This certainly wasn't the ethos of Internal Feng Shui. Carolyn went upstairs and knocked on the door of the other room. There was no reply. She didn't want to wake Helen if she was having a lie-in, but now she was slightly concerned. She decided to go back to the breakfast room and found Bea sitting with Marion. They were both very subdued.

"No Helen?" asked Marion. "No" snarled Carolyn. "She might be traumatised." They all walked in silence to the morning's seminar.

****

Roberta was full of the joys of spring. "Slept well then?" grumbled Marion. Roberta had. She was suddenly confronted by the faces of three very grumpy middle-aged women. Roberta sidled over to Priyanka. "Well, they obviously had a really good time last night...." Priyanka tried to stifle a giggle. Marion sighed deeply as she noticed how fresh Peter, Priyanka and Roberta looked. Young people always did. Perhaps it was time to accept at last that she was just too old to stay up all night, or drink that much, or....Marion shuddered as the thought crossed her mind. Perhaps she just shouldn't be doing this kind of thing anymore.

Perhaps it was the time of life to be "sensible". Marion had found herself getting more and more tired of late. There was so much work to do at the University and the job had been getting more and more stifling, as well as pressurised as younger lecturers pushed their way up the career ladder. Marion felt she had no energy to compete. She needed to slow down and hardly bounced out of bed with joie de vivre on her days off. As it was, she often found it hard to lift her head off the pillow. She decided to visit the doctor, who much to her chagrin, told her it was "just what happens at her age" and suggested caffeine tablets.

Disillusioned and depressed, Marion had decided to try homeopathy. Bea had told her there was a nice lady in Muswell Hill who was "bloody marvellous".

It was pricey, but worth a go. Marion at first felt dubious when the homeopath came to the reception area to fetch her. A tiny Chinese lady in a starched white coat came out. She had a black bun coiled so tightly on the top of her head, that it almost looked as if it had been attached by a cruel operation.

"Mrs Green?" asked the Chinese lady, looking up from her folder. Marion debated not answering, but then realised she was the only person in the waiting area. Carefully putting down the copy of the health magazine she had been reading, Marion felt her legs tremble slightly as she entered the surgery. The homeopath didn't look up or smile as she took a potted medical history from Marion.

"You *don't* smoke?" asked the homeopath.

"No. Not at all" replied Marion.

The Chinese lady gave a Samurai stare. "But there are signs" she said, "Especially round the eyes and jaw region that tell me otherwise..." Marion was exasperated.

"But I *don't* smoke!" she protested.

"Hmmm..." the homeopath prodded around Marion's chin. "Recreational?" she asked.

"Recre....? Oh...yes cannabis. But only a bit. Really only a very very little bit. You see, my boss has really been stressing me out and anyway, I can't really get my hands on pot, I mean cannabis these days as most of my student suppliers have left and I mean, er....I only really have a tiny bit....no more than.....a couple of joints a day sometimes...sometimes only one. Really, really...."

The Chinese homeopath made some notes on her clipboard and placed it firmly on the side of her desk. "Ok Mrs Green...." she sighed. "You want to stop feeling so tired? You stop smoking pot." Marion paid £120 to be told this. She wondered how many joints she could have rolled for that...

****

The morning's Internal Feng Shui seminar had already started, but there was still no sign of Helen. Two hours and a coffee break later, Carolyn started to feel a bit worried. She told her friends she was going to wander back to the bed and breakfast. Back there, the landlady said she thought Helen must still be in her room as she hadn't seen her wander out or even come down for breakfast.

 Carolyn was let into the room, but there was no sign of Helen. Carolyn went into the bathroom, where Helen was lying in the bath, her eyes closed. Her reading book was face downwards in the water. Carolyn plunged her hand into the water to see if there were any empty pill bottles, slung the soaking book onto the bathmat, and shook Helen violently.

Helen screamed. "Jesus! Fuck! Carolyn - what the fuck are you doing?!"

Carolyn gasped. "Oh my God, thank fuck. You're OK."

"Of course I'm bloody ok! Just fell asleep. I didn't exactly sleep well last night, what with all that crap going on." At this point, the landlady sensing that no one had actually died but that there were indeed some very bad vibes in the room, crept quietly back downstairs. Carolyn decided not to go back to Peter's seminar, but to take Helen out for coffee. She felt responsible, somehow.

Back on the course however, Marion and Bea were becoming increasingly irritated by the amount of time Roberta and Priyanka kept looking at them and giggling. Bea, still feeling raw and vulnerable from events of the previous evening, became especially paranoid. She was sure that everyone in the room knew what had happened with her and Helen. She didn't even stop to think that the majority of people who attended an Internal Feng Shui course would be so self-absorbed, they wouldn't even notice *her* anyway. As Marion later pointed out, the clue was in the "Internal" bit.....

Bea blew on her camomile tea and lowered her voice as she spoke to Marion. "Does it show?" she asked.

"Does w*hat* show?" said Marion.

"That I haven't had sex for *ages*" said Bea, lowering her voice to a tiny whisper.

" God, yeah!" said Marion "The whole world can see it!"

"Oh Marion, I'm serious" said Bea. "It's imprinted in my aura, isn't it? People can sense these kind of things, can't they? D'ya think that's why Helen came on to me? Because she sort of felt sorry for me? "

"I think she came on to you, because she fancies you" said Marion.

Bea sighed deeply. "Maybe it's just men that don't fancy me anymore...." Marion looked at her beautiful, funny, lovely friend, and wondered what it was that had made this woman's self-esteem drop so low. All she could see in front of her was a very attractive, attentive and articulate lady – someone who had the "aura" of an extremely interesting person. Sex didn't come into it. Plenty of people wanted to get to know Bea – she was warm and engaging, but sure enough on this particular morning she had closed herself off and no one approached her. Marion realized Bea had been very shaken by the Helen incident. She didn't know exactly what deep, existential angst had been triggered, but this wasn't good.

Sensing the need to be gentle, Marion suggested Bea return to the bed and breakfast to have a little lie down, but Bea protested. First of all, Helen might be there and secondly she really needed some distraction, which was the whole point of this course. Glancing at the whiteboard, Marion saw that people were going to need to pair up after the break. With half her group of friends not talking to each other, that wasn't boding very well.

"I can work with you, can't I?" Bea asked Marion shakily. Marion said of course she could. Peter was concerned about that, however. He didn't feel that either Marion or Bea would be getting the best out of the course if they didn't work with other people. Peter asked where Marion's other friends were, but that involved too much explaining....

****

"We're visiting some friends who live just outside of Glastonbury" Priyanka told Roberta later. "It'd be lovely if you can join us". Roberta beamed. These highly enlightened beings thought of her as a friend. She could hardly believe her luck. She'd come to Glastonbury because she was interested in the course and general ambience. She'd never expected to meet such genuine soul-mates. How wonderful that they were so "elevated" – so knowledgeable and spiritual, so warm and welcoming. Roberta knew that she definitely wanted to get to know Priyanka and Peter better – meeting their friends was just an added bonus.

****

Carolyn very much wanted everyone to get together for lunch and talk. Life, not to mention the weekend was too short for everyone to be falling out. Bea, however, wanted a bit of time on her own. The incense in the lecture room made her feel very heady and dry-throated. She wanted some fresh air – some peace. Somewhere quiet and undisturbed that was away from other people's thoughts, and where she could just sit quietly with her own. It might have been a bit much to ask for in Glastonbury at the height of the spring equinox, but at least it was a pretty town to walk around.

Bea found herself heading towards the Chalice Well and found a little bench just in front of the entrance. She read some leaflets she'd collected. Glastonbury was steeped in myth and folklore and Christ and Mary Magdalene were said to have visited the Chalice Well and blessed the waters. Bea found the spiritual mythology fascinating. She wondered about how much time she'd also have to visit the Abbey and the little crystal shop, and...perhaps she really ought to just forgive Helen. It had all been a silly misunderstanding, quite comical really if she thought about it. She thought about the long absence of sexual encounters in her life, but if only Bea hadn't thought about it at that precise moment...

In a split second, across the street, Bea's past caught up with her. All the peace and lightness and gentle spring breeze she felt whilst going through her reading material was destroyed in an instant, as she caught a glimpse of a man over the road. There he was. Michael. The same Michael who had broken her heart nearly a decade ago, and left her feeling she could never make love to anyone else, ever again.

Bea hadn't expected this sighting to be quite so painful. At first she barely recognised him; the designer stubble had given way to a full, bushy beard, but the loud, luscious laugh was unmistakeably his. He was holding hands with a petite oriental woman who reminded Bea a bit of a young Yoko Ono. The woman was wearing a silver belly dancers belt and every time she laughed, the belt jangled in unison with Michael's laugh.

Much as Bea didn't want to see this, she couldn't help staring. A battle of head and heart ensued. Her head said, "Keep looking down. Just read your leaflets and they'll go away." Her heart said, "Look! Look! I am shattered all over again! I can't bear it, but I am compelled to look – I must, I have to....I have to endure such pain to the end of my days." Her heart won.

Just as Bea believed by her very sitting near the Chalice well and witnessing this, that some stigmata-type blood would seep through her blouse, Michael saw her. He froze in his tracks. The oriental woman tugged at his hand, anxious to know what had made him stop so abruptly. Bea tried to look neutral and not register any emotion and was surprised to see Michael look so nervous. Eventually he pulled his girlfriend over the road.

"Mi-Ling...this is an old friend of mine. Wasn't expecting to see her *here*...." Friend, thought Mi-Ling, friend? What a hideous, shallow, pathetic lie. Something had gone on here – maybe something long ago, but it was pretty obvious. People didn't look at each other like that unless "something had gone on." The something had gone on for well over a decade; that is, when Michael wasn't sleeping with other women or constantly criticising Bea and totally eroding her self-esteem, callously, cruelly and without remorse or redemption.

This was a relationship that really should have been put paid to the moment Bea realised just how calculating and manipulative the "love of her life" really was, but...that was just it. He *was* the love of her life. She had never had such powerful feelings for anyone – alas, they weren't requited. Whilst Bea felt a real "merging of souls", it was debateable whether or not Michael was actually capable of finding his soul, let alone merging it.

He looked happy with Mi-Ling, but then he looked pretty happy in the presence of any beautiful woman. As he had so frequently pointed out to her, Bea was not beautiful and it was heartbreaking how she believed him. He subtly chipped away at Bea's self-belief, until all that was left was an empty shell of her former self. It was only thanks to friends like Marion that Bea found the strength to hunt out that former self again.

Bea felt a sharp, stabbing pain somewhere around her solar plexus and had the urge to flee, but she was metaphysically glued to the ground beneath her.

"Bea? How are you?" Michael broke into a painful smile. It was a rhetorical question, if ever there was. But there was only one answer required – a sort of unspoken etiquette.

"Michael! I'm fine thank you – how are you?" Bea felt proud of herself that she could look her ex directly in the eye and answer him so clearly.

"Well...that's great!" said Michael, looking slightly disappointed. Mi-Ling tugged at Michael's hand again – she didn't like this exchange. "Anyway, we must get on" said Michael, without introducing Mi-Ling properly, "Got friends coming for dinner!" Bea stared. Michael now lived in Glastonbury? She quickly checked his and Mi-Ling's hands for wedding rings, but that would have been too weird. No – he would never commit to that. Bea stayed on the bench as Michael and Mi-Ling headed down the road, trying to understand her feelings. She'd seen him again. He was real. He seemed sort of – less handsome, somehow....

****

Helen was relieved that Bea smiled at her as the afternoon session commenced. At least it was a start to a reconciliation. Maybe doing some intensive healing work and working together that afternoon would help the women bond – help to clear up the tensions. It was Carolyn who felt unusually guilty. She felt bad about how she'd spoken to Marion, especially as it was Marion who was trying to resolve things. But the smell of wafting neroli oil and gentle flute music soon calmed everyone down, especially when Peter introduced the "Chanting Chakras" meditation.

He explained about the seven sacred chakras or energy centres and told everyone to visualise each chakra as though it were a spinning disc. Bea began to feel a bit queasy and grabbed Marion's arm. "I think you might be spinning your chakras too fast" whispered Marion. "They're chakras remember, not plates in a Greek restaurant...." Bea slowed down.

Carolyn felt an incredible spiral of energy circle up and through her body, almost knocking her out as it left somewhere through the middle of her forehead. Wow, I'll have a bit of that, she thought. What she didn't know at the time was that she had just experienced "Kundalini Rising", as Peter later explained to her.

In lay terminology, that meant you had activated some very powerful electrical circuiting in your own body which could quite literally be "mind blowing." In Carolyn's terminology, she had just had the best orgasm of her life.....

The previous day, Peter had spoken about how the energy surrounding your "aura" attracted similar energies. For example, if you were feeling down and depressed, then depressed people would be attracted to you. As Carolyn had had her "kundalini orgasm", a man over the other side of the room had been shuffling uncomfortably....

Marion wasn't entirely convinced by Peter's pontificating. She seemed to attract depressed and needy people when she was feeling particularly buoyant and uplifted. Perhaps the next lot of "open sessions" could shed some light on that. Course participants were asked to sit facing each other, cross-legged on the floor, whilst the person who was going to speak first had to place their hands on the up-turned palms of their partner.

"Something happened today" said Bea, as she placed her hands in Marion's. Peter looked across the room "But I can't tell you here. Later." Peter was practically sitting on top of them. "One of you needs to come and work with me" he said. "This is an exercise in openness and you already know each other pretty well." He took Bea to the other side of the room and Priyanka came and sat opposite Marion. Marion looked over at Bea and wondered if she really knew her as well as she thought she did. The environment was supposed to be protective and supportive. Maybe Marion would end up telling Priyanka intimate things about herself and Peter would know what had happened to Bea earlier...

****

The man who had been rather unsettled by Carolyn's orgasm was actually rather delighted to be partnered up with her. Placing her hands down on his, she said, "Psst – wanna know something really intimate about me?" The man nodded, hopefully. "Well, I've just had the best orgasm of my life."

"What, just now?" gasped the man.

"Shhh!" said Carolyn "Keep it down, or everyone will want one! Anyway, you're supposed to stay silent and let me talk until I've finished." The man nodded, excitedly. He'd definitely lucked out, getting to do this exercise with Carolyn. Much to his surprise and delight, he got to listen whilst Carolyn explained the history of her orgasms and how they always came very easily to her. He was dying to ask questions, but the instructions were to sit and listen and support the person talking.

This particular man had done these types of exercises in many workshops, many times before. He always seemed to wind up with a woman who would drone on about how abused she was in her last relationship or how hard she found it to find a suitable and committed partner, so partnering Carolyn was like a breath of fresh air. Across the other side of the room, Bea had decided to be disarmingly honest with Peter. He was right, she decided – sometimes it was better to tell your troubles to a stranger. She told Peter how she was still having issues with a long passed relationship, but didn't seem to have time to get to the bit where she'd just seen Michael in the street. Peter gently held Bea's hands and listened without judgement and complete neutrality.

This wasn't as easy as it seemed. Simply sitting and listening to someone – *really* listening in that way, without passing comment or registering emotion was much harder than it looked. Bea felt a tremendous release after opening up to Peter. It wasn't exactly that those seven years of pain melted away – more like the edges on them weren't so sharp.

Marion didn't have any particularly deep, dark secrets, at least not ones she felt she wanted to tell Priyanka. She leant forward and instead told Priyanka how she was feeling right now – how she was very irritated and annoyed with her friends. Priyanka registered no emotion, but was secretly delighted. It confirmed her thoughts about the "silly women group" and that she could go and have a good laugh about them with Roberta, later. Once Marion had finished speaking, Priyanka squeezed her hands, gently bowed her head, walked to the front of the room and rang a bell.

Peter explained this meant the couples should now swap around, so the other one could listen. Both Marion and Bea looked forward to what intimacies Priyanka and Peter might share with them, respectively.

Priyanka began. "I sometimes get annoyed with myself, when I fail to listen properly to what someone else is really telling me." Marion waited for more, but Priyanka then just seemed to continue talking without actually saying anything.

"You know when someone says something, but you know much more is hidden underneath? Well, I do sometimes beat myself up about that. After all, I'm trained. I'm a facilitator for spiritual work. Then, I have to remind myself that I am an evolving soul – that I am still learning, that I am still on my journey and it isn't the result." Then, Priyanka smiled and let go of Marion's hand.

That was *it*? That was Priyanka's most intimate stuff? Well, the girl was young, thought Marion. She obviously hadn't had much life experience. Ironically, across the other side of the room, Peter had said pretty much the same thing to Bea. Bea was very disappointed. She was glad she'd been able to voice her own pent-up emotions, but she was a caring person as well and had really wanted to take on the role of listener. What Peter had to share, if she was perfectly honest, seemed like a bit of a cliché. Priyanka rang the bell again, signalling the end of the session.

Bea and Marion held each other's gaze and knew what the other was thinking. They had trusted their teachers, but their teachers hadn't opened up to *them*. Neither of them quite knew what to make of this. It was a weird feeling – a bit like going for therapy. That was something Marion had done, prior to her interest in the Esoteric. She remembered baring her soul to a stranger shortly after her divorce, who quite frankly spent most of the hour looking extremely bored. Unfortunately, in a difficult emotional state at the time, Marion was persuaded this was part of the process and was advised to persevere. Many months later, much poorer and far more disturbed by her personal issues than she ever was before she began the therapy, Marion felt extremely grateful for the people who later became her personal therapists and only ever asked for a cup of tea as payment. Bea and Carolyn.

Friends had helped her through her deepest, darkest hours, as she had them. Roberta, keen to collate information on everything, briefly asked Marion about therapy. Marion just said it hadn't worked for her. Roberta gave her a look as if to say, well, you are just too old and fucked up now, anyway. So Marion gave Roberta the ex-therapist's number. Feeling belittled and angry, she wanted Roberta to suffer the painful extractions of her own emotions and bank account.

When Roberta asked Marion why she hadn't continued , Marion just said it had gotten too expensive. That was when Roberta came out with that horrible new age cliché about "finding the money if you *really* wanted to do something." Well, I obviously fucking well didn't want to do it then, did I? Thought Marion.

There were many things she could have done if she'd really wanted to do them. Like selling her flat, sorting her job out, looking for her son.... Sometimes Marion didn't know what she really wanted to do. She'd sometimes lose sight of how much was her own mind, and how much was the conditioning of society and what was expected of a woman her age.

As far as society was concerned, she had well outlived her use. She'd been a wife and mother and fitted in a career in between. She wanted to carry on working, but could feel the pressure to move out of the way to make place for someone younger and at a time in her life when she felt she could really give the most of herself – all her years of experience and wisdom and learning.....it seemed there was nowhere for her to go.

Not having a family to care for and not really wanting a life of allotments and cats, Marion spent time with friends, travelled, carried on working whilst she could. At least at the University she could pretend she was just some eccentric old professor and therefore worth listening to.

Marion swung the conversation back round to Roberta, seeing as she didn't really want to talk about herself anymore. It was too depressing.

"How are you getting on?"

"Brilliant" said Roberta. "Absolutely loving it. I'm so glad Bea let me know about this – I've wanted to come to Glastonbury for ages."

"You seem to be getting on very well with Priyanka" Marion said with a slight hint of derision. Roberta reddened slightly. "Yes...we do get on well. And actually, that's what I was coming to talk to you about. I won't be joining you girls for the end of course get-together."

"What?" said Marion, taken aback "But this is our last evening. It's traditional that we all go for something to eat together, and discuss the course."

"I know....." Roberta looked downwards. "But I'm not part of your tradition, am I? I'm a new comer and I've just met these wonderful people, and...." Marion grunted. They hadn't seen Roberta outside of the course all weekend, anyway. Would it really be such a loss? Besides, Priyanka was much closer to Roberta in age and maybe she really needed to hang out with some younger people who were full of joie de vivre and naivety – not cynical, "grumpy old women."

"So" asked Marion, "What is it you're doing that you can't join us?"

Roberta looked a bit awkward, yet pleased with herself at the same time. "Well....Peter and Priyanka have invited me for dinner. Actually, to the house of some of their friends."

"I see" said Marion. "Well, enjoy it. I'll see you at the coach stop in morning, then."

Roberta nodded. After her "intimate" one-to-one session with Priyanka, Marion was glad to be going out to dinner with her own friends. Roberta was in for one hell of a dull evening, if Priyanka's "confessions" had been anything to go by. Marion thought she'd better go and break the news to Bea, Carolyn and Helen.

Just before Peter led the wrap-up session, Roberta told Priyanka she was really looking forward to their evening. "Me too" said Priyanka. "I can't wait for you to meet Michael and Mi-Ling."

****

CHAPTER 4

STILL GLASTONBURY

It was a beautiful spring evening as Peter opened the sun roof of his car and drove along little country lanes to reach Michael and Mi-Ling's house. "It's so kind of you to invite me" said Roberta, unable to believe that she alone out of everyone on the course had received the special treatment.

"The cottage isn't far" said Peter, "But I usually get lost around the back of these windy lanes, so Priyanka always has to remind me which way to go."

Priyanka sighed. "We've only been coming here for three years now. Michael is an ex-student of Peter's." Roberta was feeling very excited now. She had gotten thoroughly into the whole Internal Feng Shui concept and the thought of meeting more spiritually advanced people really excited her. Eventually, after only one nearly-wrong turning, Peter pulled up in front of the most idyllic little home, complete with thatched roof and wisteria.

"I know, gorgeous, isn't it?" said Priyanka. Roberta gasped. If she could ever picture in the deepest recesses of her imagination her dream home, then this would be it. She breathed in deeply as she stepped out the car. A heady aroma of jasmine, honeysuckle and fresh country air hit her nostrils as she surveyed the beautiful front garden.

It had been lovingly and carefully attended by an expert gardener with all the colours and flowers planted by someone who looked like they knew a lot about Feng Shui. As Priyanka led Roberta into the cottage, the aroma changed to that of a most delicious stew. Mi-Ling immediately threw her arms around Priyanka and kissed her on both cheeks, then greeted Roberta as if she were also an old friend. Roberta immediately felt at home.

"Where's Michael?" asked Priyanka.

"At the store – he shouldn't be long" replied Mi-Ling. "You know him – can never have enough Cider!"

Priyanka laughed, "But Peter and I have bought loads!" Roberta started to feel guilty. She hadn't brought anything for her hosts.

"No worry – no worry at all" said Mi-Ling. "Your company is more than enough." Then she smiled the warmest, twinkly smile and returned to her cooking.

"Shall I show you around?" asked Priyanka, "You don't mind, do you Mi-Ling?" Mi-Ling shook her head and Priyanka led Roberta forward into the front living room that was much larger than it appeared from the outside of the compact cottage. Beautiful wooden ornaments and crystals bedecked the shelves and coffee table and books about the solar system, travel and religions were dotted strategically around the room. Roberta sighed and thought how perfect it would be to live there. Whilst Priyanka and Roberta sat in the living room, Peter started to unload some herbs and vegetables from his bag.

He went into the kitchen, ostensibly to help Mi-Ling. He knew his way around his friends' kitchen well. As Peter started chopping ingredients to prepare some kind of broth, Roberta commented on how good the food smelt. "Always does" said Priyanka. Then, she leaned in. "You know, I'd *really* like to get to know you better, Roberta. I know we've only had a short bit of time together this weekend, but I really feel like we're soul-mates, y'know? Why don't you tell me a bit more about yourself whilst we're waiting for Michael to get back?"

Roberta felt honoured. Priyanka wasn't only assistant to Peter, one of the most renowned spiritual course leaders of the day, but she also knew many other amazing people and could have been a gateway to that kind of lifestyle. Roberta started telling Priyanka about her studies, where she lived and who she'd been dating. Priyanka smiled sweetly, but that wasn't really what she wanted to know.

"I mean" she asked, "Tell me -what *really* makes you tick. You strike me as being a very sensual sort of woman." Then, she took a cup of what looked like some soup from Peter and handed the pottery goblet to Roberta, telling her to drink. It was like something from a magical fairy tale.

****

Marion shuffled in her seat as she drank her organic latte in Avachar. Not many places were open for dinner on Glastonbury High Street and you had to get there early if you wanted a full dinner. "What's up?" asked Helen. "Changed your mind about the ethically sourced Bean Bonanza? I wouldn't blame you. Get caught short on the coach tomorrow, and you'll be in real trouble."

Normally Marion would have laughed, but she just shrugged and stared out the window. She'd been thinking about Roberta." I do think it's rather rude of her", she said. "She's not made any effort , and even if she was making a new friend with that sullen Priyanka girl, I think she could at least have been with us this evening. Especially as Carolyn went to all that trouble to get her the last place on the course – she seems like a very ungracious girl, to me."

Bea defended her friend. "I'm not bothered she's not here. I have all of your company, and besides, why shouldn't Roberta make new friends? When in Glastonbury, do as Glastonbury does, n' all that. She's probably just in awe of all the things we've done and the people she's met. She's not as old and cynical as us, remember? Don't you remember when you were like that, Marion?" Marion couldn't deny that she'd been enamoured of her first "Glastonbury experience." When the coach had first pulled in at the bus stop near the Abbey, the town seemed completely dead in the grey gloom and wet. Once she'd sat down in a cafe, everything came along. She sat besides several lively Portuguese women about to partake in a "Mother, Maiden, Crone" course and as she got talking to them, Marion had realised there was no such thing as small talk in this town.

She rarely knew what people did for a living or even what their names were – everyone was far more interested in knowing if you'd ever astral travelled and what your plans were for the new age of Lightworkers. It made a refreshing change from offices and banks and stressful lives back home. Even though Marion remembered how she felt as a young woman in the town, she was still unhappy.

For some reason, Roberta's behaviour felt like a personal snub to her. She tried to put her finger on it. Was it really that now she had reached this time of life, Marion had become a grumpy old woman? Was she really so resentful of the young and beautiful? Surely all the workshops and spiritual training she'd done would have alerted her to the fact that youth and physical beauty were just an illusion and would fade.

But that knowledge did not help her in her present moment. Marion pushed her plate aside, declining to eat as she realised what was actually really eating *her*. She wanted a man. She'd tried to deny it and jollied along in her single life, pretending she enjoyed her work and social life so much that she really didn't have a great big void in her heart, but that was one fat, dirty lie.

She longed for the warmth and intimacy again and wondered why it was ok for Bea to wear her heart on her sleeve whilst she was supposed to tuck hers firmly away. Marion was supposed to be the strong one – the older, wiser woman; the supportive friend. What about *her* when *she* needed support?

Marion suddenly felt very ungracious. She had these wonderful friends and that should have been enough, but it wasn't. Helen noticed how glum Marion was looking and also looked hungrily at the left over dinner. Marion pushed it towards her. "Blimey, Marion, you're miles away. What's up?" asked Carolyn. Marion sighed deeply. She just didn't want to go into it – it sounded so, sort of – trite.

"Oh girls...you know how much I like being here with all of you. It's just the thought of going home to all that marking and research and it being such a long time before I can be here again."

Carolyn leaned towards her friend. "You know the girls will always be around, whether in Glastonbury or elsewhere. You know we'll have cappuccinos on the table for you any time of day, along with tissues, wine and big shoulders." But Carolyn knew her friend and she knew there was something else wrong. She decided to shake Marion up a bit. "Maybe...maybe it's time for you to move on." That did shake Marion.

"Move on? At *my* age?" She knew she was lucky to still be working at the University. Many younger colleagues had no jobs and yet were expected to be able to work for another twenty years or so before being anywhere close to drawing pensions. Carolyn, however, wasn't going to take any prisoners.

"Move on at *any* age" she said. "Don't you remember what Peter said on our first day, in the first lesson? Whatever age you are, it's no excuse to remain stuck. Remember the "seven excuses?" They should all be on that list – *if* you were taking notes, that is..." Marion wasn't in the mood for this.

"Carolyn...I'm depressed. Don't you get that? I took copious notes as it happens, but no positive affirmations are gonna shift this. Right now, I just need alcohol. And for you to stop being so bloody positive." Carolyn looked agitated, but she also knew Marion didn't stay in these moods for long.

"I'll get the bill" said Carolyn, "Some pubs might be open near the Backpackers hostel, otherwise we'll just have to hitch-hike out of town."

"Hitch-hiking? What fun!" said Bea. Helen was less happy. She'd just wanted an early night, what with the coach departing early the following morning. She wasn't sure she could cope with three hung-over friends at that time in the morning, and for a four hour coach journey. Perhaps if they were in for a heavy night she could just feign a headache, and sneak back. Besides, all that stuff with Bea had been incredibly awkward, even though Bea seemed to have gotten over it. Reluctantly, Helen followed the others out of the somewhat disappointing restaurant and down the high street to some more appropriate refreshment for the occasion.

****

Roberta's head started to spin. She had no idea why she was suddenly starting to feel dizzy as she felt so well and relaxed the rest of the evening. "Why don't you go and have a little lie down?" suggested Mi-Ling. "Let me show you upstairs." Roberta had to lean on the banister as she followed Mi-Ling up, and then she collapsed on the quilted bed the minute she reached it. "Oh dear" muttered Roberta, "I really can't think what this is. I'm not usually ill."

"Its ok" said Mi-Ling gently. "You just stay there as long as you like. Maybe it's the Glastonbury air...." Roberta tried to laugh, but felt like she was going to throw up. She covered her mouth with her hand and Mi-Ling went back downstairs. Peter was rolling a huge spliff.

"Bloody magic mushroom virgin" he muttered, "Didn't take her for that type."

"Maybe it's just as well" said Michael, "We can start the evening quicker, if you get my drift..." Peter gave a nasty leer and wry smile. He got the drift, all right. Michael walked across the room and put his arms around Mi-Ling's waist, then started to kiss the back of her neck. "You think she's pretty, don't you?" he said as he stroked his girlfriend's shoulders. Mi-Ling nodded in affirmation. "Well, darling – I might just go and check on our guest... Priyanka's done well, don't you think?"

Mi-Ling really didn't like these evenings, but she went along with them to please Michael. She had to. After all, she was so very far away from home....It was no secret that Michael liked to have sex with lots of people. He always promised Mi-Ling that everything he practiced was very safe and he wanted her to join in. At first she'd seemed like his dream girlfriend, throwing off her clothes with gusto at *those* parties, and then coming home and cooking for him.

He chuckled to himself as he thought about bumping into Bea earlier that afternoon. Poor, naive Bea. She was oh, so in love with him. Michael doubted he could ever be in love with anyone, but he could charm anyone into thinking he might be. He found Mi-Ling attractive and engaging, but he didn't love her. They'd been an item for almost five years, which wasn't unusual for him – he may have had many lovers, but alongside these were long-term girlfriends.

The security and doting was actually something Michael couldn't do without and therefore he attracted needy, dependent women. Sometimes he was upfront about his casual sex life and sometimes he'd just play ball anyway. Bea was loving, loyal, intelligent, funny and attractive, but she'd started looking her age and worst of all she was becoming very insecure. Michael never told Bea about his "other" life – she was just too emotionally fragile. Even so, she was astute and probably suspected anyway, but it made her demanding and clingy. She had to go.

Nonetheless, when Michael broke Bea's heart, it was devastating and seemed to come out the blue. She'd seemed happy enough cruising along – staying at Michael's place two or three times a week, or he'd stay with her. Even though they'd never discussed living together, Bea was sure he was "the one" and was certain, in her deluded and needy state that it was only a matter of time before Michael mentioned marriage.

Therein lay the problem. A matter of time. Bea's girlfriends seemed to put time restrictions on everything. "Two years max" said one. "If he hasn't proposed by then forget it – he never will." The same girlfriend had been living in sin for six years...Another friend was harsher.

"Leave. Go. He doesn't love you." Bea was hurt and angry. Michael bought her flowers, took her for dinner, always remembered birthdays and was charming to her friends – how could anyone say he didn't love her?

"It's something in the eye" someone once told her. "You can always spot a confirmed bachelor."

All these comments were why Bea liked hanging out with older women like Marion and Carolyn. They'd been through the mill where relationships were concerned and they weren't judgemental. Neither of them had ever banged on about Bea's biological clock and as they were both so self-sufficient and not at all desperate, they were more relaxed and fun to hang out with. Bea knew Marion didn't like Michael, even though Marion never said anything about him. When he finally admitted infidelity, it was a massive shock to Bea. And a few years later, he'd moved in with Mi-Ling......

At this very moment in time, Michael wasn't even sure the party in the cottage was going to get started. He climbed the stairs and crept into one of the bedrooms where Roberta was lying down holding her head moaning. Michael sat beside her and took her hand. "Just coming to see how you are" he said.

"Head....spinning...." murmured Roberta.

"There, there – you'll be fine" said Michael, as he moved down to the other end of the bed and propped Roberta's feet up on his lap. Then, he gently began to massage them.

"Oh – that's nice" said Roberta. The room was still spinning round as she felt his hand move up her calf muscle and then up her thigh. "What are you...what...." she muttered.

"Shh – you just relax now" said Michael as he tugged at her pants. Groggy as she was, Roberta sensed she was in trouble. She tried to push his hand away, but he was too strong and she was too weak.

"No..no...please....stop...." Peter crept upstairs, knelt across the bed and started to unbutton Roberta's blouse. Her pleas became more frantic now, although she could barely let out a stifled scream or move. She attempted to push both men away, and as Michael tried to climb on top of her, all she could make out at the end of the bed was Priyanka standing there with her arms folded and laughing.

Roberta desperately tried to reach out a hand towards Priyanka, but Peter pushed it back down and then began to caress her breasts with his free hand. "Stop...." sobbed Roberta, "Stop...", but if anyone heard her, they ignored her, anyway.

Suddenly, someone else yelled "STOP!" and at this person's command, everyone did. "Leave her alone!" shouted Mi-Ling. "She doesn't want this!" She looked angrily at the party. Reluctantly, Michael and Peter climbed off the bed.

"Frigid bitch" muttered Michael, under his breath. Somewhere, deep from within, Roberta found the strength to get up off the bed and pulling her pants back up, she shoved her way past the men and down the stairs. The front door was locked, but Mi-Ling ran down and unlocked it. Roberta tripped over the doorstep and then she ran...and ran. Her legs felt like lead, but she still ran, in any direction, anywhere, until she found a main road. There, she threw up and then sat down and sobbed.

****

"Wheershh the bloody hotel?" Helen slurred her words as the women trundled up the high street. She hadn't meant to drink, but that plan never quite manifested....

Carolyn roared with laughter. "Hotel? Ha ha! It's a miniature b&b – the only one in Glastonbury where you can get sausages!"

"Zozages" said Marion, stumbling up the hill.

"Gaaah" said Bea, "Who put rocks in my rucksack?"

"What rocks?" asked Marion.

"I'm sure it wasn't this heavy when we went *in* the pub" said Bea.

"That's your body that's got heavier" said Carolyn, "Always does after a few pints of stout!" The others laughed, raucously. Helen burped loudly.

"I think we're losssht!"

"Na" said Carolyn, "Just a few steps more." Bea pulled her rucksack off and begged everyone to slow down for a moment. She rummaged in the bag and to her surprise, found three bottles of wine.

"How the hell did these get in here?" she asked .

Carolyn roared with laughter again. "Silly landlord, making merry with his chums...turned his back and voila!"

"Oh my God – you *stole* them?" said Bea.

"Oh yes!" said Carolyn.

"We'll get arrested!" gasped Bea. She suddenly slumped down by the side of the road and too exhausted to move any more, moved the rucksack beneath her head and made a little bed right in the middle of the street. Marion tried kicking her feet.

"C'mon sweetie – we've got comfy beds to go to. Not comfy down there." Bea moaned and reluctantly got up. The women huffed and puffed uphill until they reached a grassy verge. In the distance, Marion heard what sounded like sobbing. "My God – what's that?" she said, sobering up a little.

"Must be a cat or somethin' this time of night" said Carolyn.

"No...no" said Marion, listening more closely. "It's a person. I'm sure of it. A woman." Helen, relieved that she could find a reason to get down on her hands and knees, pushed her way through some blades of grass and sure enough found a person. It was a young woman sitting slumped over, crying into her lap. Her skirt looked ripped and she didn't have any shoes on.

"You alright?" asked Helen. The woman looked up. "Oh Christ – *Roberta!*" Hearing that, Carolyn, Marion and Bea immediately rushed into the grass, although there wasn't much light at the side of the road. Roberta was just about visible by the shape of her bob and flowery skirt. No one was really in a fit state to look after her, but seeing her like that sobered them all up pretty fast.

"My God – what happened?" asked Bea. It was quite clear that Roberta had been attacked. Bea put her arms around Roberta and trod in a little pool of vomit. "Ugg – have you been drinking, as well?"

Roberta shook her head."They gave me...something....it tasted funny. Made me feel dizzy..." Bea really didn't want to think about it. It looked like some kind of date rape. But Roberta was going out with Peter and Priyanka, so what had happened after she had left? Helping Roberta onto her feet, Bea put her arm around her waist and dragged her down the road as Helen went to get help. "Gotta get back to the room..." muttered Roberta.

"Yes, but ours. Not yours" said Bea. "You can't be on your own tonight."

Bea offered Roberta her bed whilst she made up one of blankets on the floor. She was so heady from the alcohol anyway, that she slept right through the night. It was unspoken that no one would try and question Roberta until the light of morning. Marion, however, felt uncomfortable about that. She thought that they should go to the police as quickly as possible, but they'd all been drinking and Roberta was asleep...she needed to sleep.

Marion tossed and turned uneasily as she had a feeling she shouldn't go back to London in the morning. She felt like she needed to stay in Glastonbury a while longer, but couldn't pin point why. It made no sense – there was a pile of work waiting at the University and a house that badly needed cleaning. But if visits to this unique little town had taught her anything, then it was to trust her instincts.

She got up earlier than the others, crept down to reception and then asked if she might be able to stay on another few nights. As luck would have it, the bed and breakfast wasn't busy the following week. Quite what had compelled Marion to do this, she had no idea. But the weekend course and training kept playing over in her head, as of course so did what had just happened to Roberta.

One of her meditations during the weekend had been particularly intense. It involved the letting go mentally of all your "must do's" and surrendering, totally. What was your inner self telling you? For Marion, it was telling her to stay – if she did, something would come to light. "I'm not coming back with you" she told the others, as she unpacked her case in the morning.

"What?" said Carolyn "What do you mean? Just now, or not ever?"

"I want to stay – just for a little while" replied Marion. "I feel....I feel like I *need* to be here. I can't explain why, exactly – it's just something that I'm being guided to do."

"Are you going to look for somewhere to buy here?" asked Bea. Roberta sat up. As far as she was concerned, buying a cottage in Glastonbury was not a good idea.

"Good grief, no" said Marion. "All I said was, a few days. I know I've been here loads of times before, but there's so much happening – so much to explore. I feel like we've all been cooped up in a room navel gazing over the weekend and I really want to get out and about a bit...go shopping, go walking, sit in cafes and talk to new people....."

"Are we not enough for you?" asked Bea.

"Oh, don't be silly" said Marion. "You girls mean the world to me. You know that. But I need a bit of 'Marion time'. I've been so bogged down with work and finances, that this is probably going to be my only get-away all year. The old bank account isn't looking that good, so I can't afford another holiday."

"I wonder if Holis are still going" said Bea, "I heard they were in trouble." A little smile formed in the corner of Marion's mouth. Roberta looked away. Bea sat on the corner of the bed and gently pushed Roberta's hair back off her face.

"Are you ok?" she asked. "I'm sorry we were all a bit useless last night. We were all a bit the worse for the wear. Are you feeling up to the coach?"

"I'm not an invalid – just got a few scratches" Roberta retorted. She wasn't ready to disclose the full story of the evening – she felt a bit ashamed. She'd abandoned her friends and paid a rather large price.

"I meant, how are you feeling?" asked Bea.

"Sorry to snap" said Roberta. "I'm feeling a bit nauseous. I took something last night... don't know what it was...."

No one pushed Roberta for details, but Bea was concerned that they should do more. "Should we call anyone? The police?" she asked. Roberta shook her head. She could vaguely remember being groped, but thanks to Mi-Ling nothing worse had happened. It was her own fault for trusting people she didn't even know and drinking that funny smelling "tea." She actually felt quite embarrassed now, and what would the police say, anyway?

She was off her head, had taken drugs – just another young woman who had foolishly got herself caught up in the laid-back atmosphere of the place and workshop and gone home with strangers. It was her word against theirs. Anyway, Peter was a renowned teacher with a long established reputation.

Some of the evening came back to her.....she remembered Mi-Ling telling the men to stop and Priyanka just standing there grinning in an almost manipulative, evil sort of way... Priyanka, her friend.... She'd strung Roberta along. Groomed her. Made her feel singled out and special and...chosen. She wondered why Mi-Ling had "saved" her. Did she feel sorry for Roberta, or was she fed up with doing this?

Roberta tried to remember Mi-Ling. She was different to the others – something about her... she seemed somehow, kind of....trapped... But the image of Mi-Ling and the whole bedroom scenario faded and with such a hazy image, how could she be sure – how could she tell the police anything... Suddenly Roberta felt like she was going to be sick, cupped her hand over her mouth and ran into the bathroom.

"Oh dear" said Carolyn. "Mushrooms. Can be a bugger first time you take them." Marion looked shocked.

Roberta came out the bathroom. "I wouldn't have drunk it if I'd known" she said.

"Look" said Helen "Why don't we all go down for breakfast? I'm sure if we pay for Roberta, she can have some too. That is, if you feel like eating anything, Roberta...." Roberta surprisingly nodded.

"Full English might be just the ticket. Especially if they do sausages." Carolyn affirmed that they did and that the breakfast was pretty good. As they all edged downstairs, Bea was curious about Marion. Why had she decided to stay on? Marion could still only put it down to a feeling. All she could say was that she felt she was about to meet someone really important. Bea asked if she thought she was about to meet her soul-mate.

"Soul-mate?" asked Marion. She hadn't thought of it.

"Well, just make sure he has a younger brother for me!" Bea laughed and trotted down the rickety staircase. Who *am* I going to meet, thought Marion.

****

As the National Express coach trundled beyond rural areas and picked up speed on the motorway, so Roberta finally felt like telling her friends some details of the previous evening. When she mentioned the names Michael and Mi-Ling and that it was their cottage she had been to, it was Bea's turn to feel sick....

****

Marion didn't want to admit to it, but she was feeling a glorious feeling of freedom being on her own. Just being able to wander through that little bit of West Country unencumbered by other people with their emotions or deadlines, was a wonderful feeling. She decided to explore a little further afield that day and take an excursion into the nearby town of Street.

She'd heard that the entire town contained streets full of shoe shops, but couldn't quite believe that. There must have been other things to buy, surely? Marion had a local bus map, but instead decided to walk. A tinge of wetness hung in the air as it always seemed to do in that part of the world, no matter the time of year.

As she walked, Marion actually enjoyed the coolness. Lacing up her walking boots and throwing her rucksack over her shoulder, she walked on the grass verges alongside the main "A" road, and followed the traffic out of town. A car horn beeped and a little white van pulled in at the side of the road. Stephen the Wizard was the driver.

Marion found something incongruous about that – a Wizard driving a van. If Stephen did have transport of any kind, surely it would have been a white horse and not a white van? Nonetheless, it was definitely him.

"Hello there!" he called out. "Need a lift?"

"Well, hello!" said Marion. "I thought you were only here for the solstice."

"I thought you were, too!" said Stephen, "Where are you off to?" Marion replied that she wasn't entirely sure. A disembodied female voice suddenly came from the back of the van, saying there was plenty of room. The back doors pushed open, and Marion saw four young hippy girls wearing very little and smoking joints.

"Um thanks, but I need some air" said Marion. So, that was what druids got up to....no wonder Stephen had stayed beyond the solstice....

"Well, if you're sure" said Stephen. "Might see you around, then?" Marion nodded and waved goodbye to the girls. She thought what Bea had said about meeting her soul-mate. Well, it definitely wasn't Stephen. As she walked on, fears and self-doubt crept up on her. She was sixty years old. She might have been in "beautiful condition" as Michael Caine the actor had once described an older woman in a film, but so many women these days were beautiful, goddamit.

How could she have come this far in her life, never met "the one" and yet still believe she would? Marion stopped walking and let her rucksack fall off her back, as she spied a wooden bench by the side of the road. Thinking about your love life demanded the stillness of quiet contemplation. She thought back to her husband and wondered if she had ever truly been in love.

Was it just strong physical attraction or had there been more? Did she really get married because her ovaries were getting out of control, even though by the standards of modern women she was still quite young when she gave birth? It had seemed late to have a child, back then.

After all, Marion loved her husband, didn't she....? How could she not? He was handsome, intelligent, a good provider...he wanted to be a father, he was popular with the neighbours...he liked weekend walks and cosy dinner parties... he was a good catch. It was all there on paper, beautifully laid out. All Marion had to do was sign on the dotted line.

She did that the day she walked down the aisle at St Mary's in Buckingham. Most brides will say their wedding day passed by in a blurry haze, but Marion remembered every last detail. Five minutes before the ceremony, she was in the rose gardens with Carolyn, her then bridesmaid, heaving up over some Damasks. Carolyn said it was natural to feel nervous. All the formality of the occasion was daunting, after all and although not a huge wedding, Marion had chosen a traditional ceremony with a Church of England service. Alan had chosen the hymns. Marion knew them all from school, but wasn't sure that the lyrics, "He closed the yawning gates of hell" were quite right for the occasion....

She, however, had chosen the church, bridesmaids, flowers and most of the guest list, so it was only right that Alan should choose something. He was the wrong man. Marion knew as she went up the aisle. But, like so many before her, she felt she couldn't let everyone down, never mind herself. Her father having passed away some years previously, Marion was given away by her uncle and as she stood beside her husband-to-be, everyone was smiling.

It should be the most wonderful moment, but it seemed to play in slow motion like a nightmare. Marion kept thinking someone would shout, "It's ok – you can wake up now", but before she knew it, she was saying "I do" and a gold band was on her finger. She trembled as Alan slid the ring onto her.

"Keep still" he said, somewhat angrily, "Or I can't get a hold on you...." A hold on you. She seemed to be determined that this ring should not go on – that she should not be owned. The more Alan told her to relax, the more she tensed her hand, so that it felt like rigor mortis was setting in. Alan faced the congregation, and red-faced, tried to make a joke.

The vicar tried to jolly things along, and in the moment when Marion let her determined concentration slip, Alan got her and the deed was done. Marion closed her eyes....her wedding....yes...she remembered it well....

The reception, the dancing, the honeymoon.....they'd had a good marriage, hadn't they? Despite the wedding, it was love, wasn't it? A little beam of sunshine tried to force its way through the West Country cloud. A little sunbeam of hope. So, her marriage had failed. So what. Many marriages failed. Marion had been a wife and mother, even if she was no longer a wife and had no communication with her only son.

Years of disappointment may have made her cynical, but she was still an optimist, by nature. The air was clear and fresh and unpolluted and the smell of freshly cut grass was quite delicious. Marion placed aside thoughts of her ex-husband, her past lovers....all these years of attending courses and reading spiritual matter; a man in her life for a spot of recreation now just seemed empty, and meaningless...

There needed to be more. Until that moment came, however, she was going to buy some shoes.

****

Half-way between the West of England and London, Roberta slowly unravelled more about what had happened. Knowing that their "spiritual mentor" was their friends' abuser, made the women feel ill. They'd paid a lot of hard-earned money to study that weekend with Peter, took the lessons seriously and were all there for the purpose of self-development and to improve their lives.

Helen pointed out that whilst Peter wasn't exactly holier than thou, he had still been a very good teacher. Certainly his behaviour was abhorrent, but they shouldn't view the weekend as a complete waste of time. They could take the learning, and leave the teacher. Diplomatic as she was trying to be, this didn't go down too well. Carolyn became pensive for a moment.

She asked Roberta if she had any contact details for Priyanka. "We can bombard her mercilessly" said Carolyn. Sadly Roberta had no contacts. It was only just now that she realised how careful Priyanka had been about that. "I feel strongly" continued Carolyn, "That we ought to expose these people so that other young women don't end up in the same situation." She was angry.

Roberta sighed. "If people don't want to be found, they won't be. We have Peter's website details, but that's all. They can fold their company, resurrect it under a different name – anything."

"Wait a minute...." said Helen. "You said you went round to some friends of theirs, right? A cottage? Maybe we can't find Peter and Priyanka, but we could find the friends. Do you remember anything about where it was? " Roberta nodded. Bea shuddered as she realised this was all becoming a very nasty reality. Michael. Her Michael. This was who he really was.

****

Marion had never seen so many shoe shops in her life. The town of Street should have been re-named "Foot." These were not shops for a city girl who needed killer stilettos, but the most perfect little independent shops for cheap and basic leather sandals, granny type moccasins and walking footwear. Marion tried to imagine what kind of people came here, but they must have been quite different to the types that flocked to Glastonbury.

In Glastonbury everywhere sold crystals – here they sold shoes. One town was for the esoteric and spiritual part of your life and the other for the solid, practical part of your body on which everything else balanced....

After the headiness of the weekend training, Marion found it refreshing to be somewhere more normal. Most people walking around seemed to be about her age, which was hardly surprising, given the old-fashioned styles of footwear. Marion went into a shop and tried on some slip-ons. The shop assistant told Marion about the huge retail village, only a short walk away. They sold all kinds of items here.

Marion had never been to a "retail village." That sounded like a shopping woman's dream, and also a bit scary at the same time. A village of commercial hype and credit cards. There would be all sorts of interesting things to buy in close proximity, yet Marion could not quite concede the greedy consumerism. The juxtapositions played in her head. Still, here she was, so why not pay a visit?

The retail village turned out to be everything and more. There were even more shoes, but there was also a plethora of leather handbags, hundreds of shoppers and weary children on their school holidays, being dragged around for school bags. It reminded Marion too much of London. Marion decided that one pair of sandals was actually enough, and the perfect way to wear them in, would be to walk back to Glastonbury.

It was late afternoon and her tummy was rumbling. The organic bread and home-made cheeses at 'Avachar' were worth a hike back for. Marion slipped off her back pack and sat down to pull on her new sandals. As she did up one strap over her ankle, she heard a man's voice.

"Very pretty" he said. She looked up to see a swarthy-looking, not too tall a man with a thin black moustache and a little bit of goatee beard. He had big, brown, very twinkly eyes and Marion immediately noticed that his skin was incredibly smooth.

"Thank you" said Marion.

"May I?" asked the man, pointing to the spare seat beside Marion. Marion smiled and showed an upturned palm, to indicate that yes, he was welcome to sit. It was unspoken that you spoke to strangers in Glastonbury – probably less so in a heaving retail village. "I couldn't help noticing" the man said, "That your buckle does up with a little flower. A fleur de lis, in fact. I wondered if that was the reason you bought the sandals....?"

Marion stared at the stranger. What an odd thing to ask. He had a slight hint of a foreign accent which Marion couldn't quite place and he must have had impeccable eyesight if he noticed something as small as a shoe buckle, because the flowers really were tiny. "Do you know what?" she said, "I really hadn't noticed these were fleur de lis. Not until you mentioned it. So, to answer your question – no. That wasn't why I bought them. I bought them because they were comfortable, a good price and I like the colour."

The man laughed. "Perfectly good reasons" he said.

"I'm curious...." said Marion. "What is it about this flower?"

"Ah...." the man took a long, deep sigh. "It is of deep significance. At least, to people like me. No matter, just thought I'd ask." Who was he? Who was this strange, stranger? It was rare that you could look someone you had only just met directly in the eye and immediately warm to them. Marion felt very comfortable with this man. He extended his hand by way of introduction.

"I'm Salvatore" he said.

"Marion" said Marion. An incredible warmth emanated from the man's hand – it was almost like an electrical charge going down Marion's arm. She looked directly at him again, this time studiously taking in his face. "Have we met before?" she asked.

"Not unless you've been to Tuscany" said Salvatore. Marion hadn't. "It's where my spaceship is parked most of the time" he said, ready to gauge Marion's reaction. She laughed.

"So – you're Italian" she said. "Do they have many fleur de lis there? I thought they were French. What do they mean for you?"

"We eat them" said Salvatore, after which he chuckled deeply and warmly and Marion did too.

"I hope you're not going to eat my footwear" she said.

"No – they're leather" said Salvatore, "I'm vegetarian."

"In that case, I'll keep them on" said Marion. "Talking of eating.....actually, I'm really hungry. I don't know any nice vegetarian places around here. Come to think of it, I don't know any places around here at all. I was about to walk back into Glastonbury where I'm staying, for some lunch."

"Well, what do you know?" said Salvatore. "I'm staying in Glastonbury as well. "Shall we walk together?"

****

The coach pulled into Victoria station. Bea's head and stomach churned simultaneously, as she thought about Michael and what he had done. Her beloved ex was colluding with a corrupt spiritual mentor to groom young women for orgies. It was all a bit much. Bea had dealt with bumping into Michael again – how she'd cope with this, she wasn't quite sure.

She felt quite sickened by the behaviour of the women, as well. Priyanka had befriended Roberta and taken her away from the rest of them, impressing her with her "other worldly-ness." She'd gotten Roberta to trust her, and then completely betrayed her. Confusion overwhelmed Bea. Like Helen had suggested, she had actually got a lot out of the course and ironically, the exercises Peter had suggested were helping her deal with getting over Michael.

The affirmations and chanting were not dissimilar to the healing work that an alleged Red Indian Shaman had done with her. Bea knew that New Age methods worked for her, but she'd never stopped to consider the corruption or charlatans of the movement. Only Marion did that. It was Carolyn who finally helped Bea relieve some of her inner turmoil. She told Bea to remember what Peter had said about "taking what you need and leaving the rest." Some teachings were beneficial and sound. Sadly, the behaviour of some of the teachers wasn't. It was important to learn to discern which was which.

****

Marion and Salvatore reached Avachar by 1pm which was a perfect time for lunch, but terrible timing for Marion to remember that she had forgotten to phone the University. She was supposed to be in Brighton at 3pm. Immediately flying into a panic, Marion tore out of the cafe and rummaged in her bag for her mobile. Salvatore ran out after her. "Marion – are you ok? Can I help?"

"Oh my God, Oh my God" was all Marion kept repeating, as she realised she must have left her phone in the bed and breakfast. Salvatore got her to calm down as Marion tried to think up her story. Could she possibly borrow his phone, she asked? What could she say? That there were no trains, or that she'd been taken ill or...what? It was one thing planning to stay in Glastonbury for a few days extra. Quite another forgetting to tell your boss. Marion couldn't believe she hadn't called in – it was most unlike her to be so irresponsible.

"I'm sorry" said Salvatore gently, "I don't have a phone."

"You don't?" said Marion, surprised.

"I don't really need one" he said. "But why don't we go back into the cafe and see it they have a landline you can use?" He was so calm, so helpful. Suddenly Marion felt that everything would be alright. And it was. She phoned the University and was surprised how calm her boss was when she told him she needed to take some days off. He told her not to worry about coming in until the following Tuesday, which was exactly how much time she'd wanted, anyway. Everything had worked out perfectly.

"I guess" said Marion, as she ordered some fruit juice, "As they say in these parts, I am *meant* to be here." Salvatore shook his head and laughed.

"You are meant to be wherever you are at that moment" he said. He ordered a black coffee.

"Aren't you eating?" asked Marion.

"I don't need to, very much" said Salvatore, offering no more in the way of explanation. He was quite stocky in build, but didn't look like he had any surplus flesh on him. He was probably one of those annoying people who ate exactly the amount they needed quite naturally.

Marion looked pensive for a moment, then she asked Salvatore, "Do you mind watching me eat? I'm ravenous."

"Goodness, no" he replied. "*You* need to eat." Marion was slim, but it still seemed a rather odd thing to say. It struck her that Salvatore was rather odd, but in the nicest possible way. Not many people would come and chat you up by asking you about the flowers on your new shoes. She felt she just had to ask him more about the flowers. He explained.

"Where I come from, they represent perfection, light and life. They are significant in the joining of the sexes and their union. So you see, by their symbol, I know where to find others who represent and pertain to these things." Marion wasn't quite sure she understood, but it didn't matter. This charming man had found her. He added a large spoonful of white sugar to his coffee and said no more about it. As Marion would later find out about him, he only ever said what he needed to say.

****

Bea was adamant that Peter should be reported somehow, somewhere to a regulating board. Only, he wasn't actually regulated....he'd never needed to be. All his students came by word of mouth, leafleting and the internet. Bea had tried to call Marion several times, but she wasn't picking up her phone, so Bea got angry and demanded that her other friends took action.

Helen sensed that Roberta, even though the victim of the whole affair was quite frankly feeling awkward about it all and just wanting to leave the whole incident behind her. She was fed up with Bea and her wanting to "rally the troops", but Bea stomped off the coach, refused to speak to anyone and disappeared down into the tube station with her suitcase.

Carolyn tried to pacify Roberta. "I know Bea is a new friend and you don't know her all that well, but when Bea gets a *bee* in her bonnet, it'll be buzzing around for ages. She means well, she really does, but she's not always the best at seeing another person's point of view."

"Point of view?" spat Helen "She wasn't even listening to you. She just got up on her moral high horse and decided she was going to fight all corrupt

New Age practitioners everywhere. Christ, I mean Bea against an army *that* size." Roberta looked horrified.

"You mean.....lots of these people are corrupt?" she asked.

"Bloody hell, yeah" said Helen, "If you ask me – most of them."

"So why the hell did you decide to come, if you have that attitude?" said Carolyn, angrily.

"Well...." said Helen "Personally, I find it all a bit of a hoot. Fancied a girls weekend away, anyway....."

"I'm bloody glad you can chuck £250 at a hoot" said Carolyn. "Frankly I'd rather spend the money on something I really want to do. Something productive. And I *did* get a lot out of the course."

"Oo, enlighten me." Helen was practically asking to be slapped. Instead, demonstrating that she really did understand the 'universal method of controlling anger,' Carolyn took a deep breath and put her arm around Roberta, who she could see was going into a quiet moment of despair.

"I'm going to take Roberta home" said Carolyn calmly "You can call me if you've decided not to viciously attack people who don't agree with you. As it happened, Roberta was in agreement with you, but you just decided to lash out. Maybe next time you want to chuck your money at something that won't isolate you from all your friends."

Carolyn led Roberta away from the coach station and towards a cafe. National Express tea and coffee was a national disaster and didn't blend at all well with Glastonbury's diet of pure, wholesome and organic cuisine. Roberta had more than learnt her lesson about abandoning her friends all weekend and could have experienced a lot worse. Right now, she really appreciated the comfort and wisdom of an older friend.

Helen stuck her head in the air and walked off with a malevolent chuckle. Carolyn couldn't help herself. "You're just pissed off Bea rejected your sexual advances." Helen stopped laughing and Roberta started.

****

Marion was very pleased Salvatore wanted to meet up with her the next day. He had headed out of town for some specific organic foods and left her to explore the Chalice Well on her own. It seemed odd that he had to travel so much for such specific foods, as Glastonbury catered to most forms of vegetarians, vegans and extreme diets.

Marion remembered reading about a group of people called the "Breatharians" who claimed to derive all they needed to live on from air alone. Whilst she couldn't believe that was true; for a start, they looked too healthy and well-fed, Marion was nonetheless fascinated by their guru. She was an elderly Indian lady who claimed that no food had passed her lips for a decade.

She remembered about Salvatore saying he didn't need to eat much and wondered if he might be a Breatharian himself...then again, he had still had coffee and sugar....also, he said he was going to buy food, so that couldn't have been the case. The afternoon air was humid and Marion slipped off her cardigan as she went to pay her entrance fee to the grounds of the Well.

Once, everything was free – now she wouldn't be surprised if someone stood over her and asked for a couple of quid, every time she filled her water bottle up from one of the springs. Once inside the gardens, some kind of mystical, benevolent presence definitely prevailed. It was said that the Chalice well had been visited by Jesus and Mary Magdalene and some believed Jesus was actually a spaceman, sent to save the blackened souls of humanity.

A Spaceman. Bea believed lots of people were aliens. Marion thought she'd better give Bea a call as soon as she got back to the bed and breakfast and her phone and get an update on the girls. She'd been a bit distracted. Doing a last lap of the pretty little springs and flowers, Marion pushed the wooden exit gate aside and looked up to see....Peter.

They were both shocked, but Peter's face registered fear and Marion's anger. They held each other's gaze for a moment, both of them unable to speak or move. Peter had expected Marion to be back in London by now and Marion had temporarily forgotten all about him. Fortunately, she was saved by a metaphoric bell.

"Hey, Marion!" Salvatore chirped from the other side of the gate "The store was closed, so I decided to come back into town."

"Excuse me, I must go" said Marion pushing past a man she really didn't want to see and towards a man she could not have been more glad to see again.

****

CHAPTER 5

BRIGHTON

There were essays to read on the train journey, but Marion was distracted. The journey from London Victoria to Brighton was the time in which she did most of her marking, catching up and general preparation for the week. Today, her mind was fixated on a man she had just met, called Salvatore. That was all she knew about him. She didn't know his surname, where he lived, how old he was, where he worked....all Marion knew about Salvatore was that he seemed to reside in either Glastonbury or Tuscany, or somewhere in between...

He'd picked her up in a retail outlet, and she couldn't stop thinking about him. Salvatore had offered no phone number or email contact – he was terribly elusive. Maybe he didn't want to keep in touch. When Marion hastily scribbled down her contact details and handed them to him, Salvatore had declined. "Don't worry – I will find you" was all he had said, "Next time."

Then, he'd simply waved and disappeared down the long hill into town. Marion's heart told her this was the mysterious stranger she'd always longed to meet – the man she'd been waiting for and who'd been waiting for her. Half an hour later, Marion had convinced herself that Salvatore was married, a philanderer, a scrounger with no money, and that she had been fooled by his Italian charm. Italian men had always been a little bit of a fantasy where Marion was concerned – she adored Italy and always seemed to develop an unusual interest in international football whenever the Italian team were doing well....

That there was absolutely no way of knowing if she'd ever see Salvatore again, frustrated Marion immensely. Being elusive and mysterious was one thing – doing a complete disappearing act was another. She pondered on his last, simple words to her. He'd never mentioned anything clichéd, like "trust the universe" or that they'd see each other again if "it was meant to be."

Were they meant to be? This question plagued Marion. She reached into her travel bag for some work to look at and to distract her – Picasso prints for her next lecture. Laying a print down flat on the Formica train table in front of her, Marion couldn't believe what she saw. There, tiny though it was in the corner of the painting, was a clearly distinguishable little fleur de lis.....

****

Professor David Pepper was far too happy for his own good. Something was obviously very wrong. "Good morning Marion, beautiful out, isn't it?" David had his feet up on his desk and a book in his hand. Marion peered closer at the book cover. He was reading "Creative Visualisation." It was one of the first new age books Marion had ever read when she began her "spiritual quest." What on earth was David doing with it? Marion asked him. "Ah yes, bloody marvellous stuff" he said "If I picture what I want first, then I can manifest it later."

It doesn't quite work exactly like that, thought Marion. At first, she thought he was taking the proverbial piss, but then she wondered where he had got the book from. Perhaps he was having a dig at her, taking time out to do one of her courses....

"Ok....look...." Marion was quite flustered. "I know I took more time out than planned, but...." Marion was interrupted as David flicked over a page.

"Did you know, Marion, that if you visualise what you want in a little pink bubble, it strengthens the intensity of your desire?" She realised this wasn't something David was reading off the page. He had memorised it, which she found deeply disturbing.

"Oh, David – *why* are you reading that?" Marion had to know. David sat up and swung his legs back off his desk.

"Well, because quite frankly, it's terrific" he replied, simply. "Can't wait to finish it. I've got 'Feel the Fear and Do it Anyway', lined up next." He indicated another book lying face up on his desk. Marion looked at her boss quizzically and soon the reason for his new found interest in personal development became apparent. "Mira recommended I read these. Talking of which, I have to say she was bloody marvellous at the conference – didn't miss you one little bit...."

As Marion took a sharp intake of breath, who should walk in the room, but the devil herself. "Hi Marion, good trip?" asked Mira, all pearly white smiles and flowing blonde locks.

"It was....good" said Marion.

"That's great" said Mira. "I have to say, it was wonderful that I had the opportunity to take your place at the conference. I met Theolonius Poole! Oh my God, what an amazing man! His knowledge about the modern art world is something else." It certainly was something else, thought Marion. In the circles she moved in, this art critic was well known as a pompous, up himself prat who had made a great deal of money purely by being a pompous, up himself prat.

Marion wanted to scream, but instead she gritted her teeth and said, "Gosh. That's great. Such an honour." David knew Marion hated the critic, but he didn't raise an eyebrow. Mira continued.

"And....guess what? I'm going to be working with him! Can you believe it? He told me how impressed he was with my knowledge of the Cubists! I credit you with that, Marion – it was on your wonderful lectures I learnt about them!" And if you hadn't been one of my students, then you wouldn't know so well how to do my job, thought Marion.

It was inevitable, really. Marion should have known that. She hadn't been there and even if she had been working all hours and diligently arse-licking, there would always be some up and coming young thing wanting to step into her shoes, well before Marion was ready to put her slippers on....

What really grated on Marion the most was that New Age philosophy was *her* thing. David had always been really sarcastic about this and yet now Mira was introducing him to this world at a fledgling level and he thought he could already fly. "Well" said Marion, trying not to let out a prolonged and painful sigh which would state the obvious, "I'll just grab my material for the Matisse lecture, this afternoon."

"Ah – no need" said David. "Mira will do it. She covered some of your lectures whilst you were away. If I were you, I'd just go to the library for a while, or put your feet up in the canteen. You've got plenty of time until your M.A lot appear – or possibly not...." Marion managed a half smile. Student attendance hadn't been so good of late – something they all knew. She exited David's office, wondering how much longer she would be employed.

It was foolish to just have spontaneously taken that time off, and she knew it. Would it really have made much difference, however? This year's batch of students were an erratic lot, that was for sure. Sometimes they'd turn up, sometimes they'd feel an "artistic need" to stay in bed. But Marion had been working, and hard. She'd been planning lectures, reading, marking and – for what? Maybe this was nature's way of showing her she had to slow down – cut back.

Or maybe she should walk right back into David's office and demand that she should take the Matisse lecture, seeing as she had spent so much time planning it. As a member of canteen staff brought a coffee over to her table, Marion suddenly leapt up, leaving the coffee and defiantly walking back to her boss. She had a right to know what was being planned. Marion swung around the long corridor and took a sharp left turn towards David's door, then shoved it open, ready to vent spleen.

David and Mira were kissing. Marion could see David had his hand a long way up Mira's skirt. Thankfully, so embroiled in this were the couple, that they didn't see Marion. She fled back to the canteen, distressed to see that her coffee had been removed. She asked for another one, as the canteen lady shook her head. Marion stared at the milk and sugar, and then she stared at the wall in front of her for quite some time.

Noticing that Marion had gone catatonic, the canteen lady approached, tentatively. "Dr Green....are you ok?" Marion looked at her.

"What would you do if you'd just seen something you shouldn't?" asked Marion. Fortunately this particular canteen lady had been very long-serving, largely because she was so discreet.

"Well...." she replied, "That would depend upon what I saw, where it was happening and who was involved..." She was far too astute to be serving up soggy Shepherd's Pie. But she was right.

"Thank you" said Marion. "Thank you. I'll think about that." And Marion would think about it. But what on earth she was going to do about it, she really didn't know.

****

Carolyn was thinking about where to plant her new tomato plants when her mobile started to vibrate in her pocket. She felt frustrated when she saw Marion's number flash up, because much as she loved her friend, she really needed to get her vegetables sorted. She decided to ignore the call. When the phone buzzed again, she realised the call must be urgent – Marion would usually leave a message.

"It's tough, isn't it?" said Carolyn before Marion had even said anything. "I mean, getting back to work after a break, that is."

"How would you know?" asked Marion, "You retired ages ago, you lady of leisure."

"Lady of leisure?" spat Carolyn. "I'll have you know it's hardly leisurely when your sodding cucumbers refuse to grow. Between you and me, I think it's because they don't like the cabbages. They were doing fine until I moved them to the same bed."

"Well, I guess some vegetables are not good bedfellows" said Marion, irritated with the small talk. Carolyn could tell Marion wasn't in a good mood. There was a slight pause before Carolyn started to mention the coach trip back home and how Roberta had revealed more of what had happened to her. In turn, this had also affected Bea, and Carolyn had been grappling with her feelings of really enjoying Peter's teachings, but also being well aware of what he had done.

"Anyway, what did you get up to in your extra time off?" Carolyn eventually asked Marion. The answer to that deserved coffee and cake, as soon as Marion was back from Brighton and the University.

Marion sat slumped over her coffee table, surrounded by prints and books by French artists. Knee deep in Picassos, Monets, and Chagalls, she felt a migraine coming on. Normally, these paintings were her passion, her life-blood. Not only had she lectured on them for many years, but she'd visited The Louvre, Vatican, Van Gogh Museum, Guggenheim and numerous other international galleries of revered art forms.

It was in these large, spacious rooms that she could feel the full impact of the work and soak up something which she would describe as the "essence" of the paintings to her students. It was here that Marion really came into her own as a lecturer. For years she had studied the brush techniques, delved into the politics and sociologies of the eras which produced such fine artists. But it seemed few other University lecturers touched on the way the paintings really made you feel or what you could really see in them or went into anything like the depth Marion would take her students to. For this, they loved her. And for this, her other colleagues sometimes felt threatened....

Today, all the art work which had made her feel alive and adventurous and inspired her personal position, was giving her a headache from hell. Everything just clashed – the bright, bold colours of the abstract Kandinskys, the interlocking squares and triangles of the Miros, were just too painful, and in the end, Marion couldn't bear to look at them.

What on earth had brought this on? Marion wondered if she had the kind of headache that needed a lie down in bed with the curtains drawn, or just a walk. Had it been brought on by recent stresses or was it something physical, like the start of a very bad sinus cold or flu? Against the odds, Marion switched on her computer. The flickering screen made the headache worse, but Marion felt compelled to look at it. If that little Polish tart could take over all her lectures, then Marion could take over hers. She was going to know everything about Dutch painters by the end of the evening, even if it gave her a headache the size of Holland.

****

Bea had a day off and wanted to meet Marion in Brighton. She was concerned about her friend, assuming Marion had been given a very hard time by David on her return to the University. Hard as it was, Marion decided to keep to herself the incident she had witnessed between David and Mira - she hadn't quite decided what to do about that yet, if anything at all.

Whilst she waited for Bea to join her at their favourite tea place in The Lanes, Marion perused the Picasso print again. She hadn't imagined it – there was definitely a fleur de lis in the top right hand corner. She turned the print around and examined it carefully, trying to decipher if the flower was part of the painting, or embossed by the printer. Marion sighed, deeply. She hadn't thought about Salvatore for a while, but now here was a clear reminder of him.

Having just a little snippet of information about him was so frustrating. "I will find you", he'd said. Should she just take that as rejection? Was it Italian for "don't call me, I'll call you?" Marion didn't even know if Salvatore *was* Italian. She had just assumed that because of his name, looks and faint trace of some kind of Mediterranean accent.

Men. They accused women of being elusive, but Marion had never met anyone quite as elusive as Salvatore. She'd felt a connection with him at a very deep level and couldn't quite believe they would never meet again. If they didn't, then why on earth had they met in the first place? What was that all about? Such thoughts were interrupted by the arrival of Bea. She kissed Marion lightly on both cheeks. "Problems back at work?" she said, as she slung her bag over the back of her chair.

"Oh, I don't want to talk about *that*" said Marion. "Update me on what happened with Roberta. I missed all that, not getting the coach back with you." It soon became clear that Marion wasn't the only one with a man on her mind. She was shocked to hear about Michael's involvement with the Roberta incident and even more surprised to see how that had affected Bea.

Suddenly, it was as if Bea had been released from her prison. Knowing he could do something like that to her friend seemed to ignite Bea's logic and rational and her long stored feelings of love for him had suddenly gone into reverse. It seemed she had completely gotten over him – just like that. Seeing

Bea like this, was quite wonderful. "You look different" said Marion, "Like you've had a face lift – like some big weight has been taken off your shoulders."

Bea beamed a big smile. It was the first time Marion had seen her do that in years. "Chocolate cake on the agenda" said Bea. "Let us celebrate me being ready to meet a new man!" Marion leaned in close.

"Bea...." Marion looked as if she were about to reveal some very deep secret. "I think....I think *I* may have met a new man." Bea's eyes lit up.

"Heavens! Tell me! *Everything!*"

"I wish I could" replied Marion, "Only, I don't really know very much about him. And I don't even know where he is now." Bea frowned.

"Marion....I thought you knew better. You haven't...?"

"Good Lord no" said Marion, "Haven't even held hands. He just seems like.... he *knows* me. And I know him. And we had this sort of – instant connection. Talking to him is so easy, so natural. It's like the conversation just flows and I lose all track of time. I wish...I wish I could see him again."

"Oh...My.....God...." said Bea, very slowly. "Marion, can you believe it? Can you really believe this has happened to us? I've gotten over Michael and you've met somebody. All in the same week. Forget chocolate cake – this calls for champers! Let's crack open a bottle on the pier and go on some scary rides!" Marion paid for the coffee.

Bea grabbed Marion's hand and skipped down the road with her, her floral skirt twirling in a sort of hula hoop. "Whee!" sung Bea as she spun and skipped, regardless of who might stop or stare. But people in Brighton didn't really bother staring. Marion smiled. If there was one place where Bea could truly release all that agony pent up inside of seven years previously, then this was the place to do it.

She could be a grown woman riding on the carousel, skim pebbles across the windy waves, twirl down the street, showing off frilly underwear if she really wanted to....it was a place where nothing really mattered. Marion never went into the town centre much, except to catch her train home. She usually wanted to get home as quickly as possible, after work. This afternoon however, it was enjoyable to end the day in a leisurely manner, walking, eating ice cream, being silly....today it was Bea who would be getting the early train back, as Marion had two consecutive days work at the University and would stay overnight at the house of a fellow lecturer.

After she'd dropped Bea off, she was aiming to head over there and write up some more notes for her Picasso lecture. It was then that she thought of what she had seen in David's office. Then that she felt an overwhelming urge to tell someone else about it. If Marion could confide in anyone, then it was Bea. A best friend was the best person to have to hand when one couldn't figure out on one's own what to do.

Apart from affecting her job, Marion knew that this would affect David's wife, Julia, and it was Julia that Marion felt for. All the years that Marion had known David, she had never known of another indiscretion, but perhaps she had just never known....

He was pompous and arrogant yes, but Marion would never have had him down as one to fraternise with younger women. Besides, he wasn't attractive enough....She decided to tell Bea, who looked visibly shocked. "Oh my God" said Bea, "With Mira? The pretty one? What on earth does she see in *him*?"

"My job" said Marion, quite simply. "I don't see there's very much I can do about it. If the University want to get rid of me, then they'll find a way. Any excuse will do. Anyway, you can see it's been happening for some time now. The voice of experience is no longer valued. They just want young, trendy lecturers. Apart from David, I'm the oldest member of staff in the department. No one wants an argumentative old harridan thwarting their plans to seduce young things, or telling them what they can and can't have on the annual syllabus."

"Now stop that at once" Bea scolded. "You are not an old harridan. You're my lovely, clever friend and besides, you are an excellent lecturer and you know it. What does Mira know only two seconds after having completed her Masters? All she's got is her looks, and they'll go."

Marion sighed deeply. "Alas, that isn't true. Mira is a very thorough researcher and she does a pretty good job. She's also very nice. And pretty. And now she's screwing my boss."

"Gah" replied Bea, "A quadruple threat! Oh Marion, I can see what you're up against."

"I'm too old for this" sighed Marion. "I'm in no position to fight. If my job's gonna go, then it's gonna go."

Bea inhaled sharply. "Marion....this should be up to you. Hang on in there."

Marion muttered that her head was just too full of stuff. There was the Feng Shui course, stuff that had happened to Roberta, seeing David and Mira in flagrante and... Bea smiled, a wry little smile. "You're thinking about that man, aren't you?" she said. "C'mon, spill. More."

"What?" said Marion. "I already told you, there is no more. I don't even know where he is. No point in my thinking about him if I don't know if I'll ever see him again. Come to think of it, he knows very little about me. He knows I live in London, but he doesn't know which part. There must be thousands of Marion Greens in the directory. Actually, he doesn't even know my surname....off to a good start, aren't we?"

Bea frowned so hard that her eyebrows almost met in the middle. "I can't believe you let him go so easily. You spent two whole days talking to him and you haven't swapped any contact details at all. Do you know his surname? What he does for a living? Can't you Google him?"

Marion spoke softly. "Bea....you know what Glastonbury is like. You reveal your most intimate stuff to complete strangers and you never see them again. How many people are going to keep in touch from the Feng Shui course, eh? Quite."

"But...but this is different" said Bea, tears forming in her eyes. Deny it as she might, Marion also started to get quite tearful.

"Yes....yes Bea, you're right. It is." She started to sob a little.

"Oh Marion" said Bea, " I *do* hope you find him again."

"Well" said Marion, "He did say he would find *me*....."

****

It was dusk when Marion walked Bea back up to the station. She kissed her lightly on both cheeks and then waved her off on the platform as Bea disappeared into a haze of commuters. It was a mild evening and the air was very still. Seagulls cooed softly as they flew across the cool blue and pink sky and people coming home from work looked relaxed instead of red-faced and angry and stressed, jostling round trying to find a seat.

A child of about four or five looked at his ice cream like it was the best thing in the world that he had ever seen and a young couple ordered coffees from the stall in the centre of the station, still gazing into each other's eyes and holding hands as they ordered, not hearing when the attendant asked them twice if they wanted chocolate sprinkles on top....

It was the kind of evening that was perfect for lovers. If you had a lover, and if you had time, then you could wind down the hill for a bottle of wine, then head down to the beach to sit entwined until the sun set. If you didn't have a lover but you wanted one and on that particular evening could not cope with the feelings of jealousy or loneliness or both, then it was a pretty crappy evening.

Marion became quite alarmed that these feelings suddenly seemed to overwhelm her – she didn't think she was the type. She rarely felt lonely, nor was she jealous of anyone else in a relationship, but this feeling was strangely new to her and at the same time very familiar...she wanted this to be part of her life again.

She headed down the Queen's Road, ostensibly to go and catch the last bit of the sun's rays on her own. It was a bit too early to walk over to her colleague's place. Half way down the hill, Marion stopped and turned round. She'd drunk almost her body weight in cappuccino's with Bea that afternoon, but why shouldn't she go and get one with chocolate sprinkles, just because she was on her own?

Marion debated getting a bottle of wine, but that alone on the beach was simply too sad. The coffee stall people knew her well. It was her regular stop en route home. They always made her coffee exactly how she liked it, not too strong, milky and with half a teaspoon of sugar. "You're late tonight" said the man as he handed her a cardboard cup.

"Staying over tonight" replied Marion.

The man laughed. "And you came all the way up here to get coffee?"

Marion laughed. "Well, no one else makes it quite like you do." She lifted the cup off the counter. A second later, Marion did something she had never done before, which was to gaze up at the ceiling of the station. Usually she'd just observe the passengers, shop assistants, people coming to collect or drop off other people.

This time, something had made Marion look up. She noticed a border around the main decoration of the ceiling and then noticed it was decorated with little fleur de lis. Goddamit, there they were again. How could she ever get Salvatore out of her mind, when "signs" of him kept appearing everywhere?

She walked straight ahead, before noticing a man with a dark moustache and rucksack on his back. As he looked at her and grinned broadly, Marion almost dropped her coffee. "S.....Salvatore?" she gasped.

****

"I can't think we've had a better idea since 1990" said David as he leaned back on his leather chair and propped his feet up on his desk.

"1990?" queried Mira, "You've been working here that long?"

"Actually, longer than that......" David paused, not really wanting to consider the searing age gap between himself and his new lover. He went back to the idea. "Its sheer genius, you know – this idea of linking in Esoteric Studies with the art department. It's all the rage these days and yet so few universities offer anything like it. I think we'd be doing a great service to the place if we set it up. Just think about the revenue it would bring in as well – we'd be heroes, saving this old place from decline and debt!"

Mira coughed. "The University is in debt?"

"No, I mean....not the whole University. Just the Art Department. Used to be only slightly behind English and History in popularity. But numbers have declined as young people have thought they should be doing things like Computer Studies, or that old chestnut, Astro Physics."

"Old....Chestnut....?" Mira didn't have a sufficient grasp of the English language nor the reference in which to frame this somewhat old-fashioned saying. But she was rather frustrated. The Esoteric studies were her idea. Sure she needed David to implement them – she'd even thrown all her dignity out of the window and slept with him; no way was he going to take credit for this course.

She stood up and walked to the other side of the office. "I left you a list of possible lectures" she said. "Have you even looked at it?" David couldn't resist.

"Gosh, you are damned attractive when you're angry. Has anyone ever told you that?" This just served to make Mira even more angry. David was old and English. His stupid sayings. Why wasn't he taking her seriously? Seeing her irritation, he reached over for her hand. Mira pulled away, grabbed her notebook and pen and sat down.

"Enough talking" she said. "You need to make some phone calls – now."

****

A seagull swooped down very low as Marion and Salvatore wended their way through the antique shops on The Lanes, close to the sea front. "What made you decide to have a few days in Brighton?" asked Marion, astonished that she and this mysterious man had made acquaintance again.

"I've never been before" replied Salvatore, simply. "I've heard a lot about it. I always seem to meet some people from Brighton whenever I go to Glastonbury. Thought I'd like to come and see it for myself." Marion definitely hadn't told Salvatore that she worked there – she would have remembered. Besides, she was usually half on the main campus and quite often in Falmouth, half an hour outside of town. She very rarely spent time in the town centre, other than commuting to and from the train station.

It seemed very strangely co-incidental that he was here now and that it was only just after Marion had waved Bea off that she had seen him. She thought back. She remembered seeing the fleur de lis on the station ceiling. Suddenly. Something had "impulsed" her to look up. Was some peculiar force guiding the pair of them? After all, they could both have spent days in Brighton and not "accidentally" bumped into each other at all...

As fortune might have it, Salvatore's bed and breakfast was very near to the location of Marion's colleague. Salvatore tried to re-assure Marion that none of this was strange and appeared very relaxed about it all himself and then much to her surprise, explained to her in truly scientific terms by the laws of averages and chance, how easy it was that such a thing could happen.

Whilst Marion could not grasp all of what Salvatore was saying, it did all sound very feasible and by the end of the conversation she believed that the fact they were sitting together on the beach watching the sunset together was all purely to do with physics. Salvatore looked at his watch. "I'd better go and check in" he said, "But then, I was wondering if you'd like to join me for dinner?"

"That sounds a lovely idea" replied Marion, "But I'm being cooked for and someone is waiting for me. It's kind of them to put me up."

"Then maybe....breakfast?" suggested Salvatore. Marion thought that might be feasible. Her first lecture wasn't until 11.30am. Then she remembered Salvatore was in a bed and breakfast. When she reminded him he'd get his breakfast there, he looked disappointed. Marion suggested early coffee, instead.

"Oh" said Salvatore. "It's just that... I'd really like to take you somewhere." Marion looked at him directly. She'd love to get to spend time with him, but he'd just arrived – literally out of the blue. Surely he didn't expect her to drop all her plans and work, just like that? Then again, he was so elusive goddamit and men like that hardly landed on her doorstep every day.

"Have you actually got yourself a mobile phone yet?" Marion asked. Much to her surprise, Salvatore pulled one from his bag. "I wasn't expecting to travel quite so much, but found it hard to make reservations without one." They swapped numbers and Marion felt a sense of relief – even if he never responded, at least she could text him.

"Meet me here tomorrow at 8.30" said Salvatore firmly. Marion looked around, trying to find a distinctive landmark for the patch of beach they were on, then noticed the little boat lock up behind them had a distinctive pale blue fleur de lis on the door panel. She laughed.

"I told you I would find you" said Salvatore.

****

Marion hadn't slept very well. Despite having her own cosy little room and a breakfast date to look forward to, something had been troubling her. Marion would like to have done her best to completely erase the disturbing image of David and Mira "at play", but also knew that the images you would best like to forget, often stay with you. They also keep annoyingly popping up when you least expect to see them.

As these images appeared just as she was on her way to meet Salvatore, she took it as a sign that she should speak to him about her work – open up to him. She was there on the dot of 8.30am. Salvatore wasn't. She waited ten minutes. At 9am, he still wasn't there. Both angry and anxious, Marion took her phone from her bag and dialled his number. It went to an anonymous voice mail.

Despite wanting to leave an angry message, Marion bit her tongue and left a calmer, but slightly cold message saying she would leave if he didn't show in the next five minutes. Hoping that he would then actually manifest, Marion waited until 9.20am, but by this time, her heart had sunk very low and she sadly started to trudge along the pebbles towards the station. He'd seemed so keen the night before. Maybe it was because she didn't invite him back with her, or he'd expected her to stay with him at his lodgings.... It hadn't appeared that way, but maybe she'd got it all wrong. Maybe it was pure co-incidence that they'd bumped into each other and he was just being polite. He didn't really want to see her at all.

A little further along the beach was a hut that looked like it might sell really greasy burgers by day time, but already had the shutters up and looked like it might do coffee and fried sandwiches for breakfast time. Marion squinted at the menu chalked up on a board and fumbled in her purse. A man with an apron around his neck was stood with his back to her, buttering bread. "White coffee and egg sandwich please" said Marion, looking down into her handbag.

"I know what you'd *like*, but it's really not that good for you" said Salvatore turning round with freshly made scrambled egg and toast on a paper plate. Marion nearly jumped out of her skin.

"What the f.......??!!"

"Please." Salvatore wiped his hand on his apron and then put his finger to his lips. "Please don't scream so loudly or everyone will want one, and I'm not actually open yet."

"What the hell are you doing here and why aren't you where you were meant to be an hour ago?" asked Marion angrily.

"I'm so sorry" said Salvatore "I was going to call you, but I knew you'd find your way here – eventually." Marion wasn't amused.

"Ok, Mister. This isn't funny. Stop being so evasive and answer my questions." Salvatore untied his apron, unlocked the door of the hut and came down the little white, wooden steps.

"It's like this..." he said. He explained, very convincingly that the landlord at his bed and breakfast owned the beach cafe and usually came down to do the breakfast run whilst his wife made breakfast back at the shack. This morning he'd been taken ill and as he was due to lose a lot of trade, Salvatore offered to help out. "After all" continued Salvatore, "It's only for a few hours and I can cook."

Marion threw her hands in the air in exasperation, then stared at the eggs waiting patiently for her on the counter. "Wait a minute" she said, "How did you know I'd order eggs? I could have asked for a bacon butty."

"Ah no" replied Salvatore. "I remember you saying you were trying to be vegetarian and loved eating organic food, but that fried egg sandwiches on thick white bread were your vice." Marion didn't remember saying this. She crunched her feet on the pebbles beneath her. "Aren't you going to eat it?" asked Salvatore. "It will go cold. Like your coffee." He looked sad.

Marion took her paper breakfast and sat. Usually she used to like sitting staring out to sea whenever she had time quietly musing on her life, but this morning the ocean held no answers. Salvatore joined her. " I...I didn't realise..." he looked embarrassed. "I thought it would amuse you. Be a surprise for you."

"I need to be at work in an hour" said Marion dryly "I thought we were going to spend some time together."

"This is together, isn't it?" said Salvatore.

"If you call plastic breakfast on cold pebbles time together" she replied. She was exasperated and yet couldn't be all that angry with this extraordinary being. He gently took her coffee cup from her and levered off the plastic lid. Marion supped. "Mmm. Well, I do have to say, you make great coffee."

"Of course" Salvatore laughed. "It's in my blood".

"So...you *are* Italian?" said Marion.

"Not exactly...." Marion threw a pebble quite hard at Salvatore's shin, but he didn't flinch. She started to laugh.

"My God, I don't know who you are or where you come from, but I don't care. You make me laugh. And, you know what, I...." Salvatore stopped her talking by pressing a finger to her lips. And then he leant forward and kissed her. He *more* than kissed her. Whatever it was he did, she suddenly felt that she was absorbed into his very being – his very soul. And the cool, grey morning air seemed to turn all kinds of different colours that Marion had never seen before and a seagull seemed so surprised that she could have sworn he froze in mid air to stop and stare at a kiss like that...even though, on Brighton beach, he must have seen so many kisses, so many times before.

****

The History of Art department definitely wasn't its usual self. There would usually be at least a few doors slamming on a Wednesday morning – either David's as he rushed back into his office after a meeting with his seniors or Marion slamming other doors after a meeting with *him*. This Wednesday morning however, was different. Everyone seemed to be floating around and smiling at each other and asking colleagues if they'd like a cup of tea – with biscuits.

"Good morning Marion!" said an extra chirpy Professor David Pepper. "I must say – you look very well this morning. Did you manage to get some sea air yesterday? You've got a real colour in your cheeks." Marion gazed somewhere at a spot on the wall behind her boss's head. She felt all floaty and distant – not her usual focussed self at all.

David wafted up from his desk and lifted the sash window, then inhaled deeply. This, he never did. The window would never be open and subsequently the air in his office was always stale and stuffy. Marion clocked an incense burner on the corner of his desk. "That's pretty" she said.

"Thank you" said David, fingering the edges of the little wooden palette, "Mira bought it for me. She has exquisite taste, don't you think?" He sighed, walked over to the window again and inhaled deeply. "The roses.... come and breathe, Marion. Come to the window. Don't you think they're quite heavenly?" Somewhat disorientated by her boss's uncharacteristic behaviour, Marion did as instructed.

"No – not like that" he told her, "Like this. Right into the centre of your stomach – into your very being." Your very being? David didn't use phrases like that. He put his arms around Marion's waist and pressed into her diaphragm. "You breathe – like this..." he said, making "oo" and "ah" noises as hc manipulated her torso.

"Ooo, Ahh" said Marion as Mira entered the room.

"David! Dr Green!"

"Mira!" beamed David as he let go of Marion and bounced across the room. "I was just about to tell Marion about your absolutely splendid idea!"

"Really?" said Mira "And you need to hug her from behind to do that, do you?"

"Ahh..." said David.

"Oooo!" said Marion, continuing the breathing exercise, in a Pavlovian dog-like response.

Mira raised an eyebrow. "Perhaps, David, you would like me to explain about our new project." David pulled up some chairs whilst Mira eyed Marion, suspiciously. Normally Marion would be far more antagonistic towards her and normally shouting at David. Today was different. Mira spread some papers out on the desk.

"Now, it has come to our attention" she said, "that we could amalgamate our department with a department of Esoteric Studies. As you know, student numbers have been in rapid decline and we need to think creatively about our intake."

Think creatively. Suddenly Marion was back in the meeting and Salvatore was relegated to the back of her mind, as Mira came to the front of it. What a bloody cheek. What did this young East European bint know about "thinking creatively?" It was just a brand name – some kind of corporate bullshit that she'd heard at meetings and tried to make it sound like her own wonderful and innovative idea. Marion had been thinking creatively since she was born.

It was part of Marion's gene pool – how she was made. She devoured works of art, painted herself, *understood* artists....All these high-powered boffins who paid lip service to the phrase couldn't think creatively if their lives depended on it. Left to their own devices for a week in a ball pond, they'd just end up throwing them at each other, getting more aggressive and crying until their mummies came to take them out. They wouldn't actually think to *play* or *climb* out if they didn't want to play....

None of them would have relished the pleasure of burying themselves in the bright, primary colours, waving their hands up through the balls of plastic, having hysterics with their friends, putting things in colour order or patterns, or types of structures, or even just playing catch. That's what Marion and her creative friends would have done. What she didn't know at that moment, was that there was much worse to come. Much worse...

Mira pulled a folder out of a plastic sleeve and started pulling out the notes tucked within. "Now... I have been doing a lot of research and I believe this man would be an excellent candidate for the Head of this new department. If you approve, David, then I will contact him immediately and see if he'd like to arrange an interview. Thereafter, we can advertise the position." As she pushed the papers forward, Marion could see a photo of Peter at the top of a C.V. Beneath that were sub-headings like "Corporate Feng Shui", "Creative Visualisation for Managers" and several initials, including a PhD.

"Feng Shui, hmm?" said David. "Perhaps I can get him in to do the office! It could be part of the interview!" Marion turned very pale. They couldn't. They wouldn't. They couldn't employ the man who'd tried to rape her friend. She couldn't possibly be anywhere near that man ever again. If she was, then she couldn't be held accountable for her actions. "S...sorry" said Marion, running from the room, "Suddenly I... I don't feel very well...."

****

On a bench, on the seafront, Salvatore held Marion tightly to his chest. "My darling – you are shaking. What has made you like this?" Marion found herself telling Salvatore everything about Peter and the Roberta incident and her friends, and completely opening up to him. Telling Salvatore everything felt easy and natural; maybe she still knew nothing about him, but somehow Marion instinctively trusted that it was ok to tell him everything about herself. He pulled away from her and frowned. "But this man cannot lecture. Let alone at *your* University."

"Unfortunately, it isn't *my* University" said Marion, "I'm not going to get much say in the matter. How my boss will see it is that the reason he shouldn't employ Peter is because a bunch of middle-aged, hormonal women with a younger friend who won't press charges, say so. It's our word against that of an internationally renowned eminent spiritual teacher with an appallingly clean track record."

Salvatore laughed. "Is that how you describe yourself? Middle-aged and hormonal?"

"Beyond even both of those now" sighed Marion. "If Roberta won't testify, then whoever will believe *me*? None of us were there. We just found her crying and bruised. It was obvious what had happened, but we can't *prove* it." Salvatore looked pensively at the sea for a while.

"Hmm...let me think now. Who will believe this beautiful, wise, funny, intelligent University lecturer... well – I will, for one. Marion.... did you say that the position is going to be advertised? I mean, Peter hasn't officially been offered the job – yet?"

"I think they have to, even if he does get offered it. University bureaucracy."

"....And your boss" said Salvatore. "His name is?" When Marion told him, Salvatore said David Pepper's name out loud, pronouncing all the vowels in a way Marion had never heard. She couldn't even say it sounded slightly Italian. It was like Salvatore was trying to lodge the name in his head, somewhere. After a short while of uttering to himself, Salvatore said, "Leave it with me."

Marion had no idea what that meant, other than that he was going to keep repeating the name until he was satisfied with his own pronunciation, but after the way he'd kissed her last night, she really didn't care...

****

She didn't want to say it. She wanted it to come from him. But forces against her will made Marion blurt out a sort of urgency in seeing Salvatore again as they walked up to the station. "I have to go back to London. I'm here next Wednesday. Where are you going? When can I see you again?"

Salvatore explained that he had to go to Italy for a while to work. "But you know, I like Brighton, Marion. Maybe we can meet here again." So much of her life had spilled out and yet – so little of his. And now he was being as elusive as always. *Where* in Italy? How long for? Could she visit? Marion suddenly felt herself becoming all the things she didn't want to be. Needy, desperate. But her feelings were growing, and that made it painful. Maybe his weren't, maybe there were other women.....the agony of not knowing was horrendous. Against her better nature, she found herself asking Salvatore to actually set their next date.

"I will" he said, "But...." Marion let out a deep sigh. He cupped her face in his hands. "My sweet one. Of *course* I want to see you again. But I just don't know when that will be. My work is, I think you say, freelance. So you see, until I know where I next need to be, it is difficult for me to make an arrangement. But I will phone you."

"Pleeeese" stressed Marion, painfully. "Please don't say you'll phone me, if you really don't want to. I would rather you weren't courteous, or polite or didn't want to hurt my feelings. I would rather you hurt them here and now than to leave me suffering helplessly. It's much better that you men put us out of our misery on the spot, than leave us so hoping and yearning until we realise, yes actually realise, that we are never going to hear from you again."

Salvatore looked desperately hurt. "Is that what you *really* think?" Marion nodded. "But I'm telling you the truth" said Salvatore. "I would never do that to you – never. I want to be with you, see you, more than anything. Only, the powers that be dictate where I will be working – the choice isn't my own. I will call you a*s soon as I know*. I absolutely promise you."

Marion realised she didn't actually know what work Salvatore did. It seemed to involve a lot of travelling, that much was certain. He tried to explain, but still did not really provide a clear answer. "I suppose you might call what I do the study of Earth Sciences. I do ecological work, but there is also an astrological, philosophical, religious and spiritual aspect to it. It's hard for me to explain...."

"You're right there" said Marion "Do you have a job title?" Salvatore's eyes lit up.

"Ah...yes. Yes. I think so. I asked my boss what the translation might be and he said he was sure it was....yes. That's it. Maestro."

"Maestro?" Marion fell about laughing. "I think something got lost in the translation. We normally have more specific titles in this country. I usually associate the term Maestro with music."

"No" said Salvatore pensively, "It *is* correct." So what now? Apart from some kind of ecological scientist, was Salvatore about to reveal that he was also an Opera singer? He went on. "In music, you conduct things, don't you? Organise the rhythms, the orchestra, the flow of life through melody..." Now he really was beginning to sound like a Maestro. Marion smiled softly.

"Very well then. I shall call you Maestro Salvatore. I have no idea what else to call you. You don't even seem to have a surname." At this conjecture, Marion had hoped Salvatore would tell her his full name, but he just smiled and said Maestro Salvatore would do perfectly well. Just at that moment, a passing seagull dropped a turd on his forehead. Salvatore gasped, but Marion laughed out loud.

"Now, *there's* an opinion" she said as she took a tissue from her handbag and gently wiped the excrement from Salvatore's brow.

****

She sat on the train back to London Victoria as the green fields blurred into a mass of buildings and anonymous shapes. Normally Marion would use the journey to catch up on research, but this time her thoughts were elsewhere. She knew she would see him again and when or where no longer mattered. The shapes outside the window may have blurred, but her mind's eye could not have been clearer. There wasn't the same anxiety, the waiting by the phone feeling. He was there. He was everywhere.

****

The receptionist at the front desk of the University building *appeared* to be very busy, but Salvatore caught her flicking through a glossy magazine. He lifted his briefcase, put it on the counter and said good afternoon. The girl could not ignore his smile that spread from one side of his face to the other or the incredible light emanating from his twinkling dark brown eyes or even the incredibly smooth, unlined skin which was so luminous, it somehow didn't look human.

Before she knew what she was doing, the girl had organised a meeting between Salvatore and Professor David Pepper in the History of Art Department. And not only that, but she faxed over Salvatore's C.V as he stood there. David Pepper would now be in no doubt whatsoever that he had to meet him and furthermore, that there wouldn't be a second to waste.

****

CHAPTER 6

CROUCH END AND BRIGHTON

It was a seriously soggy day. Even in Crouch End, if you looked out of the window, you could barely see the horizon. Marion sort of liked the pale grey colour that only ever seemed to emanate in autumn, but once it started to get cold, then it really wasn't her favourite time of year. She thought Carolyn must've been cursing the weather; a double-edged sword for keen gardeners.

The rain kept the soil moist, but then you couldn't really get out there and dig. Perhaps it would be a very good moment to call Carolyn. Perhaps she would be sitting indoors frustrated, hoping somebody would call. Carolyn saw Marion's number flash up on her caller display and she picked up the phone.

"Bitch."

"Whaaat?" gasped Marion. "What have I done to deserve that?"

"You met a man and you didn't tell me."

" I was *going* to tell you....."

"Yes. But you haven't – yet. And Bea knows and you haven't let me know. No excuse. Bitch."

"I see..." said Marion. "Well...I wonder what you're up to now. Maybe if you're free you'd like to come round and put my lead on and take me for a walk?"

"Only if I'm going to get some sordid gossip" replied Carolyn.

"Gossip yes, sordid can't promise" said Marion, as she heard Carolyn growl down the phone. Then, she thought about David and Mira. "Actually....hmm. There *is* sordid. Yes, there is. I think you should come and take me for walkies, right now." Carolyn made a strange sound which sounded like a mix between a burp and a hiccup.

Then she told Marion to give her half an hour and she'd meet her at Felice's, on the high street. As they hung up, Marion repeated the name Felice in her head. It sounded so Italian. It was Italian. Why did there always have to be reminders....? Felice's cafe was one of the last original survivors of the high street, last but not least because it always gave excellent personal service.

Felice himself must've been about one hundred and ten by now, but he was always there in person, serving cappuccino slavishly whilst his wife made carbonara to die for. When it wasn't so busy, the couple would come and sit at customer's tables and regale then with stories of their home island of Sicily. It all sounded so romantic. Why you would want to leave the sunshine and olive groves for dusty grey London was a mystery, but Felice and Mrs Felice seemed to love the local community and their cafe. And the community loved them back and provided them with a living.

Marion was frequently guilty of diving into Starbucks or some other chain coffee house when she was in a hurry, but when you had time to linger, then Felice's was the best. Only....why did she have to have constant reminders of Salvatore, even when he wasn't there...

There were friends to catch up with, University work to catch up on and the ghastly thought of going to Brighton to find Peter there. Then she remembered Salvatore saying he would "sort it out." Her skin started to crawl a little bit....Italian, mafia, "sort it out"......NO. Marion really didn't like how that phrase sounded in that context. She glanced up at the clock. She was late.

****

Carolyn was only two shops away from Felice's when she saw Helen on the other side of the road. She was holding hands with a tall, auburn-haired woman and they were laughing and chatting. It seemed like a long time since Carolyn had seen Helen. It was time to burn some bridges. She crossed the road and invited her and her girlfriend to join her.

"You go" said Helen's friend, "Got to get to work." They gazed into each other's eyes for a while and Helen eventually let go of her hand. "You'd bloody well better call me later" said Helen, before they kissed passionately in the middle of the high street. It was a good job they were quite a few yards away from Felice's. He may have been friendly enough, but staunchly Catholic Mrs Felice was most disapproving of lesbians.

Felice's was busy. Mothers dressed in clothes from expensive catalogues or the classier end of the high street, took children in and out of pushchairs and sipped cappuccinos without moving one strand of their immaculately coiffed hair. Carolyn looked at what Helen was wearing. Helen rarely wore make-up but she had beautiful, glowing skin. Carolyn never wore make up but her complexion was rough and ruddy and made her look like she had spent all day ploughing the fields rather than tending a small vegetable patch at the back of her house.

Suddenly, for maybe the first time ever, she felt a bit ashamed. These days, lesbians looked more feminine than her. A throwback to the days of ardent burn-your-bra feminism, Carolyn professed that she liked to cut her own hair, let it turn grey and dress for comfort rather than to appease men's sexual appetites.

How she looked never seemed to deter admirers – Carolyn was a woman who you might say was very comfortable in her own skin. Yet, for some strange reason this morning, something had shaken her out of it. She wasn't to know exactly what this "something" was, until sometime later. Marion hadn't arrived yet, and glancing around, Carolyn was a bit worried they wouldn't get a table. Suddenly, Helen grabbed Carolyn's arm and pushed her long, sharp elbows in between a group of yummy mummies who were dithering over where to sit. Helen focussed determinedly on a good little corner spot that had exactly three chairs. She saw a yummy mummy make a grab for one of the chairs, but with her height and ultra long legs, Helen was able to leap into the chair well before the mummy could grab the top of it.

"Mine" said Helen defiantly, crossing her arms. There then ensued a bit of a non-verbal exchange whereby the mummy glanced at Helen, then at Carolyn, then at the chair. Helen knew the woman was thinking there were only two of them, whilst she herself was in a group of three. Then the woman saw that

Helen had plonked her bag down on another chair as Carolyn moved in to sit on the other.

Helen was obviously one of those annoying woman who puts a bag or coat on a spare chair for ages and ages, allegedly reserved for a friend that never shows up, or not at least for another hour. The mummy kept up her resistance. Eventually Helen said, "It's for our friend...poor thing....she can't stand up well after her leg operation.....they may have to remove...." A crocodile tear fell from her eye as Helen glanced downwards.

The mummy looked a bit embarrassed and shuffled off saying she'd find another chair. "Wow, impressive" said Carolyn at Helen's Bafta worthy performance.

"What are lesbians for?" said Helen, "I don't do niceties with Desperate Housewives." Just then, Marion came in and spotting her, Carolyn immediately leapt off her chair and ran to greet her. Before Marion could say hello, Carolyn grabbed her by the arm.

"Quick, limp" she said.

"What?" said Marion.

"Really badly. Like your leg is almost hanging off, or something."

"But, why....?" Carolyn kicked Marion so hard in the shin so that she almost doubled-up, then put her hand over her mouth to stop her yelling and led her to her seat as the yummy mummies looked on in pity. As she sat, Marion examined her leg to see a bruise forming. Helen went to give her a hug.

"Hi Marion, lovely to see you again. So sorry, but if we didn't have at least one disabled person amongst our party, then we'd never have gotten a table." Marion couldn't talk, so exasperated was she. Then she glanced around the cafe and saw how over brimming it was with customers. It was the time of day when people were really starting to pack in. She also noticed a plethora of push chairs taking up a lot of space.

Helen tutted and shook her head. "Think they bloody own the place" she muttered.

"I take it you don't want any kids then?" said Marion.

"Christ, no" said Helen. "Look at the mucky, screeching little things. No thank you very much."

"I had one once....." said Marion, her voice growing fainter and trailing off.

"You? Sorry, I had no idea. Is he...she.....?" Helen felt very awkward as Marion had looked so sad as she said it. Marion soon enlightened her.

"I have no idea where *he* is" she said, eventually. "Must have just had his twenty-seventh birthday."

"I.... I'm so sorry" said Helen. "Do you *want* to know where he is?" Marion looked at her sadly. She hadn't spoken about Gabriel for years. It was a big thing to admit to someone that she hardly knew, but Helen seemed genuinely concerned. Besides, she had shared a weekend with Marion where baring your soul was as much common practice as sharing a glass of wine.

Before Marion could say more, Carolyn returned to the table with a tray full of cakes and coffees. She sensed some kind of meaningful exchange between Marion and Helen and immediately felt excluded. There seemed to be an ethereal "bond" between them, which Carolyn concluded was to do with them both being in new relationships. As she passed some carrot cake over to Marion, she realised Marion looked very sad. Maybe it wasn't working out with the new man, after all.

Helen looked a bit distant as she helped herself to her espresso and a slice of lemon drizzle. Carolyn sighed as she spooned up some tiramisu. She'd been gone five minutes and already a whole drama had been played out – one she wasn't part of. Carolyn decided to be jovial. "So Hels – how long you been seeing the brunette?" Helen blushed and sunk into her seat.

"Ahem. Early days. A bit of discretion, if you will."

"Discretion?" blurted Carolyn. "You were hardly dealing in that whilst you were playing tonsil hockey outside." Helen almost threw a fork at Carolyn.

"Excuse me, I need the toilet" said Helen, leaving the table.

"What the hell was all that about?" said Marion.

"No idea" said Carolyn. "Bit touchy, isn't she?"

"Not Helen – *you*. You can tell she was really embarrassed. It's nice that she's happy with someone. You don't have to be all schoolgirl about it."

"You *know* I always tell it like it is" said Carolyn crossly. " Are things a bit frosty in sunny Tuscany these days?" This was uncalled for. Marion pushed her cake away and went off to the toilet to find Helen. Carolyn looked bemused. As Marion and Helen returned to the table, Marion asked Helen if she'd like to join her in Starbucks where the lunchtime rush might be quieter, and continue their conversation there.

Now Carolyn was really left out. She sat staring at three pieces of cake and remaining dregs of coffees all to herself and the whispering, giggling gossip of numerous yummy mummies.

****

It was back home alone that Carolyn let an alien feeling of shame creep over her. That woman who'd just let rip at her friends in Felice's, wasn't her – surely? She must've been temporarily "possessed", shocked out of her own body by the presence of too many young women with prams. She'd waited at home expecting an angry Marion to phone her, but there was no call. From anyone.

Suddenly, bright, positive, feisty Carolyn who was always at parties and always the life and soul of them felt – lonely. She had only herself to blame for the isolation. Accepting that she was currently bitter, jealous and twisted was a hard pill to swallow. She'd never been that bothered about being in a relationship – something everyone else had always envied. She'd been the fun-loving, free spirit with money to travel and cherry pick lovers. But now, deep inside was an aching loneliness that no one really knew about.

That was why she did all these New age workshops and courses – she was longing to find a real soul-mate; someone she really did connect with on a very deep level. Eventually she left a very apologetic message on Marion's answer phone, saying she'd been feeling a touch grouchy, but knew that was no excuse. Later that evening she dialled Bea's number, but Bea was either out or not answering either. Carolyn had had one little moment of madness. Did that preclude her from her friends ever talking to her again....?

****

That evening, back for dinner in Felice's, Marion felt guilty. She picked at her gnocchi and pesto dish, whilst Felice looked on with concern. Bea wolfed down her seafood pizza. "I shouldn't just have walked out on Carolyn" said Marion, "She was being weird, but obviously she's not ok – I mean, in herself. If she's feeling vulnerable for any reason, I should be there to listen."

"She'll cool off" said Bea, continuing to shovel in mouthfuls of food and gulp down her prosciutto.

"Blimey" said Marion, "Kids stressing you out, or their parents?"

"No" said Bea. "I'm *enjoying* my food. I'm enjoying it because – because I'm happy." Marion put her cutlery down. She couldn't express her delight at hearing her old friend say that. She scanned Bea's face. It was true. The deep grooves that had started to appear between her eyes as a visible sign of Bea's distress had softened considerably. Her skin looked clear and her eyes which had looked sad and distant for years now had their old sparkle back. She seemed very present and in the moment, instead of wistfully nostalgic, wishing to be back in the past days of perceived happier times.

Marion felt a little tear trickle down her cheek. "Oh, please *don't*" said Bea, "I'm not *that* happy!"

Marion wiped the tear away. "Thank goodness for that! I'm not sure I can cope with a friend who is problem free." Then Marion looked pensive. "I'm just thinking....do you remember when we first met Peter in Glastonbury?" Bea nodded. "He seemed extremely happy to me. And peaceful. Sort of, 'at one' with himself. And yet....how can you be that happy and do what he did? Behave that way?"

Bea thought. "Perhaps being a nasty bastard is what *makes* him happy. All that front, giving seminars and being an expert consultant on lifestyle....I struggle with that, as well. He's a charlatan, and yet...yet, his course was really good...."

"Which makes it even more deplorable" said Marion. "And I'm afraid there's worse to come. I think Peter's coming to lecture at my university – in *my* department." Bea gasped. Marion went on to explain about the new Esoteric Studies course and how keen David and Mira were on him and his C.V.

"Well, that's unless there's someone *better*", Bea suggested.

"How can there be?" said Marion, despairingly. "He's already such a name and he has pristine qualifications. He's also extremely charming, so I'm sure he'll fly through the interview. What am I gonna do, Bea...?"

"I guess... wait until you get back to Uni" said Bea. "Tiramisu?"

Marion nodded.

****

Carolyn apologised. Marion apologised too. That was enough. Tension somewhere along the line of such long friendships wasn't unusual and as long as there was honesty, could usually be resolved. To this end, Marion invited Carolyn round for coffee and was somewhat surprised when Carolyn said she was going to the hairdressers.

That wasn't a place she had set foot in for at least twenty years. Why now? Nonetheless, Carolyn said she was free to meet in Felice's later. Felice pulled a chair up beside Marion as she waited. "Mrs Marion – why donta you move in, huh? My wife, she love to feed you all day long. Lika nothing better."

Marion laughed. "Felice, I'd be as big as a house." Felice shook his head as he glanced at her petite frame. Suddenly Marion let out a yelp as she saw the sight outside the window of the cafe. Walking past was Carolyn with bright orange hair.

"Hello!" said Felice, cheerily, saying nothing about the new "do". Carolyn nodded at him and sat down opposite Marion.

"Say nothing" she instructed. "I *asked* for this. 'Fox', it's called. A beautiful shade of auburn on the colour chart. This is more like Terry's bloody chocolate orange. I paid a fortune to look like a fruit bowl, Marion." Marion found herself lost for words. Carolyn wouldn't be the first woman to have a "hairdressing malfunction", but she'd be less used to them than most.

Carolyn had thick, beautiful, silvery hair that she had never dyed. What had brought this on? Marion remembered that Bea had once gone blonde which was a big mistake with her sallow skin and that when she herself had gone darker, she'd felt she needed lots of make-up to look alive, but...Carolyn would not have experienced colouring horrors. She didn't really look *that* bad – she just didn't look like Carolyn.

"You just need to wait until it fades a bit" said Marion. "Which it will – that's what happens when you have fresh colour applied."

"Oh Marion, what on earth possessed me?" said Carolyn.

"Yes – what *did*?" asked Marion. Carolyn knew Marion wasn't just referring to her hair. She knew she'd been behaving erratically. She confessed.

Carolyn sighed deeply. "You see....all my friends seem to be falling in love."

"And that means you need orange hair?" queried Marion.

"I'm feeling frumpy – old" said Carolyn. "I looked through my wardrobe yesterday and it's all full of smock tops and leggings. I haven't bought myself anything that isn't from Oxfam since 1999."

"But smocks and leggings are you" said Marion.

"Yes, but I don't want them to be me anymore" said Carolyn. "I'm feeling left out. Lonely. Inadequate." This surprised Marion.

"I'm sorry" said Marion, "Really sorry that you feel like this. I wasn't even aware that you wanted to be in love or even had space for anyone in your life. As for your clothes – well. I can always take you shopping."

Carolyn had never married or had children. Her clothes and demeanour suggested that she had never wanted either. It therefore came as a shock to Marion, what Carolyn offered up next.

"I think I'm grieving" she said "There's the life I have, and the life I might have had. Sometimes I look out of the window in my back room at my garden and wonder what it would have been like to have a slide and swings there and a messy old sandpit where all my neat rows of cabbages are. I wonder what it would have been like to watch a chubby, bearded man playing with these children, *our* children, and feeling...actually having that bond..."

Marion felt a little tear trickle down her cheek. She'd once had a husband. And a child. She'd once had a "bond" with her husband, but never with her son. And there were no bonds with either of them now. She was also grieving...tears started to come.

"Marion...I didn't mean to upset you..." But it was too late. Despite her new found joy, Marion still needed to grieve. Tears came trickling down the faces of both women as Felice tried to place complimentary coffees down, but then went and fetched his wife as the women cried for what they thought they may have been, were brought up to strive for and yet didn't achieve.

At the same time, they both failed to recognise the richness and privilege of their lives and so they wiped their tears away, put on their very British stiff upper lips and pulled leaflets out of their handbags to see what New Age workshop they could book themselves onto next...

****

"I...I'm not sure" said Bea.

"What do you mean not s*ure*?" asked Marion.

"I think I might like to give it a rest for a while" said Bea. This was news to Marion's ears. Bea was always the most enthusiastic when it came to workshops. It made her feel very vulnerable that Bea was feeling secure enough *not* to do one. Bea explained that she just felt a bit on "information overload", but was sure she'd come to something at a future date. At the moment, she'd rather spend some time at home researching and reading.

Marion normally didn't feel so insecure, but that morning Carolyn and her orange hair had stripped away layers of self-preservation and defence and put Marion in an unusually anxious state. In comparison, Bea was relaxed and gentle. She invited Marion over for dinner. As Marion arrived, the smell of homemade nut roast and steamed vegetables filled the air.

Marion noticed a pile of books on Bea's coffee table – some with bookmarks in, some with corners folded over and several lying upside down at the place Bea had gotten up to. Bea had been busy. Marion longed to be nosy and look at what Bea was reading, but didn't dare touch any of the literature, in case she lost a carefully marked place.

Bea put down a bowl of nuts and olives on the table. Finally Marion asked "Are you researching something?" Bea was more than researching. She was obsessed. She'd been reading practically anything she could get her hands on about aliens – books about their origins, books claiming that many lived amongst humans without them even realising it, books with drawings by people that claimed they had been abducted.

Bea had also joined some internet forums and it seemed she now wanted to spend more time on these, than come to Glastonbury or the like. Amidst all the interplanetary paraphernalia, Marion noticed another book by a well-known New Age writer. She hadn't read his stuff, but didn't think he was a specialist on aliens. She glimpsed at the name. Salvatore Rosso. It rung a bell, although Marion couldn't remember why. It wasn't because of *her* Salvatore, even though Marion realised she didn't actually know his surname. He was just "Maestro", to her.

How bizarre. She must have known him for at least a month, now. Bea offered a pot of Earl Grey tea as the delicious vegetarian dinner browned under the grill. She sat down excitedly beside Marion. "I can't get enough of it" she told her. "Just *think*....all this going on beyond this planet and helping this planet evolve and...."

Marion cut in. "And *destroying* this planet" she said.

Bea was upset. "Why are you so cynical? It's *us* who are destroying the planet. Humans can do that all by themselves. We need help."

"Well, how do you *know* these aliens are friendly?" asked Marion. "Is it because some random author says so?"

"I've read enough, and anyway, I've got my own evidence" said Bea.

"Your *own* evidence?" said Marion.

"Yes" said Bea "But I'm not going to go into that now. It's *this* that I wanted to discuss with you. Some other research I've been doing." Bea picked up the book by Salvatore Rosso, eager to divert attention from the alien discussion.

 It quickly became apparent that neither of the women wanted a row, but Marion made it quite clear that she was happy to listen, provided Bea understood that she also might not agree with her. Before she began however, Bea noticed a little bookmark sticking out of Marion's handbag that was embossed with a little fleur de lis. Then she noticed the same flower on Marion's sandals.

Bea moved forward to examine them all, as though she were carrying out some kind of forensics. "Fleur de lis..." said Bea, "Where did you get these from?" her tone was almost accusatory. Marion was surprised. She explained that she'd bought the sandals and Salvatore had given her the bookmark. Then she thought back...that was odd. Her shoe buckles were the first thing Salvatore had noticed about her. Marion told Bea that she'd noticed the symbol turning up in her life quite a lot, but thought it was just coincidence. Bea put her hand to her heart.

"Oh my gosh, Marion – do you know what that symbol means? It's just sooo romantic! As in, real *soul-mate* romantic. The left hand side of the flower represents the woman and the right hand side the male and that section in the middle is their perfect union – the strong and all abiding force." Marion didn't really know what Bea meant, but she knew she was impressed. It *sounded* nice. And it sounded romantic. Until Bea continued....

"Your man of mystery. It all makes sense now. I think I know who he is...." Marion waited whilst Bea decided to reveal the planet of his derivation. But Bea was firmly on terra firma. She picked up her book again. "He's *this* man. Salvatore Rosso, the spiritual writer. You know about him?"

"A bit" said Marion, "Never read his stuff, but wasn't there all that hullabaloo a while back about him dying in mysterious circumstances?"

"That's right" continued Bea "And the body was never found."

"Wait a minute...." said Marion slowly "And you think....you think, he's still alive?" Surely this was completely implausible. Why would he pick on her, of all people? She'd never read his books – knew nothing about him. But maybe that was a reason. The fact that he was unknown to her may have been a big part of the attraction – she'd never suspect anything. As Marion, with Bea's help began to piece together sections of Salvatore's elusive jigsaw – his disappearing and re-manifesting acts, his intelligence and knowledge about the esoteric worlds - some of the colour started to drain from Marion's face.

Bea was so intoxicated with her new findings, that she didn't notice. Finally Marion asked Bea what Salvatore wrote about. "Oh my gosh" said Bea. "The most incredible, beautiful things. Can I read you some?" Bea read out a description of the Italian countryside which sounded like a storyboard for a film script. You could almost taste the olives growing on the trees, so vivid was the writing. And then there was a short story about a boy skipping who could talk to animals which was presented in such a clever way that children would get it, and yet it was loaded with meaning and allegory. This sounded like Marion's Salvatore, alright.

He may have been effusive and frustrating, but he also had a way of explaining things with a great clarity and with imagery. He was also gentle and funny and the more Bea read, the more convinced Marion became that she had found her man. "You say he died in mysterious circumstances?" Marion asked.

Bea nodded "I'm surprised you've never read him. He's highly underrated, but ever since he allegedly died, his books have shot up in the posthumous ratings."

"So – you think it was all a marketing ploy?" asked Marion.

"Well....there's a bit more to it than that. There was a rival who claimed Salvatore Rosso plagiarised all his work. But then that's quite another story in itself."

Marion took a deep gulp. "Good grief, Bea – do you think I've found the missing body....?"

****

Marion dreaded heading to Brighton that morning and not just because she hadn't completed two research documents, that had completely slipped her mind in her loved-up state. It was because she also knew that Peter would be introduced as the new Head of Esoteric Studies, and she was going to have to pretend she had never met him. She'd had a sleepless night wondering what would happen if Peter said he already knew *her*.

Her heart pounded as the train passed Preston Park, drawing closer to her destination. She badly needed a distraction – she should look at those papers. As she took the prints from her briefcase, the little fleur de lis on the corners of the pages seemed to be glowing and leaping off the page. Now they stood out more than the colours and shapes of the print itself.

The first thing Salvatore had ever noticed about her. If only Marion knew more about the symbology of this little flower, but she only knew it as a design in heraldry. She'd have to ask Salvatore when she next saw him – whenever that might be. Once she reached the double doors that led to David Pepper's office, images of little flowers had left her mind and been replaced by an entire field of butterflies in her stomach.

Marion hesitated before pushing open the already ajar door. "Ah! Marion! Do come in! I'd like you to meet our new Head of Esoteric Studies" said David.

"I've heard a lot about you, Dr Green...." said Salvatore, as he stood up to shake the hand of a completely astonished Marion.

****

There wasn't even time to speak to Salvatore. David and Mira needed to spend the whole day going through official paperwork with him, leaving Marion to marvel at what he had done. This convinced her that he was indeed, Salvatore Rosso. Who else would have the background and knowledge? Gaining the prestigious lecturer's position had been perfectly executed. He must have had an impeccable C.V to have been chosen over Peter, not to mention that his charm obviously won over the History of Art Department. Peter must've been seething.

Marion however, was smiling from ear to ear. Her lover was there – working at her University. He couldn't disappear with such alarming alacrity, if he had a regular job to attend. Eventually, Marion found a second free with David to ask why he had chosen Salvatore over all the other applicants. David told her that CV aside, the interview had been outstanding.

Salvatore had explained both intricate facts and abstract ideas to both David and Mira with such clarity, that it had left them in no doubt that young students would adore him. With him at the helm, they expected a healthy intake of applicants. It couldn't have worked out better. Peter was good and he was well known, but when it came to delivering a lecture, no one quite had the charisma of Salvatore.

Marion smiled to herself. How funny it would be when David and Mira discovered she and Salvatore were an item. "Yes" said David. "Salvatore Campo de' Fiori has been a real find."

"*Campo de' Fiori?*" said Marion "But I thought his surname was....no. Never mind." Of course. If Salvatore Rosso wanted people to think he was dead he was hardly going to come back to life under the mantle of his own name...

****

Salvatore wasn't the only surprise at The University of Sussex. Whilst helping to put out some leaflets for Fresher's Week, Marion bumped into Roberta. She barely recognised her. The sharp, Louise Brooks style bob was still evident, but it was now dyed purple with some flashes of scarlet highlights. She still wore a knitted hat and lacy shirt, but she looked much thinner, paler and subdued. As Marion approached, Roberta looked at the ground, awkwardly.

"I'm sorry" said Marion. "I'm sorry about what you went through. I know I've been rather harsh on you in the past, but no one should have to experience that." Roberta's big brown eyes suddenly looked very sad. It seemed like she had learnt a sudden and shocking lesson and knew there was some place she'd never visit again. Marion sat beside her. "So – what brings you to my place of work?"

"I'm just signing up for an M.A." said Roberta as she fished around in her bag for her application form. "I'm going to be doing Esoteric Studies. Can't wait. There are only two courses in the country."

"Well then – I'll be seeing a lot of you" said Marion. "And the course is being run by ...by a very dear friend of mine. I have every reason to suspect it will be excellent."

Roberta beamed. Then Marion added, "I have to say, you've had a bloody lucky escape, in that respect."

"What do you mean?" asked Roberta. Marion told her that Peter was almost her lecturer, but that he got pipped to the post at the last minute. "Christ" said Roberta "Peter, lecturing me. Perish the thought. I'd have had to leave in my first week."

"Well, that won't be necessary now" said Marion. How perfectly everything had worked out...

****

"Living in the Now courses start in October" said Carolyn down the phone, without the slightest hint of irony. Then she added, "In Glastonbury. I'm really missing my home town."

"Glastonbury *isn't* your home town" retorted Marion "Basingstoke is."

"Yes, but you know what I mean" said Carolyn "My *spiritual* home town. Where I really feel at home." Marion hesitated about signing up. She felt like she was coming to the end of this phase and besides – she only really wanted to be with Salvatore. But not joining Carolyn felt like a betrayal. Were it not for the love of her female friends, then Marion would never have gotten through the times before Salvatore had come into her life. These were the friendships that had endured – the tears, laughter, traumas, adventures...tragedies...all of life was in these friendships.

Marion thought about the men in her life. She thought she had loved, but the feeling she had for Salvatore – that all consuming, passionate, can't-live-without-you love, was something she had never actually known. A lump formed in her throat as she knew she had fallen deeply in love with him – somewhere deeper than the deepest well, beneath the bottom of the sea – somewhere that could only really be described as another galaxy.

But she didn't *really* know if he felt the same way back. He'd told her he loved her, that he wanted to be with her always, but...did he really *feel* the same emotions and connections and almost telepathy that she felt she had with him? Suddenly, a wash of insecurities overtook her. It was all to do with her past, but her history, her friends, her work and her country – what if she could never really let go?

For now, Salvatore was nearby, but this was only a temporary contract. Never mind a Living in the Now *course,* Marion began to worry far too much about the future to enjoy her "now" time. What if he wanted her to come and live in Italy with him, what then? She still didn't really know who he was. Then again, surely you sacrificed *everything* for the greatest love of your life...didn't you..? She grabbed her coat, realising she was late for work.

****

Marion burst into the office. She needed to find Salvatore. She couldn't believe she'd actually forgotten to ask him where he would be staying, and went to find out if she could help him with finding accommodation. "Salvatore's not in today" said Mira dryly. "It's Tuesday." As if Marion should know which days the Esoteric course ran on. She'd been left out of the whole process, except perhaps by manifesting the best lecturer ever.

The irony. Marion was sure neither David nor Mira had read or studied anything spiritual in their lives – that they were just doing this because it was "trendy" and had no real feel for the training. Here they were, however, pioneering one of the highest level courses ever on the subject. Marion made a mental note to borrow what Salvatore Rosso books she could from Bea. She thought it'd be a blast to ask Salvatore to sign them.

"Marion?" said Mira "You seem to be miles away. Everything OK?"

"Oh - it's nothing" said Marion.

"I can pass a message onto Salvatore if you like" said Mira.

"No worries – I'm sure I'll bump into him sooner or later" said Marion, chuckling to herself as she closed the door behind her.

****

David seemed rather bemused that Salvatore came to the University with not one single file or book, and questioned him awkwardly. "Good morning! You ready to um, roll today?" Salvatore cocked his head on one side, as though he were a small puppy trying to understand. David concluded that he didn't really understand the English slang expression. "You...are....ready...to start?" he asked, insultingly slowly. "First lecture 10.30." Salvatore smiled.

"Absolutely."

"I don't like to interfere" said David, "But can't help noticing you don't seem to have any materials with you – at all. Just wondered if you'd left your notes, er...." Salvatore simply smiled again and pointed to his head. "In there?" asked David, "You keep *everything* in there?" Salvatore nodded.

"But that simply isn't possible!" David protested. "I've been lecturing for over thirty years and I still have notes. At least for reference. I really don't know how you're just going to go into that room and give a lecture to a group of unknown students with a brand new syllabus and not use any notes."

"Well, I shall" replied Salvatore gently. "I have an idea which I start with, but the nature of things can change and if it does, then I run with the new idea, and so on. I'm absolutely confident it'll be fine."

David laughed nervously. "Well, it'd better be. After all, we did, ha, chose you over some very well qualified people. And I must warn you – the first lecture is always extremely testing, however experienced you are. The sort of students we have here – they will test you to the extreme." Salvatore noticed little beads of sweat forming on David's brow. He simply smiled again. The calmer Salvatore appeared to be, the more agitated David became. Finally Salvatore moved over to the window and pointed at some coffee and biscuits on a trolley – then to a little hip flask that David had forgotten to remove. He asked David if he'd like something poured. David nodded and cleared his throat.

"Do er, ahem. Do help yourself" said David.

"No thank you" said Salvatore, "Stimulants....they dull the mind..."

****

Marion really hoped Bea was about – she was excited and wanted to speak to her. She blurted out about Salvatore's first day at the University and giggling, asked Bea if she could borrow some books which she would get signed. She thought it might be a good idea to browse, if not read a couple of them first. It would hardly be form to never have read anything Salvatore had written and yet at the same time declare she knew who he was.

Bea sounded hesitant. "Well, I'll lend you the books, but..."

"But what?" asked Marion.

Bea began to sound more grave. She decided, however, that Marion must know. She had just read the last book in the series, and it was obvious, reading between the lines, that the author was going to die.

"I don't understand" said Marion. "Do you mean that Salvatore has predicted his own death?"

"He might be on the run" warned Bea. Marion could not digest this. The enigmatic, funny, other worldly Salvatore who had completely captured Marion's heart could surely not be a fugitive. Unfortunately, it did all make sense. He was aloof and effusive for the same reason he had registered at the University under a different name. David or Mira could never have recognised his identity. Their knowledge of spiritual matters was scant, and anyway – Salvatore Rosso, despite his "death" was still not awfully commercial and little known in the New Age worlds.

If anybody *was* well read enough to set up the Esoteric studies course, then it was Marion. For years she had read books and articles and attended numerous seminars. Apart from her love of art, the study of the unseen worlds was her life-blood. It was part of being with her closest friends, it was part of *her*.

And now, after all these years, she had met a soul-mate who could identify with her passion. Everyone thought he was dead, but he wasn't – yet. Marion felt thick stomach acid rise to her throat. She swallowed hard and felt her oesophagus burn. It couldn't be that Salvatore, *her* Salvatore would be taken away from her. Not now, not when she had only just found him.

Bea could sense the panic rising in Marion's body, but Bea didn't know what to do either. Her best friend's lover was on the run – not from the law, but from a potential assassin. How the hell did Marion think Bea would know what to do? It wasn't exactly a problem either of them had come up against before. Bea felt herself panicking, but she didn't want to let Marion see it.

All those years when she had been incapable of functioning, lovesick with pain for Michael, it was Marion who had held her up, come over, cooked for her and made her eat when she could barely face food. Now Bea owed Marion her full support. But what should they do? Should they confront Salvatore or go to the police or might they endanger his life? Bea did the only thing she could think of to do in such circumstances. She took Marion shopping.

****

It was an understatement to say that Salvatore was concerned about Marion's demeanour the next time he saw her at the University. Perhaps she was unwell, or tired, or over-stressed. She seemed pale and wan as opposed to her usual self, and very quiet. He approached her one day in the canteen. Marion barely looked at him.

"My little petal" said Salvatore, trying to take Marion's hand in his. "Whatever is wrong? Is it me?" he took a large gulp, starting to feel very anxious about her answer. Perhaps, suddenly – cruelly, she had fallen out of love with him. Slowly, Marion looked up, her skin sallow and yellow and her lips dry.

Eventually, she spoke. "Salvatore...I know who you are." Salvatore's smooth, tanned skin turned several shades of varying colours that Marion could swear she had never seen before.

****

Carolyn, rabbiting down the phone about the "Living in the Now" course was no help whatsoever. Eventually, Marion just said, "I can't go."

"Whaaat? But I've already booked it for you! You told me you wanted to go!" said a surprised Carolyn.

"Carolyn.....I can't explain. I really am living in the NOW. Like, right at this moment. So, I don't need a course – I need protection." Carolyn could immediately hear that something was very wrong. She tried to pacify Marion and once she had gauged that the outburst was about Salvatore, immediately concluded that they had split up.

If this was the case however, then surely the course would be good for Marion? It would help take her mind off him – keep her focussed elsewhere. "We'll protect you" said Carolyn softly and was happy as Marion grumpily relented. It may have been running away from her problems, but there were times when that was an acceptable solution to all of them.

****

When Marion announced her mini-break to Salvatore, he was crest-fallen. How could she have possibly found out about him and only in the space of a few days, at that? It wasn't possible. There was no way she could have known, unless...No. If that was the case, then they would have contacted him..It was too early. Way too soon. Why then was she so upset and refusing to talk to him?

No – it must've been something else. Maybe she'd heard something, assumed he'd been unfaithful, or maybe, maybe...she just couldn't quite tell him that *she* had met someone else. But that couldn't be. He couldn't have come all that way for *that* to happen...

****

"Marion – STOP!" commanded Carolyn. "Stop the car. You're definitely in no fit state to drive. Let me take over." Reluctantly, Marion pulled in.

"It's not right, Carolyn – I shouldn't be here. I should have said something to him before I left – not just have left him in the lurch. What if something happens, and I'm not there?"

"What if something happens and you *are* there?" asked Carolyn. "Salvatore's a grown man. I'm sure he can manage without you for a weekend." She looked at Marion's face. "But...oh, good grief, no. Please don't tell me you can't manage without *him*. You will. You can. You're with us and together we will all manage."

Marion slumped forward over the steering wheel and Carolyn pressed on the hazard lights button as they sat on the hard shoulder. It was a grey gloomy day and even if Marion felt like curling up in a ball, they needed to be seen on the motorway. Gently, Carolyn persuaded Marion to let her drive and continue their journey. They spent the next two hours in silence as Marion reached into her handbag, switched off her mobile and stared blankly and miserably at the long stretch of road ahead in the distance.

****

A short while after Marion and Carolyn reached their bed and breakfast in Glastonbury, Bea and Roberta pulled up. Bea had also relented. She'd been enthused and driven by her alien research, but the zest for her research ebbed and flowed and she didn't want to feel left out of a girlie gathering. Helen and her girlfriend were going to make their way down by coach, deciding to link it in with a visit to the Bristol Art Gallery.

This exhibition was something Marion had wanted to see, but she was hardly in the mood now. Carolyn had managed to book rooms in an Ashram, at the bottom of the Tor. She'd spent months on Ashrams in India, liked them and also this was cheaper than their usual accommodation. The others weren't so sure about staying there.

Breakfast was at 7am, after early morning meditation. Bea considered lying in and skipping breakfast, but then thought she couldn't possibly get through a morning of intensive workshops without any food. Once beds had all been allocated, Carolyn said she was going to pop out for five minutes. Her friends surveyed their surroundings.

The place was rather stark and basic. Not that they needed anything else, but they'd all got used to material comforts. Bea lifted a very thin duvet off the bed and shook her head, just as Carolyn came back, rushing into the room with a bottle of Shiraz and a stack of plastic cups. "Quick girls, get that down you. Not meant to have any alcohol in here."

"Oh my goodness" said Bea sarcastically, "If I'd known we weren't going to get gin for breakfast, then I never would have come..."

Carolyn ignored her. "I think Marion could use a tipple. Go on Mrs – get that down your neck. It'll make everything better. For a while..." Bea folded her arms and frowned. She protested that booze wasn't the answer. She said that what Marion needed was support and a cup of herbal tea.

"Are you joking?" said Carolyn, "We've only been in Glastonbury five minutes, I've spent a tenner on medicine and you've gone all bloody hippy on me. Loosen up, will you? We're in the hippiest b&b I could find. There'll be plenty of time for herbal tea at 7am."

"I can't believe you're doing this" said Bea. "Marion is really cut up and you come into a sacred Ashram with cheap wine..."

"It *wasn't* cheap", Carolyn cut in. Bea continued.

"You come into a sacred Ashram with wine thinking that getting pissed is going to make all the pain go away. Have you no respect?"

"I respect Marion" spat back Carolyn "Which is why I've brought her here and why I'm going to look after her."

"You call that respect?" screeched Bea, "She needs T.L.C. Not inebriation." The women's voices rose at volume as Marion just sat on the bed, observing the bickering. When it reached fever pitch, an alarmed looking, petite Indian girl bedecked in a fuchsia pink sari and holding a bowl of incense, walked into the room without knocking.

"Ladies! You are disturbing the other guests. We do ask you to respect the rules of the Ashram, which includes keeping the noise down. Is there a problem with anything?"

"No, there's no problem" said Marion as she picked up her handbag and walked out. "I could use some peace and quiet."

****

Somewhat shamefacedly, Carolyn and Bea made up. They apologised to the Indian girl and offered to help her "space clear" the rooms. When Bea rung a little bell, it chimed out loud and clear. "That's because the atmosphere in here is so clean" explained the Indian girl. "Most of the people who stay here meditate regularly and purify themselves. Some of my personal work involves going into offices and doing cleanses in there. There is much, sticky energy if you will, in these places. It requires much intensive sound cleansing and often exorcisms of dark spirits, too."

Carolyn looked shocked. She used to work for large, corporate firms. "I do a lot of work in London" said the girl "And then I can come back and settle here." She collected her smoking cones and Tibetan cymbals and rolled up some rugs before heading back down the stairs.

"I like it here" said Bea, turning to Carolyn. "Thank you for finding us this place. You'd better go and hide the wine, though....."

****

CHAPTER 7

GLASTONBURY

Why on earth Marion had decided to use alcohol to clear her mind, was anybody's guess. An excess of Pear cider was making her hallucinate. She could swear that the two women sitting opposite had grown pink wings and fairy crowns, and then she remembered that she was in Glastonbury. Staggering across the pub to the toilets, the pictures of male and female signs blurred into one, and desperate for a pee and concluding that she was wearing trousers and not a skirt, Marion shoved open the door of the Gents.

Seeing a man with very long hair standing at a urinal, Marion thought she was in the Ladies, and stumbled towards a cubicle. The man turned round. "M...Marion?" It was Stephen the Wizard. Marion could barely make out the shape, but the voice was distinctive.

"Whaaara you doing in the Ladies?" she asked. Hastily pushing down his gown over his exposed privates, Stephen went to catch Marion as she nearly fell headlong into a urinal. "Shotoppit!" she protested, "I need to pissshhh!" Stephen gently guided her out the door and into the Ladies. A black figure on the door appeared to be wearing a skirt. She looked at Stephen again and he looked like he was wearing a skirt, which made things terribly confusing.

However, Marion's accumulated consumption of cider over-rode everything else at that moment and after a loud noise of gushing water, she let out a long "Ahhh" sound. After that, she sat on the loo for a long while, her head in her hands, trying to stop it from spinning round so much. Eventually there was an angry knock on the door.

"For Godsake, hurry up love. Have you fallen down the hole?"

"I....I don't feel very well....." slurred Marion.

"Oh Christ...." the voice outside the door had a broad Somerset accent. "Do I need to get you help?"

"No, I...." Marion unlocked the door and stumbled out, still pulling her jeans up.

"Alright, alright my lovely" said the woman, seeing Marion, who was not exactly a spring chicken in her worse for wear state. "Where do you live? We'll get you back OK." Marion blurted that she didn't live anywhere – she was doing a course. "A course?" said the woman. "Well, I don't know what made you come in here and do this to yourself tonight, but you might want to think about taking the morning off this course you're doing...I do consultancy work myself, and...." an awful thought struck the woman who now found she was trying to hold Marion upright. This inebriated wreck might be signed up for *her* course.

She led Marion out of the lavatories, and Stephen helped the woman drag Marion over to the woman's car. "Do you know her?" asked the woman. "Said she's doing a course. Hope it's not my one...."

"Yes, so do I" said Stephen, anxiously peering into the back seat as Marion was belted in.

****

Marion peered out sheepishly from under the bed covers. "Drunk and disorderly in an Ashram" muttered Carolyn. "Disgraceful."

"But it was *your* idea to drink" protested Marion "Bet you polished off that bottle of wine, n'all".

"We were going to come and look for you" said Bea, "But you didn't give us much time. I can't believe you downed that amount of cider so quickly."

"I can't believe you weren't puking your guts out" said Carolyn. "It's potent stuff."

"Leave me alone – I'm suffering" moaned Marion.

"It's just fortuitous that such a nice, helpful lady also needed a piss and brought you back here. We really should try and find out who she was, so that we can thank her" said Carolyn.

"Glastonbury is a small place" added Bea, "We're bound to bump into her. She was pretty distinct looking anyway, with all that pink hair. Anyway, I need some grub. Think you can face it, Marion?" Marion groaned again and shook her head. Herb tea and macrobiotic seaweed pancakes were hardly her idea of hair of the dog.

"No moving until we get back from breakfast then" said Bea. "I'm not letting you out of my sight again the rest of the weekend." As they descended the staircase, Carolyn said she couldn't believe Marion had gotten so drunk. She didn't think she was *that* gutted over Salvatore.

"In fact" said Carolyn, "I thought they were just taking a bit of a break. They haven't actually split up, have they?"

"Who knows?" said Bea "He, I mean it, is all a bit of a mystery....."

****

People, including the cleaning staff at the Bakshi Ashram were not late risers. Marion had to fake illness just to be allowed to get up and get dressed. Then she realised she'd already been put into bed with all her clothes on. There was just caked on make up to wash off and lipstick smears on the sheets. The last time Marion had woken up in that sort of state, she was probably about eighteen.

On the bedside table, she saw that Carolyn had written down the address and directions for the venue of the "Living in the Now" course. She tucked it into her handbag and tried to sneak out the door unnoticed. The little pink-sari clad Indian girl was there. She looked Marion up and down and gave her a look that seemed to be like tutting, although she was making no sound.

"Good morning" she said "You're rather late for breakfast, but if you go in the kitchen and speak to the chef he may have some bread left or get some cereal for you." Marion thanked the girl, but said she'd probably just skip breakfast. She got a filthy look. Why did we have to stay somewhere so bloody devout, she thought.

There was a bracing wind outside – perfect for clearing her fuzzy head. Maybe there was even time to climb up the Tor. As she climbed, it seemed to take longer to reach the top than she had remembered. Panting and looking for a resting place, Marion looked around to see a lady with long speckled grey and Titian hair, meditating in her long purple velvet robe.

In her mind's eye, Marion saw a vision of long ago. When she had first come to Glastonbury as a young woman, when her heart had first been broken – this was where she'd sat. Marion stared out over the fields and watched a herd of cows keep moving around, making oddly symmetrical shapes. There was a church spire and some distant haystacks – the omnipresent view.

Marion let out a long sigh as the woman beside her continued to meditate. All those years of life, hopes and dreams, bereavements and traumas. Marion was no longer a girl desperate to find the love of her life. She wondered if her feelings for Salvatore were fuelled by simple fantasy – by all the teachings she had grown up with; fed as a young woman. Was any of that happy ever after stuff for real?

Marion's relationship with Salvatore went far beyond the realms of physical attraction and the romantic knight in armour who came to the rescue from loneliness. It was hard for her to articulate, but she thought of it as a "meeting of minds", that they seemed to be so like each other – so in touch with each other's thoughts and feelings. Amidst her long-forged female friendships, he was her best male friend and yet also the most tender lover she had ever met.

How the world had changed since she was a little girl, dressing up in Princess clothes. She'd done the getting married and having a baby bit. That was what her parents had done. Now, where was her son? What was he doing? As Marion felt some tears trickle down her cheeks, the woman next to her took hold of her hand. Marion didn't resist. It felt right. There was a powerful moment next when Marion realised the woman she really was.

She was strong, she could be on her own and she could be peaceful. She may not have fulfilled the expectations of her younger self, but looking back, she had achieved so much. Marion felt the energy of the other woman flow into her palm and right inside her body. A perfect stranger giving her exactly what she needed on the crest of Glastonbury Tor, without paying for an expensive course, booking hotels or being at the bottom of a Shaman's waiting list.

There, on the hill, was a pure act of humanity. An act whereby Marion received exactly the kind of healing she needed.

****

"Heavenly Health" housed a room that was bedecked in a not dissimilar fashion to the Internal Feng Shui course. The fashionable incense burned, as did the "Sounds of the Sea" CD. Next to the CD player sat a wooden Buddha, who looked like he might have liked to listen to something else.

The course leader came in the room and Bea and Carolyn gasped – as did she. It was the woman who had brought Marion back the night before. Anxiously, the lady glanced round the room and then seemed relieved to see that Marion wasn't there. Helen and her partner didn't know what had happened – they'd been in a room on another floor of the Ashram.

Lynn, the course leader introduced herself. "Good morning everyone and thank you for being here so early. As you know, I believe in Living In the Now and I believe that now is the best time to have a cup of tea. I believe that Now should be easy and comfortable and that you should all be refreshed. Please do help yourselves to a selection of English Breakfast, Earl Grey and various herb teas and begin the morning with seeing just how pleasant Living in the Now really is."

"I like *her*" Carolyn whispered to Helen. At the tea urn, Roberta wanted to know what had happened with Marion the previous evening, but Lynn made everyone return to their seats quickly.

Marion had left the woman-on-the-Tor with just a parting smile and few small tears. Neither of them had said a word to each other. Whatever it was that Marion had had to face in herself, she had just sat and looked at it and put it aside – for now, at least. The urge to attend the course at this moment was not exactly huge, but the urge for a big, frothy cappuccino was.

Luckily, "Avachar" was open, full of early morning visitors. Stephen the Wizard was in there peering at a leaflet over the top of his spectacles. "Hello!" said Marion cheerily, not remembering anything about the incident the night before. He coloured, looked away awkwardly and removed his glasses.

"H...hello Marion" he eventually said softly, trying to keep his voice down. "You're ok....?"

"Sure" said Marion, "Why shouldn't I be?"

"Oh, no reason – no reason at all" said Stephen, heaving a sigh of relief that Marion had not remembered seeing him "exposed", so to speak. "Here – why don't you join me?" Marion did so and ordered some coffee and a granola bar. Somehow, without any lead up to it, she found herself telling Stephen all about Salvatore. Fortunately for her, he turned out to be a very good listener and offered advice without judgement.

"So, my friend – you have fallen in love. And deeply." Marion's eyes became moist.

"Yes – yes, I believe I have" she said, trying not to cry.

"It's quite alright to cry" said Stephen "Emotions shouldn't be bottled up." He sounded like a woman. "Furthermore, whatever you say to me stays with me, OK?" Here was a good man. A trustworthy friend with several metres of hair. He was just the right stranger to tell your troubles to.

It transpired that Stephen knew quite a lot about Salvatore Rosso and was fascinated to hear that he might indeed be alive. "A fascinating man, yet highly underrated. He was the sort of person you heard about via word of mouth – there's little about him on the internet. He was, is, if current rumours are to be believed, apparently very private." That sounded like Marion's Salvatore alright.

She started to get quite jittery. She was certain now – his face when she'd told him "she knew who he was...." Well. That said it all. "You have confronted him about this, haven't you?" said Stephen. "Did he deny it?

Hmm....At the moment we're just speculating. I mean, as you said, he's using a different surname so if I were you I wouldn't really assume anything." Stephen could see Marion was desperate.

"Why don't you go to the Blue Cove bookshop. If they don't have a book by a top spiritual writer in there then it doesn't exist. I'm sure if you read more about him, you may be able to get more clues – piece more things together." Marion agreed that this would be a good idea. Suddenly, she remembered why she was in Glastonbury – she was meant to be at a workshop right now. She told Stephen she couldn't face going, even though she'd paid good money to do it.

"Then don't go" said Stephen. "You're the customer – they've already got your money. If you change your mind, then it's your shout. Maybe you're a bit workshopped-out. Maybe you just need to sit with friends at the moment, and drink tea." Stephen *was* a good man. A very good man. Any man who knew the vital importance of tea and friends, was a good man.

****

Marion was extremely disappointed not to find a single book by Salvatore Rosso in Blue Cove. Either he was extremely popular in Glastonbury, or Stephen had been too optimistic about what may still have been in stock. She was recommended to try another bookstore, but that was way out of town. Even so, she trekked out there but it was still to no avail. It seemed like only Bea and Stephen had heard of Salvatore Rosso. Marion stopped by a bench, to ponder on the fact that there was something very peculiar about this.

She was in the "world headquarters" of New Age study, so it seemed most odd that the writer largely remained an unknown. How, when he had such miraculous, incredible things to say could he be so little read? That was complete madness – a madness of the world. It was only during a chance meeting at the Chalice Well that Marion found someone who *had* heard of him, and really wished she hadn't......

****

"Marion's really missing out" said Helen, "I think Lynn is great."

"I hope she's ok" said Bea "Maybe I should give her a call?"

"Maybe just let her be" said Carolyn "She's living in *her* Now. Christ, I'm glad I'm not in a relationship."

"But she'd really like Lynn, don't you think?" said Bea. "She's right on our wavelength – funny and really sussed." Carolyn and Helen had to agree that everyone had warmed to her. There was no pretension – just a warm, earthy women who'd introduced herself by telling everyone about her impoverished childhood and how she'd come to be a Life Coach. Bea said she thought she might like some sessions with her.

"I think it's time I started to nurture myself more" said Bea, "I really do think I've moved on mentally now, and I'd like to start putting that to practical use." Carolyn looked at her. Bea really was a different woman to the one who'd done the Internal Feng Shui course with her. After nearly a decade of grieving an empty relationship, it seemed that Bea's "awakening" had come, and she realised the man of her dreams was in fact a nightmare.

Many times Marion had pointed out that Michael could not be the man of Bea's dreams because she wasn't the woman of *his* – he had dumped her, but this detail didn't even seem to go in one of Bea's ears, before it came out the other. She had a need to believe in true love. In soul-mates. She'd created a little enclosed bubble around her life that was more fantasy than real. Living in denial just seemed so much easier than facing the grim reality of life.

But bubbles burst. After a few years of living together, Michael told Bea he "needed space" to practise his own spiritual development. He wanted to stay in the relationship – just not be in it as much. Everyone could see where this was leading – Michael could continue all his other affairs and yet still go round and see Bea when he wanted a hot vegetarian meal, someone to run him a bath and massage him, tell him how adorable he was, encourage his career and always be up for sex in case other wells ran a bit dry.

He was bored and wanted to go. Bea agreed to the deal. By this time, Michael was a very successful coach and Neuro Linguistic Programmer, meeting Peter whilst organising a management team. He could afford his own, separate place. When he was struggling to pay rent on his own, he'd happily moved into Bea's for a short while. He happily leeched without offering anything in return. During this period in Bea's life, Carolyn had tried to be subtle in lending her a book called "Living With the Vampires."

Of course this wasn't actually about the gothic, blood-sucking creatures beloved of horror films, but was in fact a psychology book about people who literally suck you dry, taking everything you have and leaving you exhausted, or as the book said – anaemic. Carolyn had surreptitiously left the book on Bea's kitchen table, knowing she would look at it. What she didn't realise was that it would cause a huge row, with Marion stuck in the middle.

Bea couldn't possibly see Michael as someone who "drained her life blood" – they were good together. Couldn't her friends see that....? What her friends could see was their enthusiastic, funny and vibrant friend becoming more and more down on herself and withdrawn. More and more Michael started staying away from home saying he was helping out on seminars or had been invited abroad for talks on his work.

Once he'd found a new home, he unceremoniously dumped Bea. He told her he needed more space for personal development than he thought he did, even though he took with him a great deal of her furniture. Seven long years had passed since then, seven years for Bea to get over her "loss." But it was in Glastonbury where her healing had begun and it seemed she was starting to return to her former self. Only now she wasn't particularly interested in being in a relationship – her all absorbing thought now was to meet an alien.

Bea had never had much reading time, but now it seemed she was devouring everything on the subject and it just so happened that it was something Salvatore Rosso had written about a lot. During the break, she eavesdropped on Lynn telling Roberta that if only people could be more aware, beings from other planets were actually living all around, all the time. Lynn said that sort of awareness would be the best possible example of "living in the now" that she could possibly think of.

"Sorry to butt in" said Bea "It just sounded so interesting – what you were saying about aliens."

"Well" Lynn continued, "There have been many alleged sightings of UFOs in Glastonbury – if you didn't already know...." She put down her cup of tea then put her arms around Roberta and Bea's shoulders. "Ladies, I'm not really supposed to reveal this, but sometime between very soon and next spring, those in the know are saying that aliens will finally reveal themselves to us. Rumour has it that will happen in this very town." Bea gasped.

"Why here?" asked Roberta "Who's been saying this?"

"Everyone" said Lynn "Druids, Lightworkers, Shamans – anyone working with earth energies. People who have been doing this work for years have been receiving channelled messages. These messages have sometimes been unclear but now it seems there is enough evidence that an actual spaceship will land on this planet." Roberta looked bemused. Bea was delighted. Then she looked crestfallen. "B...but...that means anytime between now and another six months – I can't stay here for six months, just in case. Yet – I wouldn't want to miss something like that."

"If you truly apply yourself to the Living In the Now, then you won't" said Lynn, somewhat annoyingly. "You'll sense when it will happen – align with it. Then you'll make the necessary arrangements. If you are a human who is meant to witness this, then you'll be here. Just trust the Universe." Bea was beginning to go off Lynn a bit. She'd enjoyed the morning, but break time was descending into clichés.

Carolyn found Bea and said that maybe they ought to check up on Marion. Marion hadn't even started the course and now it might be time for them to leave it. They might all find it more fruitful at that moment to be in the Now with friends, discussing their own versions of life and the universe, rather than some cobbled version imposed upon them by a New Age teacher.

Carolyn knew she could talk "real talk" with Marion. For example, sometimes when Marion asked her how she was feeling she would just say "Shit, thanks" and know that Marion would be comfortable with that. She felt grateful for a friend she could be her "true" self with. But a New Age teacher would ask her to "reframe" her answer. Carolyn felt like she had to walk on eggshells.

Expressive, earthy and honest, she felt like her own answer was a perfectly good one and to say "Actually, I am not feeling aligned with the Universe at the moment" was well – a shit answer. Bullshit answer, to be precise. This moment of personal revelation was actually a very uncomfortable moment for Carolyn as she shuffled around the soft-cushioned, incense-filled, angel-statue bedecked type of room, in which she was used to spending so many of her weekends.....

****

Marion sat alone on a bench near the Chalice Well. She'd spent the last half hour talking to an Italian lady about Salvatore Rosso. His books may have been elusive in the UK, but in Italy he was very well known. In criminal circles and Mafia activities. When the woman saw all the colour drain from Marion's face as she was telling her about this, she asked if Marion knew him personally.

When Marion said she might do, the woman advised her to stay as far away as possible. The previous week Marion had suspected her lover had a terminal illness. Now he might be a murderer. He might be on the run. Exactly *how* was Marion to deal with this information? All she knew was that she needed to move, run – way down the High Street, past all the shops and towards the venue where Living in the Now was going on and where her friends where. She knew she needed them more than ever. She didn't need a guru, a man or the path to enlightenment. Just her friends. She needed to be with that which she loved.

****

"Marion.. ..don't" pleaded Carolyn. "It'll be too much for you. You just need to go back to the Ashram and lie down."

"Lie down *there* ?"said Marion. "I'll be turfed out within ten minutes by someone wanting to do some space clearing or ring some Tibetan bells or smoke me out with incense. They don't believe in lie-downs there."

"I'm not so sure you should be involving yourself in intensive lectures right now" said Carolyn, "We can just go and sit down somewhere."

"I've paid to Live in the Now, so I'm damn well going to" said Marion with all the feistiness of the Marion her friends knew and loved. Then she added, "I need to be somewhere, doing something. I need to have my mind diverted, otherwise I won't be able to stop thinking about him." Bea knew exactly how that felt. She spent years thinking about a man who was no longer in her life. Then a new thought popped into her mind – people should know about Michael....

People should know about Peter and Mi-Ling and all of it. She knew Roberta just wanted it all quietly forgotten, but in the light of Salvatore also maybe being a member of the Mafia, this now just seemed plain wrong. These people would carry on living their privileged lives, Salvatore would carry on playing Marion, and everything would remain hidden in pretty little cottages in the West of England.

And these people would carry on abusing other people, unless they couldn't any longer....How could Bea personally deal with this? Suddenly she seemed miles away. "You alright?" asked Marion.

"Yeah. Yeah" said Bea. "It's just that that arrogant, pompous, ignorant twat Michael, suddenly popped into my head." Marion and Carolyn looked shocked. Bea hadn't spoken about him like that before.

"Seems like the Glastonbury air has been doing you good" said Carolyn.

"I've just been thinking...." said Bea "About the whole thing with Roberta. She seems fine about it now, but I'm not sure I am. Isn't it all very weird? And how Marion thought Peter might start teaching at the University, then Salvatore coming along and getting the job and oh..Marion, I'm so sorry....I....I'm rambling."

Suddenly, without warning, Marion burst into tears. Carolyn put her arm around her. "Oh my darling, you really do love him, don't you?" Marion nodded. "I mean, deeply – for real. I can see it." Marion thought back to the first time she met Salvatore. She could have met someone in Avachar, on top of the Tor or on a workshop, but it was in that little town full of shoes that he had found her. Everything she had ever read or work-shopped on laws of attraction about putting yourself "in the right place for love to find you", could never have sent her here.

Suddenly, her tears stopped as she had a revelation. Whoever he was, whatever he had done, surely real love was about finding a connection. The connection with him was the fleur de lis which had started showing up everywhere. Marion had never had much chance to ask Salvatore about the symbolism, but someone else might know about it. It was all she had to go on. Marion hadn't called Salvatore, and at her request he hadn't called her. But that just made her yearn for him all the more.

****

It turned out that Lynn was the person who knew about fleur de lis. "Gosh, he's a spiritual man, alright" said Lynn. "That little flower is very powerful." She drew a diagram of the flower in three parts. " It's strange...it seems like....it seems like this Salvatore man already knew you were going to get together, just from looking at your feet....." Marion laughed, but Lynn was dead serious.

She was adamant that it was the magnetic power of the symbol bringing them together, even though Marion had only bought the sandals because they were comfy. Lynn said the very fact Marion had decided to stay on in Glastonbury back then and spend some time on her own was very significant. She'd been "guided" towards, Street, towards the particular shoe shop that stocked those sandals. They were a one-off, not mass produced. And she'd therefore been spotted by a "one-off" type of man....

This was the stuff dreams were made of. It had been such a long time since Marion had felt that way about anyone, and if truth be told, she had never really felt *this* way about anyone. Salvatore had switched something on at the very core of her being and it was almost like Marion couldn't turn back –

couldn't run from him. Her friends would protest, but Marion wasn't ready to completely leave this man alone...

Lynn suggested the group started the following morning with a walk on the Tor, if it wasn't too cold. It was alleged that a crop of fleurs de lis had started growing there, amongst an unusually large amount of four-leaved clovers. Scientists had been investigating up there, and Lynn thought they should go before they were all removed. Marion wondered how fleurs de lis had come to be growing at the top of the Tor.

"French visiting hippies" suggested Carolyn, making Marion laugh for the first time in a long time.

"Or they're not from earth" said Bea quite nonchalantly, making everyone look at her in a bemused, yet pensive sort of way.

Before they set off for the Tor, Marion thought about Stephen the Wizard. He had been so kind to her and she wanted to get him a little something, but she had no contact details for him. Still, she felt certain she would bump into him. What sort of gift did you get a wizard? At least she was in the right place. The shops were closed, but Marion carefully scrutinized their windows. "What do you think I should get?" she asked Bea.

"Hmmm..." Bea surveyed the window displays of expensive looking velvet cloaks, skulls on sticks, pestles and mortars and other weird and wonderful objects and then said quite simply, "Flowers."

"Flowers?" said Marion.

"Not any flowers" said Bea. "Fleur de lis flowers."

"They're not exactly going to have them at the local florists" said Marion.

"If you find one or two on the Tor, those will make the perfect present for Stephen" said Bea. Marion looked at her, quizzically. "Well, he's a wizard, isn't he?" Bea continued. "He probably appreciates being given unusual things, especially if he buys his own brews and potions when he's here. Maybe he can alchemise the flowers into something....or other...."

The long climb up the Tor began. "Do you really think I'll find one?" asked Marion. "It's only a myth that they're growing here, after all. It's probably just a bit of fun for Lynn watching all her course participants rummaging around in the grass, looking for needles in a haystack."

Bea looked at Marion in a way that scared her. It was fixed, intense, as though Marion had just broken some great, holy vow. "*Why* are you so cynical?" she asked, "Can't you believe, just for once, that dreams can actually come true?" Marion stared at Bea. She knew that she had just come out with a very uncomfortable truth; it was presenting the sort of reality you absolutely don't want to face up to because it's way too painful.

It was painful precisely because it was self-caused. It was hard to do anything about her uncomfortable feeling, even though it was causing so much pain. Marion gulped hard. Had she deliberately sabotaged her relationship with Salvatore? Decided in her own head that true love was a myth, or that she was too old to live it, or that fairytales never come true anyway? Would they ever see each other again? It was she who had pushed him away, after all. Had he really done anything so awful? *Really*? Lost in her own thoughts, Marion followed Bea and the others up the hill until Lynn pointed to a spot where things humans thought could not exist, were waiting to be found....

****

At first, rummaging through grass and peculiar weeds was fun. But when it got to lunchtime, tummies were rumbling and everyone started to get a bit grumpy. Lynn had waxed lyrical about what an amazing morning they were all going to have, but when she jokingly said that they wouldn't be going to eat until someone found a fleur de lis, nobody was very amused.

"I'm so hungry I think I'd bloody well eat one, if I found one" said Carolyn.

"My get up and go has suddenly gone" said Marion. There were no four-leaved clovers to be found, either. But then Marion looked up and saw a familiar looking figure across the greenery. He was some distance away, but even then – the presence was unmistakable. She felt some sort of electrical surge through her body and couldn't help herself; Marion started to run. Run towards Salvatore.

It seemed as if he hadn't seen her, he was focussing on the grass in front of him with a large magnifying glass, looking downwards and surveying plant life. Even if he hadn't seen her, he must have *felt* her – felt the same surge that she did. Suddenly, Marion tripped. A rock caught beneath her foot and she fell down hard, twisting her knee and ankle.

Seeing what had happened, Lynn ran over to help, as did other people from the group. It quickly became apparent that Marion had suffered a nasty sprain, but she didn't behave the way you would expect with that type of injury – she behaved like she was delirious, like she'd had a head injury.

"Salvatore – over there. I saw him" she kept muttering.

"There isn't anyone there" said Bea, trying to soothe her.

"I think we might have to get her to casualty" said Lynn "I didn't see her bang her head but..."

"Let me get up!" yelled Marion. She tried to fight off everyone trying to help her, desperate to get across to the other side of the Tor.

"Marion, *calm down*" said Carolyn "We're going to find a way to get you back down the hill..." But Marion pushed Carolyn away and amazingly got up and ran on her twisted leg towards the spot where she had seen Salvatore. Nothing was there. Nothing but grass and rocks and mud. Marion collapsed on the ground and let out a long howl.

****

"I think we should head back to London" said Bea after Marion had been examined by a local doctor. Her sprain turned out to be fairly minor, but Bea was concerned about her mental condition. It was lucky that after running across the field, Marion hadn't caused further damage to her ligaments. More worrying was that Marion was starting to hallucinate about her absent lover and whilst Bea knew that Glastonbury often did funny things to people, seeing usually very rational Marion in that kind of state was most disturbing.

Marion wanted to stay on and finish the course, but Lynn thought she needed to rest more. She kindly offered to return some course money, seeing as Marion had missed most of it. This was an unknown quantity – courses averaged at around £200-£300 per weekend and usually had to be paid up front, well in advance.

Unless some sort of expensive insurance had been taken out as well, refunds were usually non-negotiable, even in emergencies. Lynn declared that if Marion had had insurance, then she would have classified her case as "an act of God."

"Obviously you're meant to be with this man" Lynn smiled. "Anyone who can run across the Tor at such speed with a battered limb, very much wants to be with whoever they thought they saw."

Marion sunk her head into her hands. "Oh God – I was so *sure* I saw him. He was there, collecting samples or something. He's a scientist, you see. Well, that and many other things. I'm so stupid, aren't I Lynn? I don't really know him at all. I've gone and fallen in love and been completely irrational and put you and my friends to so much trouble. This just isn't me, it really isn't me at all. I'm a University lecturer you see and I *have* to be rational, and...."

Marion was starting to ramble. Lynn took hold of her hand.

"Marion....falling in love *isn't* rational, is it? I've been married to the most wonderful man for the last five years and I never thought I would meet another husband again, either. You need to talk to this man and tell him that you *must* know the truth about him. This relationship you and he have could be wonderful, I just know – I sense it. He knows about the symbol of the fleur de lis, after all......Did you know Marion, that the biggest regret most people ever have in their lives is not letting someone know how they really feel about them?"

Never had Marion known anyone to talk so positively when she had met a new man. Her friends were all very supportive, but her closest ones had never met him. Sometimes she doubted herself, if he actually existed. If love could happen for Lynn again, then why not her too?

There was Bea who was just starting to heal after seven years in denial, Carolyn who had never settled down and never seemed bothered until

Marion had fallen for someone, Helen who had a girlfriend and Roberta who was young and gorgeous and...nearly been raped. Where did Marion stand in all the middle of this male and female dysfunction and her overwhelming emotions?

Lynn started to take some cash out of her handbag, but Marion refused it. There ensued an awkward exchange whereby Lynn kept trying to give Marion the money and Marion kept shoving it back. Eventually, Lynn tucked a £50 note into Marion's coat pocket whilst she wasn't looking. Bea wanted to take Marion back to the Ashram, but Marion insisted that Bea stay and finish off the course. She felt guilty about being the centre of attention when it wasn't intentional.

Marion, however, did need to go and lie down and rest her leg and spend some time in quiet contemplation at the Ashram. Bea drove her back, tucked her up in bed and then returned to Lynn. Lying still for the first time in a long time, Marion heard her mobile ring.

"Marion....forgive me. I know you said not to call, but...I thought you might have been badly injured. Just let me know that you're ok, then I promise never to call again." Salvatore's voice was warm and soothing. But how did he know she'd been hurt?

"Because I *saw* you" said Salvatore. "I was collecting specimens and I saw you fall. It took all my strength not to run over and wrap my arms around you. Had you been alone, then I would have done." So, he was there. Marion wasn't going mad. Salvatore was really up on the Tor earlier that morning doing his thing and even at that distance, they had both identified each other.

"Salvatore.....can you meet me? I think we need to talk." Salvatore heaved a deep sigh of relief. Even if it came to nothing, at least she would see him – let him have his say. There was no getting away from it now; Salvatore had absolutely no idea how Marion could possibly have discovered his origins – when they had first met he was certain that was impossible.

Yet, if anyone could discover this about him, then it would have been her. If he was honest, then it was her perception and depth which had made him fall so deeply in love with her and know she was the one. And when he couldn't have her, when she pushed him away, it just made him want her all the more. He hadn't planned it this way.....

Marion gave Salvatore directions to the Ashram and lay back on the rather uncomfortable bed. Here she was in this place where people came to meditate and be peaceful, and she had been anything but. Hearing Salvatore's voice however, was calming and healing. She was sure that there would be a settlement of some kind, for them both. Maybe they would be together happily ever after, just like Lynn had said. But then Marion put the romantic fantasy out of her head as she rolled over on her side and saw a copy of a trash magazine with celebrity gossip that Carolyn had left in the room. That was perfect reading for the moment.

****

Bea approached Lynn later on that day. "Do you know anything about Salvatore Rosso?" she asked.

"If you're talking about one of the most incredible spiritual and esoteric writers of all time, then yes. Quite a lot."

Bea smiled. "I don't actually mean his work, you know. I mean *him*. Do you know anything about him?" Lynn rubbed her forehead, trying to find some recollection.

"Well, there are all kinds of stories concerning his whereabouts..." Bea encouraged her. Lynn said that if you read between the lines, then you could see this was a troubled man. A man in danger who feared for his life. Some said that he was actually writing about the mafia, and that if you were in the know and had the intelligence, then you could see it cleverly coded into his writing. Bea flinched a lot at that bit; a cold – blooded killer being heralded as the most forward thinking spiritual writer of their age? How could this be?

Lynn continued. "Apparently, he didn't treat women very well, either." That was it, as far as Bea was concerned. Much to Lynn's astonishment, she turned and ran out the door.

****

Bea's car was parked near the Ashram and it took her a full fifteen minutes to run back there as fast as she could. Not being as fit as she would have liked, Bea found herself wheezing and coughing as she reached the front door. "Are you ok?" asked a young Asian girl.

"Yes..." gasped Bea, "I just...needed....a jog...." Bea pushed past her and ran up the stairs. She had to warn Marion. She had to tell her never to talk to that philandering, violent, good for nothing lover of hers ever again. She pushed hard against the bedroom door, but Marion had left it unlocked so Bea fell in a heap on the floor. Choking, she spat out her words. "Marion..you have to keep away from that..that...gasp..wheeze....that....Salvatore man!"

A man put out his hand to help Bea up. "Nice to meet you, too" said Salvatore. Bea stared at him hard. This couldn't be the man she had read about or the one that Lynn had just been telling her about. He was far too gentle and soft looking and he had the deepest, warmest, most twinkling dark black eyes she had ever seen. Indeed, she stared at him for far longer than you might do when you have only just met someone.

"Bea...?" Marion questioned her being there and her outburst. Bea looked up at the two of them, somewhat shamefacedly. They were perfect together. Anyone could see that. Bea knew that she hadn't thought to question anything – she'd just wanted to protect her friend. Admittedly, bolting out of Lynn's class like that was a bit like Marion chasing off towards her mirage, except that he wasn't a mirage. Salvatore was real flesh and blood. He was *there*. If only Bea had met him in better circumstances. Fortunately, Salvatore was not in the least bit fazed. In fact, he was rather amused. "Ladies, I believe there is a small kitchen down the hallway where I can make some tea, no?" Marion nodded. "I shall make some and then we can all have a chat together. That would be good I think."

"Peppermint please" said Bea, still in shock at actually meeting the man who was never there.

****

CHAPTER 8

GLASTONBURY, BRIGHTON AND LONDON

Lynn had given up trying to second guess the tangled lives of her course participants. One had run off and nearly broke her leg and another one had just run off. Only Carolyn, Roberta and Helen and a few other women remained by the end of the course. Lynn stared around the room; she'd had to up her prices this year and wondered if that had been putting people off. Then again, there was so much competition.

Hiring venues didn't come cheap, even in Glastonbury where just about anyone who owned any property would offer it up for a bed and breakfast or New Age courses to take advantage of the many "pilgrims" who flocked to the town. Lynn surveyed her course participants. Most of them were older women with few financial concerns. Thank goodness for them, or she wouldn't have a living.

Lynn had struggled. Both her parents worked, due to the fact that they'd kept producing children and Lynn, now in her late fifties was the middle one of eight. She'd had many relationships, but no children and just met her true love a few years ago. Lynn knew what her course participants wanted to achieve. Always, people would begin by talking about their hopes for a yet to arrive future. That was when Lynn baffled everyone by saying that the only thing that existed was right now. Just what if in a year's time your life was exactly the same? What if your hopes and dreams for the year didn't manifest?

Most people recoiled in horror at the thought, but then Lynn got everyone to meditate and feel what that would really be like. She pondered on how Marion had missed this part of the course. In fact, Marion had missed most of the course and yet she lived for the moment. She knew what to do on instinct alone, with little hesitation. She didn't wistfully daydream or moan or talk of having "a better life one day" – she just went for it.

Marion felt the joy and pain of risking falling in love. Felt the sorrow, detachment, abandonment, loss. Felt things very deeply and could therefore give to another very deeply, too. And right now, really in that moment, Lynn was feeling that Marion was one of the very few people she'd ever met who didn't need a course tutor or therapist or workshops or strategies. She was wild and free and went with the flow. It made Lynn feel like a bit of a fraud. She was nowhere near as sorted and she felt unusually wobbly as she prepared to start a discussion on asking everyone what they had got from the weekend.

It was obvious what they'd got. Half of them had already left. Lynn needn't have worried. No one ever asked for money back, even though Lynn had returned money to Marion that Marion didn't want. Why on earth had she felt that Marion deserved it, more than anyone else? In a sudden frenzied moment, Lynn suddenly thought that she should declare things hadn't really worked out as she'd planned, end the course right there and then give everyone their money back. Fortunately she stopped herself. She had a mortgage and this was her job. It wasn't just some philanthropic cause. Roberta interrupted Lynn's disturbed train of thought.

"Are we starting again in a minute, Lynn? Just want to know if I've got time to make another cuppa." Lynn stared at Roberta. She was the kind of girl who would easily get the whole package – if she wanted. She'd forge a brilliant career, get married, have kids. She could just stand there and it would all come to her. If only Lynn had had Roberta's confidence that young. All of a sudden she felt pangs of jealousy which was not something she had known for a long time. Why would she suddenly be jealous of a beautiful young woman who had her whole life ahead of her? Lynn blinked as Roberta asked the question again, thinking Lynn hadn't heard her.

"Yes. Do make some tea" said Lynn as Roberta was shocked at the glare she got from Lynn for asking such a seemingly non-offensive question.

****

Bea, Marion and Salvatore walked slowly to the High Road with Bea and Salvatore supporting Marion on each side with her twisted ankle. Bea had taken to Salvatore, but she was still anxious. If he was all the things Salvatore Rosso was said to be, then surely neither she nor Marion should be anywhere near him. Yet, her instinct told her instead that this man was one of the kindest and most honest that she had ever met.

If she could put her finger on her first impressions then she would have described him as gently funny whilst at the same time being sort of "other worldly", although she knew the latter description wasn't quite the right terminology. Bea had met other people to whom this might apply; they were spiritual, knowledgeable and sometimes a bit like they weren't entirely rooted to the planet, but that wasn't the case with Salvatore.

He seemed the most human person she had ever met and he also appeared to have the utmost of respect for Marion. When he looked at Bea, she felt like he already knew everything about her. This wasn't in a scary way, but a sort of very comforting way, like she could talk to him about almost anything. It was easy to fathom Marion's attraction.

Maybe it was a good thing that Bea was there. With a relationship like this, so deep and intense and intimate, then everything was at stake. Maybe a voice of neutrality in the middle would help. Bea wondered if Marion had actually confronted Salvatore, since he'd arrived at the Ashram. She thought she might broach the subject herself, seeing as she had actually read the books he had allegedly written.

"I understand that aliens are going to reveal themselves to us much sooner than originally thought" Bea stuck her neck out. "I've been reading quite a lot of literature about people who believe this, as well as talking to some people here. *They* think they're going to land here! Can you believe it? Mind you, if aliens *were* going to land, I imagine they'd find themselves very at home in Glastonbury."

Marion shot Bea a filthy look. They'd all been doing fine. Why had she brought this up? Salvatore's golden skin turned very pale, and as Bea noticed this, she felt the colour of her complexion change as well. Their worst fears had been realised – Bea had sussed out the man. Now that he had been found out, she might as well continue to ask him all the questions she had wanted to.

"So, I don't know if *you* think they'll land here, but I know you think these beings come from somewhere very near our sun." Suddenly Salvatore looked very puzzled.

"What do you mean you know *I* think that?" asked Salvatore. Marion had already confronted Salvatore, but of course Bea didn't know this.

"Tell me, *Mr Rosso*" continued Bea, "I thought it had been proved that nothing could possibly live that near to a sun. Why do you think otherwise?"

Salvatore softened. "Before I explain that, pray tell me *Miss Hamilton* why you think I am Mr Rosso?" Now it was Bea's turn to be pale. How did he know her surname? Of course, Marion could have told him, but there seemed to be no reason she might have done. Bea looked at Marion, but she just shrugged and shook her head.

"W....well" stuttered Bea. "Are you? Are you him?" Salvatore beckoned to the two women to sit on a nearby bench. He could see Marion was struggling to stay upright.

"Miss Hamilton, or may I call you Bea?" said Salvatore, then he chuckled, "Actually, Marion did tell me your surname once. She doesn't realise that I remember most things. But to answer your question, no – I am not Salvatore Rosso. I know of him, I know he is Italian, around the same age as myself and a very eminent writer. But he is also a crook and a liar which I must say most emphatically, I am *not.*"

Bea hung her head. "I'm sorry. But you must understand my concern about Marion. It's just that you fitted his description so well – almost perfectly in every way. And Marion told me you had taken up a lecturer's position at her University in Esoteric studies. Apparently, you pipped another extremely well qualified candidate to the post, so I figured you must be someone pretty high up in that world."

"High up...." said Salvatore to himself, as if it was something he wanted to ponder upon. Then he thought about what to say to Bea. "I suppose you may say....I am high up. Much of the time. But then I am also in exactly the same place as you, some of the time....sort of..."

"Honestly" said Marion, "You are both as bewildering as each other. I'm at least glad the two people I most care about are getting on so well. And you're both into aliens." At this, Salvatore looked into the distance and Bea noticed he looked sad. It was like he was thinking of something or someone far away.

"You're thinking of home, aren't you?" said Bea. Salvatore looked at her searchingly before she added, "Which part of Italy exactly is it you're from?"

"I'm not exactly from there" said Salvatore, "Not originally, anyway."

"Salvatore's father was a pilot in the army. They lived all over the place" said Marion, somewhat proudly. "You went all over the world when you were little, didn't you?"

"Yes" said Salvatore softly and then he looked at Bea as he added, "I went *everywhere*...."

****

Lynn drew the course to a close as some people lingered, wondering if there would be a meal out or coffee in Avachar. "I guess The Herbivore" might still be open, offered Lynn.

"Herbivore?" protested Carolyn. "Suppose I fancy a bit of meat? Like a big fat juicy steak?" Several women turned round and looked at her disapprovingly. "Soddit. You can't even get breakfast sausages in this town anymore. It's just gone to the dogs. If they eat fucking grass here now, that is...."

Carolyn remembered a time when you could get burgers and freshly slaughtered lamb chops from neighbouring fields in Glastonbury. She rowed enough with Bea about the natural order of the food chain – how human beings were *meant* to eat animals, which made Bea very upset and angry.

She said that eating meat made people very aggressive, not realising just how wound up and antagonistic she was becoming whilst saying this...

All the same, Carolyn wasn't going to get a rump steak in Glastonbury. She wondered where Bea and Marion might be – it was getting late to eat out. When Lynn's group arrived at the Herbivore, it was difficult to seat them all. Many workshops had taken place that weekend and everyone wanted to eat afterwards. Always obliging, the manager went to fetch stools and bustled around fetching cutlery. It was a tight squeeze, but everyone fitted in the end.

Lynn ordered wine and cider and passed around menus, making certain recommendations. A waitress came out of the kitchen and Roberta felt her blood turn cold. It was Mi-Ling, Michael's girlfriend. One of her persecutors. Mi-Ling recognised Roberta and stood frozen to the spot for a moment.

Roberta admonished herself. Why had she expected she might never bump into any of them again? Somehow, she never expected Mi-Ling to be a waitress. The house she shared with Michael was a salubrious large cottage which may have looked bohemian and arty but in fact housed some extremely expensive furniture and artefacts. Mi-Ling surely wouldn't be waitressing to earn extra cash. Lynn noticed the interaction between the two women and visualised her own scenario. Both were in their early thirties, arty, exotic looking and beautiful. Was there a tussle over a man involved? Mi-Ling shook off the immediate situation and started taking orders at the furthest end of the table to Roberta. She didn't look up, even when she felt Roberta's eyes boring into her.

Lynn noticed, though. When Mi-Ling eventually had to take Roberta's order she smiled and leaned in, in exactly the same way as she had done with everyone else. Tactfully she managed to move in close enough to whisper in Roberta's ear. "Can I speak to you? Not here – I'll slip you my number later."

Roberta didn't know whether to nod or shake her head. She ended up nodding. When her food arrived, she started pushing it around the plate, alerting Lynn to the fact something was definitely going on between her and the waitress. "Not hungry?" Lynn asked.

"Oh, just not into veggie food that much" said Roberta "I only really came to socialise."

"Too right" said Carolyn "We need meat. Women at my time of life need iron." The table went quiet and all eyes turned to Carolyn. "Oh for God's sake" she said "Does anyone know where the nearest McDonald's is?" Slowly, people returned to their meals, but Carolyn could hear the disapproving mutters echo around the room.

Lynn laughed. "Well, that told them. I'm sorry, I thought this place might suit everyone, but it doesn't seem so. Perhaps we can go to the pub afterwards? To make up for it?" By now Carolyn had made herself a complete outcast, so going for a drink seemed irrelevant. Roberta butted in.

"Good idea. I fancy some local Scrumpy."

"That'll give you a good clear out" said Carolyn. The other ladies started to shuffle uncomfortably at all the talk of meat, alcohol and bowel movements. They put their heads down and tucked into their dinners of organic mushrooms, hemp seeds and tofu cheese, whether they liked it or not. Surprisingly, Carolyn wolfed all her food down and then asked Mi-Ling if they had a dessert menu.

"I never said I *don't like* veggie grub" explained Carolyn, "I just don't think it's good for you to eat all the time." She ordered a ginger and vanilla cheesecake whilst others had herb teas and homemade brownies. People filtered out of the restaurant and Helen and her girlfriend decided to skip drinks and head back to the Ashram for an early night.

"Pub" said Lynn. "There's only us still standing. Lets live in the now." Roberta got her bag and slipped off to the Ladies. On the way back she took a business card from Mi-Ling that Mi-Ling wrote her number on.

"Please" urged Mi-Ling "It's important."

****

Lynn got nosy after a cider, or two. "What was all that about with the waitress?" she asked Roberta.

"Uh...just someone I met...when I was doing a course here once. She wanted to catch up." Lynn didn't buy into that. She'd noticed the terse exchange between them. Roberta sidled up closer to Helen and Carolyn.

"Christ – just because we've been doing this course doesn't mean we have to reveal *all* our innermost secrets to Lynn, does it? I mean, I like her, but she isn't half nosy." Helen agreed. She advised Roberta to keep the business card tucked out of sight, but confessed she wondered what Mi-Ling wanted to see her about, as well.

"Maybe she wants to make it up to you" said Helen.

"Maybe...." said Roberta, remembering that it was Mi-Ling who had got her out of the precarious situation in the first place.

"I know you'd rather forget it all happened, but maybe she can shed some light on things" suggested Carolyn. Meanwhile, in a far dark corner of the pub, Lynn was sat with a large bottle of pear cider feeling rather lonely. All the other women were either at the bar or huddled around tables chatting. The minute she saw Roberta get up to get some more drinks, she patted the empty seat besides her.

"Oh Christ, I really don't feel like this" muttered Roberta, under her breath. Lynn may have had a lovely husband, but she was quite bereft of female gossip and missed it.

"Just make up some crap" said Carolyn as Roberta conceded. Lynn threw her heavy crocheted shawl over her shoulders and initially made way too much small talk for Roberta to feel remotely comfortable. She wished Lynn would just cut to the chase so that she could make her escape.

"You know, I wouldn't knock that back quite so fast" advised Lynn, as she clocked Roberta gulping at a scotch and diet coke. "I know it slips down easily, but remember you've not eaten much."

"I know that, but I'm a poor student now" said Roberta "I need to make the most of drinking whilst I still can – I think it'll be the last workshop I'll be able to afford for a while, as well."

"Ooo, a student?" said Lynn "Do tell me about it!" Roberta tried not to sigh quite as deeply. Now she'd have to tell Lynn about that, to try and divert her from Mi-Ling. Quickly, Roberta explained that she was just about to start the course and needed to get to Brighton the following day.

"Wow, Esoteric studies" said Lynn, "I only know of one other course in that, at Exeter University. You're lucky you got in."

"Yes" said Roberta, and then no more. Much to her alarm, at this point, Lynn put her arm around her.

"Oh dear... I can sense that you're very irritated and angry. It's difficult when you can't tell anyone, but it's ok – you can tell me. This is something to do with the girl in that restaurant, isn't it?" Roberta could no longer keep up the polite pretence.

"I'm angry because it's none of your sodding business."

Lynn looked shocked and extremely hurt. "Roberta! I'm so surprised at your sudden antagonism. We've all been so *sharing* this weekend – including me, your mentor. There must be some very disturbing issue going on in your inner psyche to suddenly react like this."

Roberta wasn't falling for it. "Bollocks" she said quite simply before getting up and walking away. "Please let's go" she urged Carolyn as she returned to the table. Carolyn knew the scenario well. She'd spent whole weekends pouring out her grief and misery and life traumas to various therapists and life coaches who would leave her all raw and exposed, without tucking any of it back in so that it at least had some grip on the edges, before she left. Sometimes she wondered what she was doing with all this stuff anymore. Maybe it was time to move on. But where to...?

****

"Please do join us for some dinner" Salvatore implored Bea, "Marion and I will have plenty of time to be on our own when we get back to Brighton. I need to look for a new flat or studio – I've just been renting a room there, as I'm not sure how temporary my post will be."

"And anyway, we need a little love nest to escape to" said Marion. She kissed Salvatore. Normally she'd never do anything so cheesy, especially in front of a friend, but she was so relieved that he was back. Bea mimed sticking her fingers down her throat.

"Sorry" said Marion as Salvatore laughed. "Salvatore will be such an amazing tutor. I just know it."

"I believe a friend of mine is going to start your course" said Bea, "A young lady called Roberta. She's very enthusiastic."

"Excellent" said Salvatore "Enthusiastic is what I like. I'm not so keen on the ones who fall asleep at the back and start snoring loudly." Bea and Marion started laughing. How could anyone *not* fall for Salvatore? He was so warm and sparkling and endearing with a gentle, slightly self-effacing sense of humour. Most of all, Bea saw the way Salvatore and Marion looked at each other. They were deeply in love – that was very much apparent. How could she deny her closest friend this opportunity late in her life? She started to feel guilty that she'd doubted Salvatore's intentions. There was no way that this particular man could have been a criminal, charlatan or member of the Mafia. Bea just knew that. She was sensitive enough to gauge this and so was Marion. And it was for this reason that Bea decided to leave them alone together that night.

****

"He's here? Really here in Glastonbury? It wasn't just a mirage then?" said Carolyn to Bea. "You simply must come here at once and tell us everything!" Bea sighed. This wasn't a moment for giddy gossip. She had just witnessed a deep and intense relationship and that had really moved her. She had seen what she thought was impossible, manifested as possible and the thought of sitting in a pub with Carolyn man-bashing really had no appeal whatsoever.

"Actually, do you know what – I'm really tired" said Bea, "Think I'm going to have an early one." Carolyn protested – they'd all taken cars to

Glastonbury this time, so could set out late the next day. Bea was adamant, however.

"Looks like it's just you and me, kiddo" said Carolyn to Roberta and was then crestfallen when Roberta said she wanted to head back to the b&b with Helen. "Jesus, what the hell's wrong with all you crystal-guzzling, India-loving vegetarians?" she cried. "What happened to the good old-fashioned earthy sorts who stayed up until 4am playing spin the bottle and downing cider?"

A male voice rang from out of a corner, "Here we are, come and join us." Normally Carolyn would have told him where to go. But he had a nice beard and big, round, jolly face.

"Go on" said Roberta " Enjoy."

****

"So sorry we can't give you a lift" said Marion to Salvatore "But we've simply got too many rucksacks. I'd love it if you could come and stay with me in London for a few days before we go back to the Uni, though. Would you? You can get a coach directly from here to Victoria and I can meet you there." Salvatore took Marion's face gently in his hands.

"I would like that very much my darling. I would hate to lose you again." Salvatore's big brown eyes resonated with a deep sadness. It was like his entire world would evaporate if he couldn't be with this woman. Marion hugged him close.

"Nor me, you" she said, "It's taken all this time to find you...If I had had one wish left in my life, then it would have been meeting a man like you whilst I still had most of my faculties..." Salvatore laughed. He loved Marion's humour, it reminded him of...suddenly he looked very sad again.

"Salvatore, what's wrong?" Salvatore shook his head in denial and said that he was delighted to be invited to Marion's home. Everything seemed to be falling beautifully into place. He had the job at the University, they could see each other regularly – why be sad? But Marion knew that he was and this clouded her joy at their re-union, making her anxious and unhappy, because...because deep inside she knew there was something he wasn't telling her...

****

Carolyn was disturbed by her evening in the pub with the Somerset farmers – mostly because she'd really enjoyed it. The men were raucous, somewhat sexist and boozy and whilst alcohol and being loud had been former components of Carolyn's life, she thought that she had really moved on since her student days.

In middle age, she turned to New Age, spending much time and money travelling around places in Asia like India, dipping her toes into many little pieces of the spiritual world. Buddhism, Hinduism, Whirling Dervishes and the Brahma Kumaris...Carolyn was a shining example of the sort of middle class lady who goes off to "find herself" amidst mass poverty.

She had a job in a City Bank in London, finally going part-time and downscaling to mini-breaks. She'd lived on a commune in Scotland, embracing living off the land, but missing central heating and realising that this sort of life was much better suited to somewhere hot... The way she carried on in the pub that night felt like a release – like a throwback to more carefree times.

At least being bought drinks all night was one of the good things about "sexist" behaviour. Carolyn enjoyed playing darts, knocking back shots and joking with the landlord and barmaids – discussing the pitiful lives of television soap characters, the state of young girls' fashion and...football.

It was actually refreshing not to have to think about the benefits of a particular yoga position, health foods or where to hang wind chimes. This left Carolyn with a certain amount of inner turmoil. Everything she thought was important to her suddenly seemed stale and samey. She cherished her friends dearly, but maybe they needed to do something a bit different together...maybe, just maybe, she wouldn't be joining them on the next Holistic course, forgetting that this one had been her idea in the first place....

****

Roberta got up early to trot off down the High Street to get some sweets for the journey home. Suddenly, there she was again. Mi-Ling. That woman got everywhere. It could have been worse – Roberta could easily have bumped into Peter or Michael and quite frankly she didn't know what she would have done if she did, but this was bad enough.

Mi-Ling looked eager to speak and Roberta could not avoid an encounter. Mi-Ling ran after her, down the hill and panted as she got her words out. "I know I'm probably the last person you want to talk to and I don't blame you, but please hear me out. I'm leaving Michael. I want to come to London and find work, because I can't bear what he's doing – what he did to you. It's so wrong...I know...when he offered me a better life in England when we were first introduced by the agency..." The agency? Roberta's ears pricked up.

"You met on the internet?" queried Roberta "A dating agency?"

"An Anglo-Thai marriage bureau" said Mi-Ling "It was deliberate. I wanted an English husband and Michael has been promising to marry me for the last three years, but it hasn't happened. He's given me a good life materially, but...I can't stand what he makes me do. Not with other young women, like you....." Roberta started to have horrible images of ping pong balls....

"And Peter and his girlfriend Priyanka, they're just as bad" continued Mi-Ling. "So cold. So indifferent. But when I met *you* Roberta, you were different to the others...you have a good brain...I don't know anyone in London...I'm hoping you can help me....."

Roberta was gob-smacked. Mi-Ling seemed to have a real cheek, but then maybe she'd had no choice but to take this path in life. She couldn't decide what to do, so just ran off saying "I'm sorry." A Thai bride. Just wait until Bea heard about this.

****

Back in Crouch End, in Marion's house, Salvatore was exploring the ornaments on the shelves in her living room. He picked up a hand carved wooden elephant and felt the smoothness of the organic substance. "What a beautiful piece" he said "Have you ever been to Africa?"

"No" said Marion "Like most of my ornaments, it comes from Glastonbury." Salvatore moved across the room and stood back from a shiny blue object. He picked it up and looked at it from all angles.

"Blue Agate" said Salvatore "Beautiful." He seemed completely taken with the little stone man Bea had bought Marion several years ago and held the object up to the fading light, twirling it between his thumb and forefinger. As he did so, Marion noticed the same sad expression on his face that she had seen before they'd left Glastonbury.

She picked up a sense of longing, but for what - she didn't know. She started to think of the sea in Brighton and how the colour of the stone reflected that. Marion deduced that wherever his homeland was, Salvatore lived somewhere near the coast – there was something in the way he looked at this stone....

Now that he was in her home, Marion felt she had every right to ask him questions. He needed to reveal his origins at last. First of all, to ease him in, Marion told Salvatore more about the stone. "Bea got me that" she said. "Apparently, it's a little spaceman, or something....she's so into all that...me, I can't really buy into it."

"Well, Bea is right" said Salvatore. "This is a Peruvian carving. There are many recorded sighting of aliens and spacecraft there. Of course, this actual carving isn't so ancient – he was made purely for the tourist industry."

"So..." said Marion, edging closer to her questions, "The spaceman isn't from Italy, then?"

"Italy?" Salvatore looked confused. "No. No – it's definitely from Peru. I've studied Geology greatly." He put the carving back down on the shelf, then looked wistfully into the distance. Marion didn't talk for a while, either. If Salvatore wasn't Salvatore Rosso, then maybe he wasn't even Italian.

Just because he said he had a base in Tuscany, dark looks and spoke with a slight trace of a European accent, she had made an assumption about him. Yet – he didn't really look Peruvian either. It was very hard to place his creed or race, except that he had an Italian name. Perhaps that was his original heritage and he had been christened, thus.

All those years of her New Age workshops and study had taught her never to make assumptions about anything, and yet she had assumed a huge amount about the man who had recently become the most important person in her life. Marion realised that wherever he was from was completely immaterial, as long as for now that wherever he was, he was with her.

He was "the one" and wherever he was going, she wanted to be with him. A sense of magic and freedom filled up her very being as she had this realisation – that she really would go anywhere, just to be with him. But first of all, he had to ask....

It was Tuesday and after spending an idyllic extended weekend together, Marion knew Salvatore had lectures on Wednesday. Everything seemed perfect right now – he didn't run away from her or give any more ambiguous answers to her questions; furthermore Marion knew exactly where Salvatore was going to be and when. They could be at her home together in London, they could even make a home in Brighton if Salvatore's work became more permanent. Perhaps she would be going on some exotic trip with him, helping him research plant life and ancient cultures and whatever else he did in Italy, Peru or somewhere else quite magnificent.

Caught up in her fantasy, Marion remembered that it was the canteen lady at the University who'd first recognised how in love she was. "Who is he then, Professor Green?" she'd asked, pulling up a chair. When she'd asked if it was anyone she knew, Marion replied that she didn't really know him herself – yet. That was true. But she was determined to know *everything* about him now.

****

Roberta loved Salvatore's lectures. He oozed enthusiasm for his subject, whilst coming across as warm and compassionate at the same time. Small wonder Marion had fallen for him. Salvatore scanned the room to see a plethora of eager faces. Apart from Roberta, he clocked a young man at the back of the room who seemed to have something about him. He was probably in his late twenties and looked a bit shy. That might have been because he was one of the few men there, but the fact that he was a man and that he was there, gave Salvatore some hope....

"I'd like to talk to you today about the Fleur de Lis" said Salvatore, showing a detailed ink drawing up on the screen. His lecture was completely fascinating as he explained the origins and symbol of the flower and then passed around some tiny samples he said he had collected from the top of Glastonbury Tor.

Salvatore backed up his theory with his own scientific evidence and his students were completely mesmerised. They'd never received tuition at this level and depth before. Their professor explained about one petal being masculine and the other feminine and the third in the middle representing a brand new way of thinking...for men and for women...

Other than the literal act of copulation and then gestation, Salvatore was suggesting something new on a much higher level. Something along the lines of ways of thinking changing for future generations. Roberta was riveted. Nothing on her New Agey courses went into this kind of depth.

Often, other speakers appeared jaded or even just not that bothered about what they were teaching. They'd throw hand-outs and website addresses at you and tell you to go away and research everything yourself. But not Salvatore. He seemed like he had studied for a hundred years. Not only did he believe in his topic, but he seemed to be completely saturated in it – like he lived, ate and breathed what he taught.

At the end of the class, as everyone filtered downstairs to the canteen, Roberta approached Salvatore. "Thank you. That was *amazing*."

"Glad you enjoyed it" said Salvatore. "Of course – this is only part one. There is much more about it and quite frankly thank goodness for that, otherwise I'd be out of a job."

Roberta looked at Salvatore quizzically. He carried on. "I'm glad I chose this job – I never wanted to be something like an accountant or architect. The answers are too exact for me. I don't like things to be too exact...." Roberta looked even more confused.

"Nothing?" she said. Suddenly, Salvatore remembered where he was and that this young lady was a friend of Bea and Marion's. He looked at her very honestly.

"Ah...I know what you are thinking. Relationships. Well, you are right. Often they are not as exact as we would like them to be..." With that, Salvatore went out the room and Roberta wasn't sure whether to follow him or not, and ask more. She might not have understood the answers, even if she did.....

****

"Do you know about this bloody ball?" Marion asked Salvatore as they walked back together to his Brighton apartment.

"Ball?" asked Salvatore. It was obvious he didn't.

"Bloody David and Mira want to hold some stupid Art Department event. Like we have the money to spend on things like that...."

"Well, I suppose there must be some celebration at times" Salvatore responded. "Why do you dislike the idea so much?" Marion explained how she never much enjoyed large functions, much less dressing up. Such an event would no doubt be extremely pretentious and merely a chance to show off, with the women flaunting their dresses and the men eyeing them up and down whilst pontificating on their own wonderfulness of their years' work.

Marion asked Salvatore if he had ever had to suffer University balls, other than when he'd been a student himself. "We don't really have them where

I'm from, but I have to say, I actually quite like the sound of it. You say dressing up. Do you mean fancy dress?" There was not a hint of joking in his voice. Salvatore actually meant it.

Marion was bewildered by his naivety. She went on to explain that such events were occasions to see which oldest, ugliest Professor could get off with the youngest, prettiest female student and that such liaisons were always fuelled by alcohol and always ended in fights and vomit.

Sometimes they would end in unwanted pregnancies. Salvatore mentioned that Professor David Hall was already having an affair with a young, pretty woman, at which point Marion remembered that David's wife would come to the ball.

"Oh God, I really don't want to go...." she groaned.

"Oh come on. Come with me" said Salvatore. "We can groan at it all together....."

"But then we've got to go and get stupid outfits and oh bugger it....we'll be expected to go, won't we, anyway? We have to show face." This wasn't an expression Salvatore knew. He seemed to take it literally.

"Just our faces? Why do we have to dress up then?" Marion burst out laughing.

"Dearest, lovely man. You are so funny. I wish...." she cut herself short.

"What do you wish, my darling?"

The rest just came pouring out of Marion in great gushing waves of emotion that she couldn't stop. "I wish – I wish that we could be together for always. There, I've said it now. I've found you so late in life and I want this to be the best time in my life. Wherever I am, wherever I go I want you to be there with me and I want you to take me with you, wherever you need to go."

Marion shocked herself, but this was the truth. Salvatore's eyes started to well up.

"Do you really mean that?"

"Yes" said Marion without any hesitation. "Yes. I do."

Now it was Salvatore's turn to say how he felt. Pulling her closely towards his chest, he told Marion that she was the love of his life and that when she left him, it hurt him more than anything ever had in his life. He'd been waiting all his life to meet her too and they could – would always be together, if...if she really meant what she'd said about going anywhere with him.

Marion knew what he was alluding to. She'd realised that Salvatore probably couldn't stay in the UK for all that long – there were probably all sorts of messy visas to sort, work permits and legal hold-ups. This was why he needed to keep disappearing. She understood.

"Do I need to get a...how do you say it – tux...edo?" asked Salvatore. Marion laughed.

"Yes. I'm afraid so. It's a very formal event. At least, on the outside. Once all the grand hand-shaking and pompous blowing of own trumpets has passed, then after the champagne it's pretty much a free for all."

"I guess I should make the effort" said Salvatore "After all, I have just started a new job. I'd like to get some feedback as well, if some of my students go. There are some interesting students in my class. One young man in particular. I'm looking forward to reading his first assignment." Then he gazed into the distance again and Marion realised she was going to have to get used to him doing that.... especially if they were going to be together forever.

****

What a dashing figure Salvatore cut in a tuxedo. Normally Marion hated formal men's clothing and normally Salvatore wore the same jeans and a slightly faded pull-over. She knew that men that always wore the same clothes usually drove their women mad, and that they were always trying to get them to go shopping with them.

But this was something Marion liked about Salvatore – outer appearances were the least of it for him. He always told her how beautiful she was – even when she was sat in front of her dressing table mirror with blobs of cream on her face. He made her *feel* beautiful. Their physical attraction may have been strong, but in the grand scheme of things it was only a tiny fraction of their love.

Every time Marion had doubted him, he had come back. In truth, she still knew little about his outer life, but the person he was – this was someone she wanted to be with very much. She went up to him and straightened his bowtie. His eyes twinkled brightly and for a moment she thought he looked like the film star, Omar Shariff. But that was more of something to do with his "essence" than actual physical resemblance. Film stars had that same kind of charisma – the same light in the eyes.

Marion decided he was the most handsome man she had ever seen, and how in a superficial sort of way, she would be proud to be on his arm, escorted to the ball. "Well" she told Salvatore, "I believe we will cut quite a dashing pair together. But then, you haven't seen my dress yet."

"Can I? Now?" asked Salvatore.

"Oh no" said Marion teasingly. "Not before the ball – it's awfully bad luck." Salvatore looked serious.

"Really? It's bad luck?"

Marion looked at him - puzzled. It seemed he hadn't got her reference to when the groom sees the bride in her dress before their wedding day. Maybe it wasn't a tradition in his culture.

"It would be awful for you to see me looking so stunning that you wouldn't be able to resist me and yet not be able to have me for several hours" said Marion, provocatively putting her finger to her lips.

Salvatore laughed. "Absolutely – I couldn't bear it. In that case you had better put it on at the last possible minute...in the car maybe.....?" And with that, they made love before they got to the ball, before Marion even had time to see if the straps needed taking up....

****

Salvatore still didn't understand if it was bad luck that Marion looked so amazingly beautiful in her dark purple ball-gown with her porcelain complexion and red hair. She was wearing more make up than usual as well, which seemed to contribute to the sparkle in her eye. At least eight years of University balls had gone by without her having had an escort.

Bea had come to a couple of balls as Marion's guest and looked hopelessly out of place in her hippy frills. Carolyn had been to one and got rip roaringly drunk. Maybe this time Marion could actually enjoy herself. This charming, divine man was taking *her* and right now he couldn't take his eyes off her. She hoped it would stay that way all night and beyond.

She and Salvatore took a cab into town, and on arrival at the University hoards of people were already filing into the main hall and quaffing champagne. In the distance, Salvatore spotted Mira with a young man on her arm. Across the room from her was Professor David Pepper with a very attractive older woman, possibly Marion's age, on his arm.

Salvatore pulled Marion to one side. "I am confused – I thought David and Mira were partners..?" Marion explained. She didn't know who Mira was with, but the woman David was with was his wife of many years – Julia. Salvatore looked visibly shocked. "You mean – he's betraying his wife? How can he do that to such a beautiful woman? How can he do it anyway? It's wrong, so wrong."

Surely, especially if he had been a lecturer, Salvatore could not have been so naive. Marion pointed out that this sort of behaviour amongst professors was common practise. Salvatore tutted and shook his head. "It's not something common where *I* come from. When we are in a relationship, we tell the truth. If David no longer desires his wife, then he must tell her." Marion looked dumbfounded, but she could also see that Salvatore was completely serious.

"But he *does* desire her. He desires her support of him, her charm, her domestic skills and intelligence and he desires how good it looks for him to be seen with a woman like that. But he desires Mira as well – he's flattered to have the attentions of her young, lithe body and the whole naughty little secret they have; doing this behind his wife's back gives him a dirty little thrill and a release from the rigid boredom of academia."

Salvatore shook his head. And they espoused the virtues of older women. Marion had never heard a man talk like that; not honestly, anyway. She was in good shape, but she remembered Bea telling her how Michael always criticised her body and told her she had let herself go. That he therefore had a "right" to not only look at younger, slimmer women, but sleep with them as well. Much as Bea would have loved to tell him where to go, by this stage in their relationship she had let herself be so abused and her self-esteem was so crushed, that she completely believed how unattractive he made her out to be.

Marion had not experienced abuse to that extent, but she had been left for younger women. Salvatore grasped both her hands in his. "Marion – you know, don't you, that I would *never* treat you this way? I would never leave you. Not unless you wanted me to...." As they looked at each other, it was hard to tell who was more surprised.

"Oh my" he exclaimed, gripping her tighter, "You *expect* to be treated this way. The way David treats Julia." Marion's face fell. It was true. As deeply as she loved Salvatore and wanted to believe that they would happily spend the rest of their lives together, she knew she hadn't really believed in fairytales since she'd discovered that Father Christmas was really her next door neighbour. Later experiences had taught her not to believe in true love, either.

Before the matter could be discussed further, a Professor from the Social Sciences department cornered Salvatore. He'd already had a great deal to drink, was spoiling for a fight, and eyeing up Marion, to boot. She walked away – Salvatore would handle it in his own inimitable way. Still holding in her head what he'd just said, she wandered over to Julia and kissed her on both cheeks. She hadn't seen her for a long time.

"Marion! Haven't seen you for ages! I must say, you look absolutely stunning!"

"Speak for yourself!" said Marion, looking at this most elegant woman with her simple emerald green number that fell off one of her very lovely shoulders.

"I must say – Mira seems like a sweet girl" said Julia. Marion tried not to choke on her canapé.

"Y...yes. Very s.....sweet" she coughed.

"Oh....it's alright darling...I know. She's just David's type. Willowy, blonde....foreign. Hardly the first and unlikely to be the last." Marion was shocked.

"Oh my God Julia, I'm so...."

"Sorry?" asked Julia. "Don't be. I know you'll say why don't I leave him, but one really did know what one was letting oneself in for, marrying a University Professor. I can't say *I'm* sorry at all. I haven't really fancied him for years and to be honest, he's quite a bore in bed. Quite relieved he leaves me alone in that department, if you get my drift."

Marion had always liked Julia and this made her feel sad. Their marriage was a farce. Salvatore seemed such the antithesis of your typical lecturer. Julia continued.

"I enjoy the lifestyle, you see. Anyway, I couldn't have brought up our three sons on my own – not without the income. All began when I was pregnant with my first, but come....I don't want to bore you about David. I think there's something you should know about Mira..."

Marion felt a little bit sick. She hadn't quite trusted this confident, beautiful young woman from day one, but wondered if that was just because she was confident, beautiful and young. She was hardly going to go unnoticed in a department full of stuffy ageing fuddy-duddies. She was like a breath of fresh air.

David was weary of arguing with wilful Marion, hardly spoke much to his wife and a woman who appeared to be in awe of his status, was hugely attractive to him. Mira also made it very clear that she was sexually available and after a very long time of having no "Sabbath", suddenly all David's Sundays had come at once...

Julia laid out what Marion had been trying to push into denial for a very long time. Mira wanted her job. It had been obvious for a long time – covering her lectures, escorting David to the weekend seminars and co-devising the new Esoteric Studies programme. "I always thought that was *your* kind of thing,

Marion – Tarot, and what have you. I'm surprised you took your eye off the ball for so long – let it slip."

Marion had to confess that she never thought David would take her seriously if she had suggested such a course. Mira had cleverly picked up on a gap in the market and was exploiting the commercial viability of such a course – it was working. Marion confessed to Julia that in some ways, it was a relief. She'd been getting more and more tired – more and more uninspired with her job and much more into her own interests.

It felt like the right time to do something completely different – drastic, even. "And this action" said Julia, "It wouldn't have anything to do with that man smiling over at you, would it...?" Marion went to walk towards Salvatore, but Julia dragged her to one side. "I'm serious, darling. Could you manage on your pension? I know you'll get a good pay off, but how long will that last? Please listen to me. I know this is the case. I've seen David's notes...."

Suddenly Marion let Salvatore stop distracting her, gulped hard and listened. Salvatore picked up on Marion's distress and went towards her, but then Mira grabbed his arm. "Professor Campo de'Fiori! I haven't had the opportunity to talk to you since you began lecturing for us! We've been getting such excellent feedback about you. I know there is only a small intake at the moment, but I believe this will change, and fast. Once word gets around, I think you may even be over-subscribed. We're going through the old CVs again for back up lecturers, as I know you really can't take this all on yourself. In a weekend or two, David and I were thinking..."

"Excuse me" said Salvatore firmly, as he walked away and left a very surprised Mira staring at him. She reddened and felt angry. Mira wasn't used to being ignored and she called after him, but to no avail. Marion was all that mattered to Salvatore.

"Please think about what I said" Julia told Marion as she left her "And please think of me as your first port of call if you need help." Marion nodded. In a split second, Salvatore was there.

"My darling! Whatever's wrong?" Marion looked at him. He was miles away when she'd been having the conversation with Julia – how could he possibly have heard anything? He wouldn't even have been able to see them properly so far across the room, so crowded was the place. How could he possibly have picked up on her distress? They'd started out the evening on a high and now it seemed to be crashing down around them. Suddenly, the things Marion really hadn't wanted to think about were turning into quite a nasty reality. And yet, in the midst of it all – here he was. Steadfast, principled, loving – right by her side, without her even asking for support. Marion realised what her principles were.

****

It was an uneasy evening back at Salvatore's Brighton apartment. Marion wavered about telling Salvatore about her conversation with Julia because she knew he would do anything for her, including putting his own job on the line. He knew she was deeply troubled by something David's wife had told her. Marion would never lie to Salvatore, but maybe for now one little tiny white lie was ok.

But Salvatore wouldn't let things lie. He wouldn't have sensed something so strongly. In this moment, Marion realised there was no room for playing any kind of games in their relationship. This time and moment called for somewhat painful openness, and the complete revealing of oneself to the other. She told him the truth.

Whilst Salvatore listened, he also seemed just as confused as she was when she'd been explaining about lecturers having affairs with younger women, earlier that evening. Salvatore seemed not able to get his head around someone with Marion's gravitas, experience and track record being replaced by a recent graduate. It hadn't even registered with him that being David's mistress was something Mira had cleverly manipulated, and that that might have a lot to do with the decision.

Even the fact that Mira had hi-jacked Marion's New Age specialisation and then claimed the idea was her own still seemed to bewilder him. Effectively, as a result of this, he now had a job, but there still seemed to be something Salvatore wasn't getting. Marion could only conclude that he had been isolated and out of the loop of Western society for a very long time. Wherever he was from must have been very remote and traditional.

Yet, that place must have been unusual because Salvatore seemed to have a huge respect for women in general. He felt that whilst there were no doubt some young people worthy of high University positions, these were not many and that they should never try to oust an older person from their post.

Carolyn had been pensioned off early, due to a whole new team, all of them at least twenty years younger than her. No one was meant to discriminate due to age, but it went on all the time. Even Bea who was the youngest of Marion's friends had started to notice younger and newer colleagues being favoured over her. This had caused Bea to leave and start her own business – something which of course her company had hoped for – they wouldn't have to pay out redundancy. Salvatore was surely very out of touch. "This is not the same...for me...it seems you have a very short time span in which to be revered, and yet we most of us live well beyond that age. What are you supposed to do after then?"

"Quite" said Marion. "It's up to us to try and fight for survival. I'm one of the lucky ones. I'll get my pay-off, but I'll need to lower my standard of living quite a bit..." Suddenly it came to her exactly how much all those New Age courses had cost.

As though he were reading her mind, Salvatore said Marion wouldn't need to do courses anymore because she had him now, and he would teach her. If she wanted... Then he cupped her face in his hands and stared at her intently. She knew something very serious and probably somewhat unnerving was coming next and also that she probably wasn't going to like hearing it.

"You know how much I love you, don't you?" said Salvatore.

"Yes" said Marion nervously.

"Well...were you really serious when you said that you wanted to be with me forever and that you would go anywhere with me?" He saw her hesitate. Marion didn't answer quite as readily, this time.

"I..." There was no doubt that Marion wanted to be with Salvatore for the rest of their natural lives, but...they hadn't exactly discussed practicalities. Could they manage together on his salary in his country? Where would they live? Could she afford to come back regularly to the UK to visit everyone?

Perhaps Marion didn't really want to break the spell. Maybe the truth was that if she agreed to go with him, their destination would be an impoverished little village where she could never contact anyone by phone or email. Would that be OK? Would a life as Mrs Campo de'Fiori suit her wherever she was? Before Marion could answer, Salvatore spoke.

"I know. Your friends. I know what they mean to you. And besides, they have been around a lot longer than I have. I wish I could stay here, but..." Marion put a finger to his lips. For now she wanted to stay in the fantasy, knowing that Salvatore had at least a few more months on his Brighton contract, if she was going to lose her own job. But when they made love again, there was a great deal of sadness in their embrace.....

****

Salvatore was probably the only lecturer who hadn't been drinking heavily the night before. He wondered if he might actually need to go to work – if any of his students would turn up. As he slowly climbed the steep concrete steps to his faculty, he stopped for a moment to pause for breath. He saw Roberta and the eager young man who had attended the first few of his lectures walking together. Salvatore smiled and headed towards his seminar room.

David Pepper was sat at his desk with an ice pack on his head, moaning. "It's your own stupid fault" said Mira, crossly. "You *knew* there would be lots to do today and yet you just knocked back all that free alcohol and God only knows what else...Yet you firmly instructed *me* to keep a clear head. Well, thank you very much. You know, maybe *I* would have liked a drink or two, but...Oh! Good morning Professor Campo de'Fiori!" Mira stopped herself short.

Salvatore smiled and went to the coffee trolley. "Anyone else?" he asked.

"Yes please" said Mira "White, no sugar. And David will have it strong and black." David groaned loudly as Salvatore tried to stifle a giggle. After pouring the coffees, Salvatore went to the lecture room. He delivered a fascinating lecture about the history of hats and how these in ancient times, such as Ancient Egypt, were said to be to do with development of the brain, psychic abilities and auras.

Roberta sat at the front not wanting to miss anything, and the young man raised his hand after the first part as he looked curiously down at his notes. As he did so, Salvatore noticed a strange tattoo on his arm. "Yes, erm....?" Salvatore looked at his class list, slightly embarrassed that he couldn't remember the young man's name.

"Gabriel" replied the student.

"Gabriel..yes..." Salvatore seemed distracted. "May I ask you a question, before you ask me something? Your tattoo.....that looks like a most unusual design of the Auric Pentagram..."

Roberta sat up. She really liked Gabriel, and now he became even more interesting. "Are you pagan?" she asked him. That was the only association she knew with a Pentagram.

"No" said Gabriel, "I mean, there are lots of ideas about it I like, but Professor is right. This is an Auric Pentagram."

"Which means – what?" asked Roberta.

"Well....that's a whole new lesson in itself" said Salvatore. He appeared to be sweating slightly and his usual calm demeanour was showing signs of slipping. "So...urm...back to hats...."

****

CHAPTER 9

BRIGHTON, CROUCH END AND GLASTONBURY

It was crisp, and slightly hopeful in the direction of spring when Roberta and Gabriel had a walk on the pier. Filled up with a sense of excitement and hope in meeting this new man, Roberta was feeling in a playful mood and wanted to grab his hand and run over to the games arcade. But his mood was sombre.

All Roberta knew about him so far was that he asked the most amazing questions in class and she was always fascinated to hear how Salvatore would answer. Suddenly, out the blue, Gabriel told Roberta some very personal information. "I'm almost thirty" he said "and I haven't seen or been in touch with my mother for nearly a decade. She doesn't know where I am and she gave up trying to trace me. I rejected her because....well, I'm not really sure why. She just started getting into all this odd stuff like tarot and that and well...now I guess I've just realised I *am* my mother's son. I'm doing this M.A. in Esoteric studies, but back then my mother rejected my father in the process of 'finding herself.'

I was an angry young man and blamed her for all sorts of things for a very long time and then...about six months ago, my best mate died. Suddenly. Which is when I thought – life's too short – I could spend the rest of my life hating my mother and never see her again." Blimey, thought Roberta. She'd gone out with people with "issues" before, but this was abusing the privilege.

Normally she would have found some selfish reason to walk away, but this man had something about him, other than his insecurities. "Have you any idea where your mother is now?" she asked.

"Yes" said Gabriel, gazing at her with an intensity. "She's here. She teaches at this University. Has done for years." Roberta gazed back at him. He continued. "She doesn't know I'm here, but...look. You're the only person who knows about this." Roberta gasped. There was only really one person who Gabriel's mother could be – teaching there, into all new age stuff...she started to search his face for features similar to Marion's, but there was nothing physically to show he was her son. Maybe she was wrong.

That didn't negate the fact that it made the situation very wrong. If he were Marion's flesh and blood, then she was in love with her friend's son. It had never been this complicated before, but then if she was honest, she'd never really felt this way about anyone before. Nor had she ever experienced the grief, heartache or uncertainty – yearning for someone, being dumped...she had never been through the pain of unrequited love.

All of these places had been visited respectively by Marion, Bea or Carolyn. Roberta was considerably younger than them and used to having any man she wanted. She was the one who was pursued and she was the one who accepted or declined at will. Now she knew she had strong feelings for someone who only seemed to want her to confide in. This was a new world full of self-doubt, uncertainty and anxiety for Roberta.

Suddenly, all her years of study of meditation, crystal healing, Feng Shui and suchlike betrayed her. She wanted to show compassion, but was crying inside. He didn't want her – not *that* way anyway, which just made him all the more desirable. To find a way of being with him and not being with him seemed impossible right now, but Roberta knew she would just have to do it. She would just have to.

****

Marion couldn't stop thinking about David's wife, Julia. She'd seemed so nonchalant, so blasé about her husband sleeping with other women. Whether David did it because he thought she no longer cared about him or just that he could get away with it was anyone's guess, but the fact was, he still did it. It brought up a lot of bad memories for Marion. Her ex-husband had been unfaithful, but only once their relationship was already crumbling.

All she could remember was that she'd thought at the time that this was only something that happened in other people's marriages, and went into denial for a while. All the clichés fitted perfectly; they'd become more like brother and sister, friends who no longer fancied each other – the truth was, the marriage was over.

But there had been a time when it was all fresh and shiny and new and this made Marion think about her future with Salvatore. A sense of dread and panic set in. Were all long-term relationships destined to end in grey, motionless landscapes, devoid of feeling and fraught with betrayal? That was always the way hers had ended up, and the ones she saw around her.

Was this why she and the girls were, as Bea had once put it, "terminally single?" That they just never wanted to go through all the heartache again? Marion wanted to be with Salvatore more than anything, but that was just it – would they feel this way about each other, always? This doubt and insecurity had no doubt been sparked off by seeing Julia.

On the surface, Julia was bubbly, glamorous and witty. She was fun company. But what lay beneath the surface? Marion would never have labelled Julia as someone so shallow as to simply live for status and soft furnishings. She had degrees and at one time, a career of her own. Nonetheless, this women's demeanour had troubled Marion greatly. She knew her feelings needed to be discussed with the guidance of a trusted girlfriend. Bea.

****

University work was piling up, so there was no time to meet in person. Several emails and one very long phone call later, Marion was still frustrated. She'd expected Bea to be more supportive and sympathetic. Marion paced the room angrily. Bea had told Marion to be grateful and that she was being over anxious. That she and Salvatore were a match made in heaven and that she wished she could meet someone the same. Marion went back to her computer.

An email from Bea pinged up that began "Dear Sweetpea." Bea's emails often began like that. Then it went on; " I've been thinking a lot about you and...I'm sorry, but I just think I'm jealous. I don't want to be jealous of my best friend, but I think I am. I yearn to meet the love of my life – pine for him. Then someone just came and walked, literally into *your* life. It pains me to say this, but we can carry on doing angel cards and self-development courses for the rest of our lives and grow into being amazing, confident, fabulous women, but...it won't really magic *the one* into most of our lives, will it?" Marion had to re-read that last bit several times.

All those years of learning, hankering, searching. At the end of the day, did it really only come down to chance? She thought back to how she'd decided to stay on in Glastonbury, taken a walk into Street – how Salvatore had allegedly come and chatted her up because of the flower on her shoes. It seemed absurd that the perfect man for her should show up in these circumstances.

Yet, she had heard it said many times that love finds you when you're not looking for it. As Bea might have responded, "When the hell is that?" That day, Marion hadn't been looking – not for love, anyway. She'd been looking for the perfect pair of shoes, but found something else that was a perfect fit.

Bea must have been wrong. Marion had *manifested* Salvatore at a time in her life when it was right to do so. Putting everything aside, including Bea's personal thoughts, Marion needed to become clear in herself about her impending future. After a while, she became sure that the future no longer lay in weekend retreats with girlfriends. Her friends would all be happy for her – eventually.

Finally, Marion realised what it was that was holding her back. Salvatore had never married or had a family, but she had a son. She may not have seen him for many years, but he was out there – somewhere. Suddenly, the thought of leaving all she knew behind made her want to know where he was and what was happening in his life. Before she went away, Gabriel had to be found. How on earth this would happen, Marion really had no idea.

****

Roberta felt a churlish mix of emotions. She knew she'd been falling for Gabriel for quite a while and it seemed that just when she thought he was reciprocating, she discovered that he had another agenda entirely. Trying to admit to the fact she may be experiencing her first broken heart was very hard for Roberta. She hated how down she was feeling and that horrible sort of sick feeling she got whenever she saw him.

There was the strong feeling combined with the not receiving, the euphoria combined with the sudden brutal truth. This was Marion's son, for goodness sake – she should have known he'd be a law unto himself. How come Marion had never mentioned him before? This wasn't a case for Roberta to meddle in. The time had come for them to meet. And maybe after that, Roberta could plan a direct hit...

****

Salvatore seemed to have adopted a cat. It had unusual colouring – mostly white but with a little black patch on its back and one beneath its nose like a Hitler moustache. "Look, Adolf has come to see me again" said Salvatore, making Marion laugh.

"Do you know what his *real* name, is or where he lives?" asked Marion.

"Hmmm" said Salvatore, "You know, I think *he* might actually be a *she.....* "

"Blimey – a transsexual cat" said Marion. With that, Adolf jumped on Salvatore's lap, as if to make a point. Marion got up to make tea. The banter between them might have been playful, but this was only pre-empting a more serious talk to come. Salvatore would say no more until he was certain that no more doubt was holding Marion back. She handed him a mug of unsweetened tea and came straight out with it.

"Salvatore, I have a son."

He looked at her and the cat meowed. "OK....and you are thinking....what?" said Salvatore nervously as he stroked Adolf. But Marion said no more. Adolf cocked her head from side to side, not quite sure if she should break the silence of the humans with more meowing or doing something drastic like digging her claws into Salvatore's lap. This was one of those moments alright – didn't humans know this was why cats sat on laps...? Eventually, Marion spoke.

"I don't know where he is. We haven't been in touch for years. I don't know what he looks like, what he's doing...I think of him sometimes and I've been thinking a lot about him recently and I'm thinking of him now, because.." Suddenly, she burst out crying. Adolf jumped onto her lap and Salvatore put his arm around Marion's shoulder. He knew. This would affect Marion's decision to go away.

Everything else wasn't such a wrench, but a mother leaving her child...unfortunately things needed to be sorted out soon. Salvatore hadn't yet mentioned to David or Mira about his wanting to end his contract and Marion hadn't tied things up with her redundancy either. Salvatore was starting to show unusual signs of anxiety – the need to move things forward was getting more urgent. He wouldn't coerce or try to manipulate Marion in any way – that wasn't how he did things. This would be entirely her choice.

He could tell her how beautiful his home was, how much he was sure she would love it and how all his family and friends would surely adore her, but this would mean giving up literally her whole own life for him. Only one thing was certain and that was that Salvatore could not stay in the U.K. for very much longer. The race to find Gabriel was on.

****

Bea had found her calling. She'd thought that all those years of expensive personal development courses were to aid her in manifesting her perfect partner, but she had discovered her true purpose instead. Marion might not have been able to make a decision about her own life, but Bea knew exactly about her own. That very day, she handed in her notice as a child psychologist at a top clinic and enrolled on a post-graduate course for U.F.O. study. She'd find some part-time work – waitressing, anything to support herself.

Bea was absolutely determined to make contact with alien life forms and not only that, but she wanted to be the first person to make live documentary news doing so. So clear and focussed was Bea with this determination, that she had no doubt in her mind it would happen – and soon.

Carolyn was less than enthusiastic. She turned up at Bea's place with strange two-tone hair; it was grey until half way down where the orange colour was growing out. Bea stared. "I'm thinking of going blonde" said Carolyn by way of a half-baked explanation. "Wanted to see if it would suit me." Bea looked puzzled. "Half and half?" said Carolyn. "I'm a bit red head and a bit grey. Mix the two together and that sort of makes blonde – doesn't it?" Bea frowned.

"Dammit" said Carolyn. "I'm actually trying to grow out this ghastly colour. It just didn't work. I'm a silver fox and I should be proud of it. I was trying to make myself look younger, but I just ended up looking ridiculous." Bea was a woman who had seemed to find her calling, but now Carolyn was a woman who couldn't even find the right hair colour.

It seemed Carolyn was having a bit of an identity crisis. She was sometimes funny, sometimes grumpy and a sometimes feisty lady who had been a really good friend. Ostensibly she had come over to Bea's to discuss Bea's new spontaneous career move, but they both knew why she was really there.

"What will we do without her?" said Bea. Carolyn had hoped that this bit wasn't coming quite so soon because she hadn't prepared an answer. Maybe they could have discussed her hair for a while longer, but Bea was in no mood to beat around the bush. She was making rapid changes to her life, even if the momentum had been building for years. Now that Marion was also about to change her life big time, Bea couldn't help but worry it would pull them apart rather than grow warmer and stronger.

Realising the discussion about Marion's departure was now due, the voice of reason kicked in with Carolyn. She spoke softly in her slightly husky tones. "Sweetheart – I know that when you get to this time in life you imagine that everything will be cosy and fixed and settled , because that's the way we've been brought up, isn't it? I know we've all had parents and siblings who have done that and still do. But do you really think that if any of us were meant to have been fixed and rigid and stay in one place for the rest of our lives that we'd have met *each other*? That we'd have become the closest, bestest friends and done all these courses together and had such a laugh? I may be an O.A.P, but I'm sure as hell not done yet!

Actually, I'm very inspired by Marion. Look at her – she's met the love of her life at sixty years old." Then, Carolyn laughed a deep throaty laugh and threw her head back. That was the real Carolyn, and that laugh was unique to her whether her hair was grey, blonde or orange. "Yep – life in the old dog yet!" she roared and then she started snorting through her laughs which in turn made Bea laugh until the two of them were hysterical.

"Thank goodness *you're* still here" said Bea."

"Marion will always be part of us" said Carolyn. "We'll always stay in touch, won't we? Wherever she is, we won't be that far away. We'll make sure we bombard her with emails and phone calls. And we can even *look* at her whilst speaking to her these days – if we want to."

Bea nodded. She felt a lump rise to her throat, because although she knew this, she would really miss Marion's physical presence. She'd miss her waving her arms around excitedly, spilling tea on her carpet as she waxed lyrical about a new lecture she'd devised, running late into Felice's - miss her hugs. Marion gave such good hugs....

"Anyway" continued Carolyn, "Marion is pretty much embedded in us now, isn't she? We've all been part of each other's lives for so long it's like we're not separate, but small parts of a whole." This sounded suspiciously like a line from one of the courses they'd done....Yet, it also kind of made sense. Each of the women did have a little bit of them in each other – the love they had for each other.

Bea realised that however diverse their lives had or would become, however physically far they were from each other, they had already attached over a series of years by way of celebrations, commiserations, bereavements, traumas and happy accidents. Everything was infused and constant and alive. Everything went on – turned over, grew, went forward. Suddenly the moment became exciting instead of sad.

Anything that had seemed like a limitation now cleared the way for infinite possibilities. Bea felt her whole spine tingle. Tears pricked the back of her eyes as she told Carolyn, "Gosh – I suddenly feel, so...so ignited." Carolyn hugged her and more tears started flowing. Whether these were tears of joy, sadness, euphoria, excitement or sudden sinking in of realities didn't matter. Without a doubt, Marion falling in love was the ultimate success story and having worked through any feelings of jealousy or bitterness, Bea and Carolyn were truly happy for her. They'd learnt about "the law of two" with psychology and spiritual matters. That everything in the world was about duality – cause and effect, black and white.

Carolyn wondered if Bea had only thought about the euphoric part of her actions. She wondered if she'd considered the bigger picture, like how she was going to pay her mortgage. "Bea....you know this course you've signed up to? I'm just wondering, well – what sort of jobs there are for people with M.A's in U.F.Os...."

Bea laughed. "Well, just look up the Ministry of Defence. They actually employ people to research such things. And surely you've heard of area 52?"

"Good Lord" said Carolyn. "Our little Bea going off to be a pioneering scientist. It'll take some years of study though, won't it? Can't you be a part-time child psychologist in the meantime?"

"Got it all sewn up" said Bea. "I really don't want to do that job anymore. I've been doing it over twenty years and my heart just isn't in it any longer. Yes, it's been good money, but if I stop shelling out for so many courses I can consolidate all my study and afford to do something that pays a bit less. Felice has offered me work at the cafe."

Carolyn couldn't quite see slightly un-coordinated, scatty Bea waitressing, but nonetheless said she thought this was a great idea. Never mind going to study the skies, Bea really was making quantum leaps in her life. Carolyn was now the only one who could completely afford to retire. She might also want to carry on studying, but if she was honest, the social bonhomie was a large part of that.

Would it be as much fun without the girls? No matter – there would always be other girls. Marion had a new love, Bea was embarking on a new career – perhaps it was time for her to make some new friends. Maybe she'd try and get in touch with her old friend who had married and emigrated to America – maybe she could visit. In their twenties, the two of them had made a pact that when they were in their seventies, they would buy Harley Davidsons and be "Hell's Grannies." Maybe they could do it a bit earlier than that.

Carolyn started to really like this idea. A bit of a dare-devil anyway, the thought of roaring into the distance following Route 66 suddenly had massive appeal. Yes. That's what she would do. She'd try and track down her friend that very afternoon. Bea had some information about U.F.Os up on her computer screen.

"You see this?" she said. Carolyn nodded. "They're coming. I need to be prepared." Bea allowed Carolyn to scroll down the screen and also observe the photos and symbols. There were alleged sightings and footage of spaceships – one bewilderingly decorated with the fleur de lis. "It's not a co-incidence" explained Bea "Salvatore was in Glastonbury studying the new growth of those flowers, and these reports say that Glastonbury is where the aliens are going to land. Soon. Next three to six months. I *have* to be there."

Carolyn cocked her head to one side. She wasn't sure whether it was genius or potty. She'd sat on the fence with this kind of stuff but an actual landing...well. She'd suspend belief. For now....Anyway, how could she think to deny Bea all that passion? After all, she hadn't had sex for years....

 Bea would either be horribly let down or discover something beautiful that would last her the rest of her life. Why not let her float around on her happy cloud for a while? Besides, Bea wasn't that far off the planet herself....They talked a bit more about the flowers, a bit more about Salvatore being a scientist. He'd be well-off then – Marion would be ok. Suddenly Carolyn found herself telling Bea, "Well, do let me know when you hear any more news – I'd like to be there too....."

****

Salvatore knew. It was obvious. The way the boy looked at him – no, deeply *inside* him when he had hooked into something that was of particular interest to him during one of the lectures. The way he cupped his head in his hand and propped up his elbow on his desk, the bright blue eyes and the light that shone out of them – eyes that showed how fast information was being absorbed and processed. This boy was his mother's son, alright.

On the one hand, this was meant to happen – Salvatore didn't believe in coincidences. On the other hand, it changed everything. What would be for the best? Should he tell her or just let her find out? For a split second, Salvatore considered whisking Marion away before she found out, but then he felt a sharp, stabbing pain in his chest and knew it was absolutely the wrong thing to do...he had been warned...

Salvatore simply had to be honest. Thoughts kept churning over in his head – mother and son, many years apart...surely they wouldn't want to part so quickly? This was a whole new ball game. Heavy hearted, Salvatore set out that morning to the University. There was at least one thing he had to do first.

David Pepper was very sorry to receive Salvatore's resignation, especially when they were about to offer him a more permanent position. Making his partner redundant however was going to be a bit awkward, so maybe it was for the best...Peter was next on the list for the job, although he may no longer have been available. David asked Mira to re-advertise the post as well as sifting through the old C.V's. Quite where they would find someone of Salvatore's calibre and qualifications, they didn't know.

Salvatore hated leaving his students in the lurch – he told David about his visa complications and work permit expiring and David asked if he'd consider returning if things didn't work out back in his home country, but Salvatore was adamant. Once he was home, he was home.

Mira had a left a message for Peter and had a while to sit and twiddle her thumbs. David wandered past. "No lectures until midday? What a coincidence, me neither... I can think of something we can do together until then, though...." Mira was getting bored with having sex with David. He'd promoted her, but not enough. When was he going to get rid of Marion, for goodness sakes? As he pulled Mira on top of him, he pulled off her jumper and shuffled her into "their" position on his lap.

It was another position that Mira had been in for too long....wearily she obliged. It wouldn't last that long, anyway....at least, that's what Mira had hoped. To try and hurry things along, she howled - ostensibly with delight, at which precise moment the office door swung open. David was absolutely certain he had locked it, but it appeared that someone else had a key.

In the doorway with two suitcases, a rucksack and her handbag stood David's wife, Julia. There was nowhere for the lovers to run, nowhere to hide. They had literally been caught in the act. Mira hastily pulled her skirt down and her knickers up. David couldn't move anything apart from his mouth which had fallen wide open in shock.

Despite having a key, Julia had never used it. Not ever. "Sorry to disturb you David" she said without batting an eyelid, "I just wanted you to know that I'm leaving you, so thought I'd better type up a list of where things are in the house as you're there so infrequently. The number of the divorce lawyer is on there, too. I'll just pop it down there, shall I?" Julia smiled cheerfully as she did this and then went to leave. David leapt up and ran after her.

"Julia, no...wait, I can....."

"Explain? There's no need, darling. Her orgasm was faked. I should know..... Gotta skedaddle now, ta ra." David continued to follow Julia down the main corridor, only managing to stop her as she was near the main exit of the building. "Please....*wait*" he pleaded. "What do you mean the orgasm was *faked*......?"

****

Roberta saw Marion in the canteen and didn't know what to say to her. She wasn't even sure she should mention Gabriel, let alone the fact she was falling in love with him. It hurt that he was far more focussed on finding his mother than asking her on a date. She looked up to see Salvatore uncharacteristically down in the dumps. When he turned round, his eyes were bloodshot and distant , like he hadn't slept at all well.

"Professor.....are you OK?" Roberta was worried.

Salvatore rarely told white lies – he just changed the subject if he felt there was a necessity to do so. "Roberta, I...I have something difficult that I need to broach with someone. It's going to make a very big difference to my life, so you see...it will be very hard. Very." Then he took hold of her hand and squeezed it tight before buying some egg on toast and yoghurt and sitting down opposite Marion.

"You look dreadful" Marion told him "Like you haven't slept all night."

"I haven't" said Salvatore. Marion started feeling little butterflies fluttering around madly in the blind darkness of her stomach, bumping into each other. There was a sudden feeling that something was about to go horribly wrong. It had to be problems with the travel, or her emigration – something to stop them being together. It couldn't be anything else. Salvatore took a deep breath and Marion waited for him to drop the bombshell. Instead he dropped an identified and not necessarily flying object.

"I think I know where your son is. He's in my class." The emotions that suddenly hit Marion were difficult for her to articulate, such a mesh of joy and hope and anxiety and anger and guilt were they. Hope that Salvatore was right. Anger that her son had abandoned her, guilt that she may have inadvertently abandoned him. Anxiety about seeing him again and how they would react to each other after all these years.

Salvatore immediately processed all this. He had anticipated how a mother might feel, how....how it might make her want to stay behind. Her child was here, for goodness sake. Could he really expect her to leave her life in England? Was he being selfish in wanting that? Still, the decision at the end of the day would not be his.

Marion stared at him, her eyes full of hope and yet prepared for disappointment. "How...do you know?" she asked him. Salvatore described the Gabriel he knew. He told her how the boy had her eyes, how he listened to him – what his essays were about. He expected the sudden euphoria of recognition, but Marion was empty.

"I don't know" she said "I haven't seen him for such a long time. He could be my son – then again, he could be anyone's." Then she said quite unexpectedly, angrily and loudly, "Why do you think this is my son? Just because his name is Gabriel. Just because he's chosen Esoteric studies. It doesn't mean anything. Nothing at all. I'm a mother who doesn't even know her own child anymore. I don't know what he looks like, I don't know how he looks at me, I don't know what he feels or smells or sounds like....Do you know what that *feels* like?" Salvatore shook his head – he wasn't a parent.

"It feels, it feels...." Marion's voice rose so that people in the canteen started looking, including Roberta. "It feels awful!" she suddenly blurted out. Then she ran out of the canteen, tears pricking the back of her eyes and heat rising in her throat. Salvatore didn't go after her. Roberta came and sat next to him.

"What was *that* about?" she said unconcerned and insensitive about the people that might be involved. Then she added. "Wait a minute...*you* were really upset earlier...has this got something to do with that?" Salvatore rose out of his chair. "It's something to do with Gabriel, isn't it?" added Roberta as Salvatore sat down in defeat.

He looked so sad that Roberta actually felt moved to apologise. "I'm sorry - I know it isn't really any of my business. It's just that I've been spending some time with Gabriel and he told me – well... he told me Professor Green is his mother."

"So, I was right" muttered Salvatore under his breath. She wouldn't have done so normally, but now that Roberta was in love with someone herself and not comfortably at that, she actually felt very deeply for the sorrow of her tutor.

"How did you know?" she asked. Salvatore mentioned Gabriel's tattoos. He didn't go into too much depth about them but it related to something Marion had studied as well – something rare. He told Roberta that Gabriel had Marion's eyes and asked questions in the same way as her – he even came up with the same answers. It became apparent to Roberta that Salvatore loved Marion very much.

"Would you like me to talk to Marion?" she asked "This must be very hard for you".

"Thank you, but I think it really should come from me" said Salvatore. "However, maybe there is something you can help me with – we must get these two to meet, don't you think?"

"Yes" replied Roberta "And sooner, rather than later."

****

Anguished banging on her front door disturbed Bea from her study. She debated opening it, but the knocking grew louder and more frantic. Tentatively, she went to peer out the window, but then heard Marion's voice, through her sobs. "Bea... please...if you're there, let me in." It was a Wednesday afternoon. Wasn't that one of Marion's lecturing afternoons? How come she wasn't in Brighton?

Reluctantly Bea shut down her laptop – she was just about to discover the date of the anticipated alien landing; something for which she had waited all her life. Then again, she might not see much more of Marion and she could always log on later. As soon as she opened the front door, Marion collapsed in her arms.

"Please forgive me, I had to see you – I just don't know what to do..."

"Marion! Whatever's happened? Come here, sit down." Bea led her to the settee.

"I shouldn't have run out" sobbed Marion, "Shouldn't have left Salvatore just like that. David doesn't even know I've come back to London – I should be lecturing a group of students right now." Bea offered to phone the faculty, make some excuse about illness, bereavement or abduction by aliens...

"I'm sorry – I just don't know what I want you to do" said Marion. " I just know that I wanted to see you. I mean, I haven't seen my son for years and now that I can, I'm terrified. Will he like me, do you think? He doesn't even know me. We don't know each other. All these years we've missed out on – will he even want to speak to me?" Bea had no idea that Gabriel was on the scene and once she'd heard the whole story she said it looked like he had deliberately come to seek Marion out. It was almost like he had a sixth sense that if he didn't find her now, then it would be too late. It would be much harder to trace her in South America, or wherever it was she was going.

"Incidentally" said Bea, "Where *are* you going?" Marion had to concede that she didn't actually know. Her passport, as requested by Salvatore, had at least several years on it – she'd even been to a letting agency about her house....she hadn't actually thought about jabs or a visa or anything like that. "Well, don't you think it's about time you found out?" asked Bea. "I mean, it's all very well this romantic notion of being whisked off somewhere for a surprise holiday, but this is the rest of your life we're talking about."

"Salvatore has promised he will show me very soon" said Marion. Bea paused for quite a while. She realised that for Marion, where in the world she might be moving was less important than the recent discovery of her only child. Bea could also see that this was tearing Marion in half. She had never seen two people more in love, more perfect for each other than Marion and Salvatore, but children – well, that could completely throw a spanner in the works.

Bea knew that Marion was tempted to just run – disappear with all denial of the fact that she knew Gabriel was nearby. But she also knew that if Marion did that then she would never forgive herself. She spoke gently. "Marion...Gabriel is a grown man now. Whatever you decide to do, he has spent many years fending for himself. I'm sure he'd be delighted for you to know that you're with such a wonderful man and anyway – you can still keep in touch, can't you? Just like we can. Meet him, Marion. *Show* him."

Dear Bea. Her head may have been in the stars but her heart was always with the earth people. Comfort and Consultation thought Marion. The phrase reminded her of an old Joni Mitchell song, "comfort and consultation, that's what he'll find" – only the song was about unrequited love. How ironic thought Marion, that Bea who had spent so many years pining for a man that didn't want her, was now so feisty and fearless and bright.

And Marion had not fallen victim to unrequited love since she healed her broken heart on her first climb up Glastonbury Tor. How much that place had to answer for. Lovers had come and gone, and... she couldn't let this one go. Whatever happened with her son, she couldn't leave Salvatore.

****

Roberta phoned Bea when she was back in London, but the last person she expected to bump into on Crouch End Broadway was Mi-Ling. This time there was no escape as Mi-Ling cornered Roberta at a table in Felice's. "Please hear me out" she urged Roberta.

"Guess I don't have a choice" said Roberta, "But then if I don't, nor does Bea. Here she is – always prompt." Mi-Ling looked very exasperated – she really wanted to spit out whatever it was she had to say. "I've left Michael" Mi-Ling said urgently. "When we met, I....I needed to come to England to try and get a job....my family are very poor... so I did what many women from my country do. I advertised myself. I would be a wife in return for a roof over my head and money. But that isn't always the way it works out...."

Bea gasped. "So....you're a mail order bride?"

"Only, Michael will never marry me" said Mi-Ling. "He's promised me he would for years, but to appease him I've had to..." Suddenly she looked crestfallen and gazed at the floor. "Look" she continued, "Let's put it this way, Roberta. You weren't the first girl to be invited back to the cottage and you won't be the last. Peter and Priyanka have been in on it for years and the girls nearly always consent..."

"What do you mean nearly always?" said Roberta angrily.

"We've always had drinks and drugs at our dinners. No secret about that" said Mi-Ling. "But Roberta, what Michael and Peter tried to do to you.....I'm afraid that with some other women, they...they succeeded."

Roberta banged her fist down on the table and swore loudly. "Well, fuck them!" she said, causing several customers to turn round. "They should be locked up!"

"I agree" said Mi-Ling "That's why I need your help. I know you wanted to leave all this behind you, but please help me Roberta – for the sake of other women. I've only agreed to these horrible things so that Michael would marry me, but I hate it – I've always hated it. I've not had anywhere else to go – nowhere to live. And he took my passport away, anyway."

"He's kept you as a slave!" gasped Bea. Mi-Ling tried very hard not to cry. More words came out through coughs and splutters.

"Women that we brought back to the cottage, they were all young, beautiful, maybe naive and a bit vulnerable. I thought, maybe I can be like this too....for him...I thought of everywhere he could possibly have my passport and then – I found it."

"Where was it?" asked Roberta.

"Under a pile of pornographic magazines" said Mi-Ling.

Bea nodded in recognition, "Michael always did like those...." Roberta looked at Bea in disbelief. Mi-Ling continued.

"Luckily, in Glastonbury I met many strong, independent women. You English ladies – you are my inspiration.....you taught me English well" Mi-Ling spoke like a native. "I now have no money and no home, but I want to get a job and I want to be free." For a while neither Roberta or Bea knew what to say. Bea could no longer be in any denial about the farce of a relationship she had once had, even if she wanted to. Michael could have had Bea.

He could have had a warm, intelligent, attractive, funny and loyal companion for life – instead he chose a life of sleaze. Now if the woman he had just exploited had anything to do with it, this would no longer be a place he could comfortably reside. Bea at least was free of him and she thanked her lucky stars for that, in more ways than one.

It was time to move on and enjoy just being with friends and prepare for the forthcoming alien landing. Roberta in the meanwhile felt very uncomfortable. She'd been prepared to be always angry with Mi-Ling, always distrust her and yet she now felt sorry for her. It was Mi-Ling who had helped her after all and now Mi-Ling would suffer....

****

As the doorbell to his little flat went, Salvatore at first inhaled with expectation, but sighed loudly as he released it with anticipated disappointment. Whatever happened now, he had no control of the situation –

all was dependent upon Marion's free will. He knew he couldn't manipulate or impose his own will upon hers – this simply wasn't in his chemical make-up.

Even though Salvatore was sure he wanted to spend the rest of his life with Marion, he nonetheless had practical, pressingly urgent matters to attend with regard to his imminent departure and not getting on with it simply wasn't an option. He looked around the flat to see what could be packed up first. He needed to see the landlord, as well. The doorbell went again.

Salvatore opened the door to find Marion there looking frustrated and confused. "Why didn't you open the door?" she said, pushing past him into the hallway.

"Sorry, I was on the ph....." Marion cut Salvatore off with her own train of thoughts.

".........so, I thought, yes – you know. I'll go and meet him. He's probably going to be very off hand with me, you know...that's what he was like the last time I saw him. He went off in such a huff.....I don't know, children. You try and do your best by them and they just walk right out that door. And then they ignore you. For years. And then, *then* they just come back thinking you'll provide a bed and dinner and comfort – just like that – just like that they can walk right back into your life."

Salvatore sat Marion down. "Well....they *can*..." he said softly.

Marion continued from where she'd left off. "God only knows what he eats these days... I don't know where he's been travelling. What if he only eats Chapattis or algae or...insects?" Salvatore couldn't help but let out a little giggle. His girlfriend could sometimes be very extreme.

"What's so bloody funny?" asked Marion.

"Of all the things to worry about...." said Salvatore. Marion tried not to, but then she started to laugh as well. Salvatore said he would be with her if she wanted him to be, but Marion was adamant that she would meet her son on her own.

****

Though she thought of Gabriel herself frequently, Roberta currently had other fish to fry. Still reeling from Mi-Ling's revelations, she was even more upset when she found out Salvatore would be leaving at the end of term. That news came from Mira, after David had quietly slunk back home earlier that morning.

Earlier, he'd asked Mira if he could talk to her and Mira replied that she was busy. This perturbed David. Mira had been snapping a lot at him of late and never seemed to have much time for him. Maybe he wasn't being romantic enough. He thought about how things were early in their relationship. Passionate liaisons, dinners – weekends in the countryside...maybe it had just gone a bit stale. It had been going on for about three months now, but David just couldn't get Julia's comment out of his head.

Did Mira *really* fake her orgasms? Had she always faked them? Surely not – she was always so willing and sounded so enthusiastic...surely she couldn't be such a good actress? It worried David to such an extent, that he started biting his fingernails. Maybe flowers or chocolates would help, but if so, then what kind? David's heart sank as he realised he really didn't know. And yet, he knew exactly what flowers and perfume and chocolate Julia liked and suddenly started to miss her desperately....

The pain of sudden realisation seeped through him until his breath got faster and more shallow and suddenly he clutched his hand to his chest and cried out, "M...Mira! I think I'm having a heart attack!" That she hesitated before running to his side made him even more fearful and his breath more shallow.

"I'll go and get someone" said Mira, fleeing the room. The less she was near him after being caught in flagrante by his wife the better, even if he was dying. David hauled himself back up onto his chair whilst Mira was gone. It turned out not to be a heart attack, but just a panic attack and all he needed was a sip of water.

Marion was the one Mira had sought out and she was bemused when she saw David looking absolutely fine. She felt his pulse. "I was really worried" said Mira. David smiled. Perhaps she did care about him, after all.

"Why did you leave him then?" asked Marion. "Why didn't you just pick up the phone and ask for an ambulance? That's what you do." Mira looked at the floor. This had to stop. Now. She wanted to further her career but she couldn't have sex with David any more. Besides, if they kept being so active, she might actually kill him off. Marion called through for someone from the medical department to attend.

She thought maybe she should just have a quiet word with Mira whilst a nurse was attending to David. As they waited, she glanced at some papers on top of Mira's desk. Whilst she couldn't see everything, she did see Peter's C.V. Why hadn't she and Salvatore even thought of it? The New Age charlatan and would-be rapist of her friend...he was next in line for Salvatore's job. Marion had to stop this happening.

Quietly she took Mira aside. "Mira...before you replace Salvatore......I need to speak to you about this man Peter...." Mira started to put pieces together. She shook her head as she realised how Salvatore had manipulated the situation to be offered the job. Marion started to panic – suppose David and Mira wanted to look further into the situation and this held up her going away with Salvatore?

Mira got cross. "Fancy telling me now, at a time like this. I don't even know if David's health is ok. You'll have to tell him about this. You know that, don't you?" Marion nodded. It was too late now. She hadn't meant it to happen like this, but then nothing much had happened to her as she'd expected in the last six months. She couldn't leave Roberta and Gabriel subjected to a new professor like Peter, or with any of the mess she had unwittingly created.

There seemed to be only one solution she could think of. Salvatore would have to fly out without her and she would join him when she'd sorted things out. After all, it was he who had to leave the UK and not her. Why should this be a problem? Yes – that's what she would do. Even though she'd had ages to get used to the idea, Marion realised how ill-prepared she was. That and the fact she still had absolutely no idea where she was going to live.

At least this way, she'd know in advance. Much as she adored him, it was time to play Salvatore at his own game. As for Mira, Mira wasn't sure what had priority – David's heart, frustration about her own position or the news she'd just heard about Peter. The nurse recommended that David go to the hospital and get an ECG done, just to be sure.

"A man his age can't be too careful" said the nurse.

That's true, thought Mira. In trying to deal with it all, Mira hardened and became unapproachable. David badly needed to be around a woman who was warm, caring and who would wrap her arms around him when he desperately needed her. He needed his wife, but she wouldn't be doing this.

CHAPTER 10

BRIGHTON, CROUCH END AND GLASTONBURY

Roberta gazed out to sea. Quiet contemplation wasn't normally her thing; she was a social butterfly who loved any excuse to be at a "happening" and University was a hot bed of activities for all tastes. Brighton was also a city of so much art and culture and lively people – she'd often wondered why Marion hadn't made it her permanent home.

Roberta felt slightly detached from herself, as if she was walking around in a body she no longer owned. True, Salvatore's lectures had really broadened her mind and changed the way she thought about almost everything, but for the first time she started to feel empathy for others who loved someone that didn't love them back.

It began as an immense sadness as she stared out across the ocean. Next, came a craving for something very sweet and comforting and she turned back to the beach to get an ice cream. Before she reached the stall, Roberta stopped herself; the thought of ice cream suddenly became unbearable, such was the pain in her stomach. It felt high up, around her solar plexus – "the seat of the soul" as Salvatore would call it.

The pain was physical, stressful mentally and emotionally. How on earth did others deal with it? She couldn't leave it continuing to eat her up – she was going to have to find Gabriel and ask him how he felt about her, one way or the other. But Gabriel was just about to meet his estranged parent and he must have been feeling quite bewildered and emotional himself.

Surely such a confession from Roberta would rock things even further and at this conjecture she realised she would have to do something she had never even conceded. She was going to have to wait for a man. She would need to gently take a back seat until he was ready. The latter was unthinkable, and yet Roberta couldn't help but think about it. And the pain was excruciating and desirable and unbearable all at once.

****

It seemed weird to Salvatore that he was the neutral party in the meeting between mother and son, because he had such a vested interest himself. Yet he and Marion had agreed that he would go to meet Gabriel first and agree to be the mediator, then, depending upon how this meeting went they would tell Gabriel about their relationship. Salvatore tried to quell his nerves and not in a very sensible way, either.

Consuming alcohol was something Salvatore did extremely rarely. It absolutely didn't agree with his constitution and he would only occasionally drink it at important meetings in his home community or for celebrations. Downing a few shots of whiskey to calm himself seemed to have the opposite effect – indeed, by the time Gabriel arrived at Salvatore's flat, he found his lecturer to be slightly inebriated. Gabriel immediately smelt the suspect liquor on Salvatore's breath, but didn't say anything. It was 11am – way too early for anyone to start drinking. He might have been expecting Salvatore to slur his words slightly, stumble a little or give him huge, inappropriate bear hugs, but Salvatore just stood in the doorway with a large frown line between his brows.

This, Gabriel knew was something most uncommon. Like most people who met Salvatore for the first time, one of the first things they noticed about him was how smooth and unlined his skin was, making it almost impossible to determine his age. His body and demeanour had the sense that he was in his late 50's or 60's, but his smile, rounded features and slightly tanned and unblemished face had the look of a much younger man.

Salvatore seemed very uncomfortable in his own home and even unwilling to let Gabriel in. Some crisis must've occurred the night before – that was all Gabriel could think. Didn't Salvatore think Gabriel might be nervous? Without waiting to be asked, he strolled into the living room, disappointed to see this other side to Salvatore.

Salvatore reached for the whiskey bottle and offered Gabriel a drink. "No thank you" said Gabriel. "It's much too early in the morning for that, but I would like a cup of tea if you have any." This seemed to sober Salvatore up dramatically. He apologised profusely and immediately boiled up the kettle whilst trying to track down a packet of biscuits he knew he had.

Gabriel just appeared to want to get the whole thing over and done with. He wouldn't need to wait long – Marion rang the doorbell. As Salvatore opened the door, she whispered "Am I here first?" Salvatore shook his head. "Ah. Ok. Well, um.....I guess I'll come in then...." Marion didn't exactly stride into the living room, but then she wasn't timid about it either.

There, on Salvatore's sofa where she and Salvatore had cuddled up, watched television, read books and made love, was her son. He looked the same, and yet different. There remained the tattoos around his upper arms of black, Celtic-style design and strange adornments in his ears that looked like they may have once belonged to sabre-toothed tigers.

His hair was no longer jet black, but grown out to his natural slightly dusky blonde colour, which stopped about an inch off the neckline of his "Nirvana" t-shirt. The look in his eyes however, was different. When he'd walked out for the last time he was cold, angry and full of hatred. Marion would not exactly say that she saw love in his eyes now, but there was definitely a softening.

And...an acceptance. A readiness. Gulping hard, Marion's body stiffened. "Gabriel...." She said his name firmly, directly, looking him straight in the eye. She could no longer describe him as a boy as he was now a young man, and what a young man. He was bright, intelligent, alert and taking an M.A. with his mother's boyfriend as his main lecturer.

Her son was studying all the things she had studied and loved and nurtured and grown into – all the things that had eventually delivered up the love of her life after having lived already for such a long time. She would never let Salvatore go. Only, Salvatore didn't know that. When he saw the look in the eyes of both mother and son, he desperately wanted to reach for the whiskey bottle again. It may not have really helped, but just knowing it was there for something to lean on was something he really needed right now.

What now? Could Salvatore honestly, really stand it if Marion chose to stay in England? The thought was too much and overwhelmed by both the thought and the whiskey, Salvatore spontaneously started to sob. Gabriel felt embarrassed. He didn't know the true extent yet of his lecturer and his mother's relationship and could have known nothing of their true feelings for each other.

Feeling decidedly awkward that his Professor was behaving this way in front of his mother, he attempted to diffuse the situation, but Marion stepped in first. Smelling the alcohol on Salvatore's breath, she was shocked. "Professor Campo de' Fiori! Please could you leave us for a moment?" This made Salvatore cry more. Nonetheless, he grabbed a bag and the whiskey and made for the front door. Marion grabbed the whiskey and sized up to him. The look in her eyes said, "Drink any more of that, and I'll kill you". He let it go and shut the door, taking only his lecturing notes with him for comfort.....

Gabriel laughed a little and smiled wryly from the corner of his mouth. He said he was relieved that Salvatore had gone out – it would give them a chance to talk properly. That was the first thing Gabriel said to his mother after all these years. She might have expected him just to say "Mum" or coldly extend his hand as if politely greeting a perfect stranger, but the second thing he said to her was "I'm sorry."

There was no look of hate in his eyes this time. Whatever had made Gabriel leave in the first place, he had come back. He told Marion how grateful he was she hadn't tried to track him down after he'd cruelly rejected her first attempts to do so. How he thought he could go out into the world and be all self-righteous and independent and not need any kind of parental guidance.

After back-packing around the world, falling in and out of love, merging with other cultures and generally learning to grow up, Gabriel couldn't help thinking about the woman he had left behind – his mum. There were so many years to catch up on. Was Gabriel still in touch with his father? Did they have a good relationship? Did Gabriel have a girlfriend? Gabriel told Marion that he was just happy he'd found *her*. As for other women, he'd made good friends with this young woman called Roberta who was on his course, but at this moment in time he didn't want to get involved with anyone.

He was just finding his feet, thinking about settling somewhere – he really liked Brighton. Marion gulped deeply. It was only that he was so settled and secure in himself and finding a way in life that Marion felt ok leaving him behind. He had been so troubled and angry and if he'd still been like that then she would have felt completely torn in two.

Satisfied that her son would still lead a full and happy life if she weren't in the country, she then proceeded to tell him about her and Salvatore. Whilst he was delighted that they were a couple, the sadness in his eyes when she told him they were going away was deep and palpable. He had grown very fond of Salvatore and only just met his mother again. But true to his word of settling down and dealing with life for himself, Gabriel gave his "blessing", verifying that Marion was doing the right thing. "How soon are you leaving?" he asked.

"Less than a month," said Marion. She couldn't be sure of the exact date – Salvatore was sorting out the flights and things back home. "Where are you going?" said Gabriel. "Maybe it's somewhere I know – somewhere I've been." He chuckled. "I've been most places, actually."

Marion felt her heart quicken as she wondered how on earth she could tell Gabriel that she really didn't know. His eyebrows made a "sad" arch. "It's far away, isn't it?" he said. Marion felt a lump in her throat that gradually grew bigger – so much so that she could barely force out the words.

"Yes. Yes, it is." Gabriel then reached out his arms to see if Marion would reciprocate with a hug. Marion did. She maybe was going far away or not that far at all, but this felt like coming home. Her boy. Her child. He was so grown up, so handsome. She told him she knew Roberta from other courses and that he'd be in safe hands with her as a friend.

Gabriel admitted that losing Salvatore would be a huge blow to his studies and wanted to know who would be taking over. Marion tried to hide what she knew about Peter and in that moment realised she'd have to do all she could to prevent him from getting the job – again. Gabriel saw the look of panic in her eyes. "Really – it's ok. Whoever it is – I'll cope."

"But I'm your *mother*" said Marion taking hold of his hand and patting it. "I need to know that you'll have a good lecturer. One I approve of."

"Well you obviously *well* approved the last one" Gabriel laughed.

"Right" Marion said adamantly. "I'm going to stick around until I know what's going on with that. Absolutely, I am."

****

Salvatore staggered down to the beach and let a biting wind tug at his few remaining strands of hair. A particularly bitter weather front was blowing in from somewhere across the sea and he could already feel the wind stinging his eyes. Salt water from sea mingled with that of his tears and Salvatore's lips tingled and dried. So near, and yet so far.

Everything seemed to change on a daily basis – one minute he was sure he'd be flying off into the sunset with his love, the next he was depressed and certain it would be the last time he ever saw her. In truth, it had pretty much been this way ever since they'd met. All the things she thought – that he was dying, that he was a con man...then, just as he thought it really would all work out, her son showed up. He'd seen the way they looked at each other. Surely Marion would never come with him now. How erratic, how beautiful, how painful were human relationships. Salvatore glared up at the sky and shook his heavy, solid fist at it. At once, there was a huge clap of thunder.

Cursing and starting to sober up, Salvatore shrugged his shoulders and looked up again. "What do you want? What am I supposed to do?" It wasn't his fault he was here, was it? *They* had sent him here – he wasn't planning to fall in love. Why did it seem so much harder than ever? He'd come to study, clarify and conclude and then return home with the results. He already knew when he'd arrived that he could never make England his permanent home.

He'd been finding it so hard to concentrate on his work; he hadn't intended to lecture in Brighton – he'd been neglecting his scientific work in Glastonbury. Whilst he'd been researching into healing flowers and herbs, he wondered how no one had ever found one to cure lovesickness.

The only cure that he had ever heard of was ironically to throw yourself into your work. Thinking he could at least do some marking before he left, he pulled Gabriel's essay from his bag. He started reading it when he spotted a tall, slim young woman with a red bob just catching the ends of whatever sun was peeping through the clouds. Cursing and starting to sober up, Salvatore shrugged his shoulders.

Maybe not all the choices had been his; he'd been allocated various locations on account of his mixed skills, but he knew he'd spent too long where he was and had to return home with his research findings. Glastonbury first, though – there was going to be a lot to do there. It was so damned hard to concentrate on his work – damn that being a cure for the "terminally in love."

In the last few weeks he had nothing to show for his final project, other than essays from his students. Dejectedly, he started to pull Gabriel's essay from his bag and looked up to see Roberta sitting a little further up the beach, crying.

He got up and walked towards her, crunching the pebbles beneath his feet. As he sat down beside her, Roberta noticed that Salvatore had been crying too. She let it all out. "Oh Professor, I'm so in love.... I don't know what to do..."

"If you're in love, then why are you crying?" asked Salvatore.

"Because he doesn't love me back" sobbed Roberta.

"Then it isn't love, my dear" said Salvatore gently. He fished in his bag for some tissues, but this comment seemed to stop the flow of Roberta's tears. She looked at him searchingly.

"Then what is it?" she asked.

"I'm not quite sure how to put it in the right English words..." Salvatore struggled. "All I know is that whatever it is, it is painful. All I can tell you is that if it isn't returned, then it isn't the real thing. I only know that I....yes, I *am* in love."

"Then why are *you* crying?" asked Roberta. Salvatore had to think. On one level there were so many reasons, but really it was because he was afraid it would be the end of his love. He took his time to answer and then realised that maybe their pain wasn't so very different.

"I'm afraid it isn't going to last" he said simply and finally.

****

Mi-Ling found employment at Felice's. She spoke good English, was polite and friendly to the customers and a good waitress. Whilst it wasn't entirely comfortable meeting Bea there in her break, she also knew that despite being Michael's ex, Bea was on her side. Bea was adamant that neither Michael nor Peter should be allowed to get away with their behaviour. This was more like helping a "sister in need", rather than ex-girlfriend revenge.

At least, this was how Bea liked to think of it. In truth, she got a little thrill in finding out what a despicable man Michael really was – maybe he always had been and she just couldn't see it. The thought she might be able to aid in his ultimate downfall excited her. Carolyn had also agreed to come, for back-up.

Mi-Ling went and joined the ladies' table. Pulling her apron off, she said, "Michael keeps calling me. He wants me to come back. Says he loves me. That he's sorry about everything and that he wants to make it up to me." Bea raised an eyebrow. Where had she heard this before, she wondered...?

Carolyn just cut to the chase. "Well, I hope you're bloody well not going to."

Mi-Ling shook her head. "Absolutely not. I don't love him any more – don't even like him. I can't. Not after what he's done." Bea was surprised. So Mi-Ling wasn't just some gold-digger? She actually had feelings? She could have used her youth and beauty to trade and use men, but it seemed she had actual feelings for the man. There must have been some good in him, then – something which made women desire him.

Sadly, he was also a sex addict and into group sex. At the same time, he expected to be in a loving, allegedly monogamous relationship that met his emotional needs.

To outsiders, he looked like the perfect boyfriend. He'd always have his arm around Bea at parties, spoke articulately and with compassion when they were in the company of others about the environment, different ecologies, love and peace...only Bea really knew the man who was cold and withdrew from her natural loving nature and made her feel terrible about herself and unworthy. She was vulnerable and he was insecure – a strong and supportive partnership, this did not make. But Bea had broken away from this now. She was free. She might not have been ready to be in another relationship, but she was ready to start loving her life again.

Mi-Ling frowned. "I have some information about Peter" she said, keeping her voice down. "He called me saying Michael had asked him to call me, because I kept ignoring Michael's calls. I mean, how low can you go? I told Peter I wasn't going to listen to him either, but he pleaded. He said that after I left, Michael realised I was the only woman he had ever really loved."

Bea gritted her teeth and then bit down so hard on her tongue, she could taste the metallic flavour of blood. Then she felt her whole spine tingle with a sudden light-headedness. Mi-Ling would not have seen the little beads of blood forming inside Bea's mouth, but she did notice all the colour suddenly draining from her face.

"Bea – are you OK?" Bea nodded and motioned to Mi-Ling to continue. She said she'd refused to hear about or have anything more to do with Michael, when Peter suddenly swung round the conversation to say he'd been offered a position as lecturer at Sussex University. He told her he was astonished he hadn't got the job in the first place – how he'd been pipped to the post at the last minute.

He was due to take up residency within the next month or so, depending upon when the current lecturer left. Bea leapt up from the table and grabbed her coat. "We've *got* to stop him" she said, with all the energy of someone who had watched too many action films.

"Bea – stop" said Carolyn. "Who do you think you are? Batman? How exactly do you think we can do this?"

"I don't know" said Bea. "I just know we have to. Call Marion. Anything. Such a horrible and utterly corrupt man cannot work there, even if Marion's leaving. What about Roberta? We absolutely can't let it happen." Mi-Ling asked Bea if she knew the heads of the apartment at the University. Bea had met David Pepper a few times, but wouldn't exactly say she knew him.

"But you know what he looks like and where we could find him?" said Mi-Ling. Bea didn't know the exact layout of the building, but she would recognise him – certainly. Mi-Ling was quite prepared to go to Brighton and reveal everything. Only – she didn't have evidence. DVD's of orgies, anything – it was all back in Glastonbury. Felice waved Mi-Ling over; her break time was up.

"Call me later" said Bea "Carolyn and I will put our heads together."

"Will we?" said Carolyn.

"Yes. We *have* to think of something" said Bea.

"You bloody well do think you're Batman, don't you?" said Carolyn.

****

The ease with which Gabriel gave his mother his blessing to go and live on the other side of the world was so natural and sincere, that it barely seemed possible. He could see how much she and Salvatore meant to each other and whilst he may have just been making a new life for himself in Brighton, he could see that Marion was ready to move on.

That she would now be hanging around a little to sort things out before she moved was a comforting thought, but he knew their time would be fleeting – their meetings scant. Once Gabriel had left Salvatore's flat, sitting alone on Salvatore's settee with the empty coffee mugs, Marion suddenly felt a sense of tremendous peace engulf her.

Suddenly she felt free of all the burdens of yesterday and ready to start a new life. She would tell Salvatore she was ready. He'd be back soon. She looked at everything packed in boxes and thought about her own home and how everything material she owned was now concealed behind cardboard. What insignificance all that she'd worked for now had.

The cosy little two- up, two- down cottage-style house that she'd bought in Crouch End decades ago for a pittance was once somewhere she would never have imagined she'd be living life as a single woman without any family around her. Life had been interesting and fun, but maybe slightly too cosy – perhaps even too safe and a touch on the drab side, if she was honest.

Salvatore hadn't sealed all his boxes and Marion had a little peep at the tops of them. They mostly consisted of his research books with very little in the way of personal artefacts. He only really had a few clothes, as well. So caught up in the whirlwind of their spiritual union had she been, that Marion realised she had paid very little attention to the practical matters of their everyday lives.

Of course, she wouldn't expect someone who was so nomadic in their work to have all that much – travelling from city to city, such as Salvatore was. Now his work was taking him back home, and she with him. Marion sighed deeply as she tried to imagine what her new home would be like. Salvatore had promised her it contained beauty beyond her imagination.

It would be easy to be cynical about such a thing, but everything Salvatore did – indeed, everything about how he *was*, might be beyond the imagination of most women. For such a long time, Marion had found herself falling into a repetitive, cynical trap of thinking he was simply too good to be true. Every negative thought about Salvatore, including that he was a member of the Mafia or on his deathbed had been proved untrue.

How awful thought Marion, that a woman should invent catastrophes, all because she'd been so conditioned to believe that true love could never really be a truth. Now, here she was – a woman to break the mould. She would prove that soul-mate relationships not only came to those who waited, but those who could finally accept that such a thing could happen.

She did sometimes wonder why she was the only one, though. Maybe Bea wasn't quite ready. Maybe Carolyn was, and it would happen soon. Maybe in a year or so, all of them would meet in Italy, or Argentina or Chile or wherever it was she going to live, all with their new partners. Maybe, just maybe as they headed towards the end of their lives, these women would have the most wonderful of endings.

As she continued gazing into the boxes, Marion noticed what appeared to be a photo frame, upturned so that the back of it was facing her. As Salvatore never spoke very much about his family or friends from back home, Marion assumed this must be his one special photo. She was surprised when she turned the frame over to see a fleur de lis. There was no writing – just what looked like a photo of the flower.

How she wondered about the significance of these in Salvatore's life. When he had climbed to the top of Glastonbury Tor to see if he could find any for his research, what a commotion this had caused. Obviously, this symbol had great significance for him and it kept showing up in their lives. When Marion had asked about it and then how she had noticed the flower showing up on documents, in architecture and other works of art since she had met him, Salvatore merely smiled and said this confirmed that she was the only woman for him. Later on, Marion came to understand that the study of this flower was extremely important to Salvatore's research, although she never exactly knew in which way.

She didn't particularly understand scientists and always preferred to base her understandings of the world on perception and instinct, but Salvatore had made her appreciate them much more, as well as their significance. Marion had always maintained that there were only two types of people in this world – artists or scientists. Artists *felt* everything to verify if something was real, whereas scientist always had to verify *it*.

To this end, she had always felt slightly superior, classifying herself in the artistic group. These were the people who were perceptive, aware, clairvoyant. Salvatore negated these theories right out of the water. He was more perceptive than anyone Marion had met in her life and yet he was a scientist.

This was what made him so attractive – not just to Marion, but to just about everyone who came across him. Salvatore had the most incredible brain, but he was also the warmest, funniest, most supportive person you could ever hope to meet.

Marion heard the front door push open. She was sure that Salvatore would return home more at peace, but he looked terribly forlorn. Best to put him out of his misery as soon as possible. Marion threw her arms around Salvatore's neck and said, "Darling – you can stop all this worrying now. I'm coming with you." Immediately, Salvatore softened. It was like the entire weight of the world had been taken off his shoulders.

He smiled and looked his sweetheart deeply in the eyes, only his relief was short lived. "Only, not yet" added Marion. Salvatore's shoulders sank and he felt his heart beating fast again. Marion put her hand on his chest to pacify him, but it felt strange – almost like she could barely feel him. It was like she could see all the signs of distress, but feel nothing.

Now it was her turn to panic. "Oh my God – what's wrong with you? Your heart..."

"I'm fine" said Salvatore. "Really. It's just that....If you *are* going to come, you *have* to come with me when I leave. It can't wait. I'm sorry." Marion looked confused. The urgency for Salvatore to return home may have been understandable, but what difference would it make to him if she came out after he had left? There was no legal requirement – not as far as she knew.

"I have to go" repeated Salvatore. " The time in which you now have to join me....it's very limited......there is only one window of opportunity and it won't come again. I'm sorry my darling – it's now or never." Marion had no idea what Salvatore was talking about. Yet, as she'd grown so accustomed to doing, she let the way he said what he said and the *essence* of this seep into her being more than his words.

Usually Salvatore was a very honest, direct and clear communicator, but there were times when he needed to express things which he found very hard to put into words. This frustrated most people who expected things to be exact, certain and correct. But Salvatore had taught Marion not to think in this way – he had told her to "think underneath" his words, when it was required. It had taken her a long time to get it, but now she understood that a kind of detection, telepathy almost, was what was required. Salvatore knew she had this ability. He'd known when he first met her.

Normally, Marion would eventually get the message loud and clear. Were it not for her warmth, charm, humour and other qualities, this alone would have made Salvatore fall for her deeply, but it was the *whole* selves and not just a part of each other which fed their desires. It was therefore unquestionable. Marion *would* go with Salvatore, and at the time he needed her to.

She was just about to tell him this when he told her that their departure would necessitate a short time apart anyway as he'd need to leave for Glastonbury to collect his pass for the Cosmic Event Conference , with whom he would consolidate the findings of his research before returning home. Marion knew about this conference via Bea. Everyone had been getting very excited about the mooted alien landing, even if Marion wasn't exactly convinced.

Salvatore handed Marion some papers. She'd need to get all her stuff packed up and join him in Glastonbury by the date stated. It felt like pressure, but in a way it needed to be. Marion wasn't concerned – she'd put all her material affairs in order, Bea would look after and effectively be landlady for her flat. It was just....Peter.....

On every rational level, Marion knew that this wasn't how you started a new life with someone. There was usually gradual build up, a getting to know each other, but that was for when you were younger. She was sixty years old – was there really time to lose? No, it had to be now or never. And anyway, she felt like she already knew Salvatore.....like she'd already known him for a very long time.

The "rational" approach had already been tried. Marion had accused Salvatore of all sorts of things, tried to find all sorts of reasons not to be with him, and yet on each occasion she had been proved wrong. Any fears she may have had, had been put to rest. Wherever they were now going, she wanted to go. Salvatore had sorted everything; all she needed to do was turn up.

"I'll be up on the Tor with the rest of the specialists" said Salvatore "Should be quite something this landing, eh?"

Marion laughed. "You really believe it then? You really think this is going to happen? I thought this was just the domain of Bea. I mean, I know some of your work involves the study of possible other planetary life forms, but what you do is of a very highly advanced scientific level. Bea's conviction only stems from the depths of her overactive imagination. Still – she's been getting very excited, especially with all the emails she's been getting."

"Well – I shall be there, nonetheless" said Salvatore. "It's in my contract, anyway. By the way, there are still a few things I need to pack. Can you help me?" He lifted the box which contained the framed photo of the fleur de lis.

"I'm not prying" said Marion, "But it sort of seems strange to me that that is the only thing you appear to have in a frame. I didn't see anything of your friends or family and..." Salvatore stopped her.

"If you come, then you will meet them" he said simply, then carried on folding things and looking around the flat. There was so much Marion wanted to ask him, but she knew he'd only answer her with more of the same and she was too tired to be telepathic....

"Well....at least tell me about the flowers" she asked him. "That's just factual. At least give me something to hold onto, before you leave." Salvatore's eyes glazed over and he gazed ahead wistfully.

"Ah, yes. My life's work. Something I have been looking into since I was a young man. It's only really been recently that I have been able to find any answers. Only since... I met you." This was still an enigma, and yet Marion could have melted into a tiny puddle on the spot. All her life there were so many things she would never have believed were possible and yet Salvatore made everything possible. Spending forever looking at one tiny bit of plant life until he got results – looking at the true meaning of things. When Marion and Salvatore looked at each other, it was never just with a cursory glance.

Before they'd officially "got it together", you could see they were searching each other – they would both frown slightly, almost like they were trying to look into each other's souls, desperate to know what the other was really thinking. Now when they looked into each other's eyes, they would both hold the moment for a very long time. Each knew what the other were thinking. They were trying to find answers, even if they were unsure of the question.

Finally, Marion realised why it had taken her so long to find the love of her life. She could never have settled for an everyday, ordinary life. All her life she had been seeking something – searching for deeper meanings. At least the last decade of that life had been spent doing this in the company of much-loved girlfriends and sometimes alone.

To this end, she had been ripped off in Greece, patronized on the Isle of Wight and had a jolly good laugh in Glastonbury. When she had reached a point when she had just about given up on finding this elusive "something", along came the man of her dreams. Before falling in love with him, she had fallen in love with life – she enjoyed, she enthused...she was attractive.

Salvatore kissed Marion lightly on the tip of her nose. It didn't exactly feel like he was kissing her goodbye, but it was slightly tentative – like he still wasn't convinced that she wouldn't change her mind. Suddenly she wanted to ask him an entire solar system of questions, but there were earthly matters to be taken care of. "I'm just going to give Bea a call...." she said.

****

Bea had many earthly matters to consider. First of all, she had promised to help Mi-Ling in thwarting Peter's plans and secondly she'd received an email from Stephen the Wizard asking if all the girls would be in Glastonbury for the Cosmic Conference. She had to read his email several times; the way it was written was just like asking them if they'd be coming down for another workshop, not the event of a lifetime.

Suddenly Bea started to feel a bit flummoxed – there were many big things in her life to sort out and all of a sudden her euphoria at changing her life became a quagmire of very little money, a mortgage and her best friend emigrating. She had hoped Salvatore with his contacts might be able to help her get a placement or put in a good word, but that was before she knew he was leaving.

Marion's number showed on the caller display. There was so much to do, but not to talk to Marion was unthinkable. Bea was delighted to hear that Marion would pop back to Crouch End before leaving for Glastonbury and beyond. She wanted to soak in her life, her friends, her memoirs. The University was fast becoming a fading memory, which was when Marion realised which things had really been of importance to her. Even though she had lectured there for over twenty years, this now became a small and insignificant part of who she was.

The sensation was strange to Marion; almost like she was in the time when there were the last things you would think about before you died. After years of putting together seminars, research, attending courses and conferences, eating in the canteen and some seriously dull weekends, it was very easy to hand in her notice.

What did remain was the memory of Brighton itself – its essence. The students. The little arty coffee shops, the old fashioned penny arcade, the unusual clothes shops and most of all the sea. Maybe her new home would be near the coast. Salvatore seemed to have as much an affinity for oceans as she did and it seemed the most natural thing that the last part of her life would be spent somewhere near water. But...what if Salvatore lived in a large sprawling city where no one could breathe and she couldn't get a job?

Quickly, Marion put the thought from her mind. He'd promised her that where they were going to live was beautiful. There must be sea and fields – he must be near nature...for his work. Her thoughts darted back to Crouch End. Her friends. In one of her "dying memories", they would be at the forefront – in Felice's, in each other's homes, travelling away.

When Marion told Bea that she would need to leave earlier than she originally thought, Bea seemed distraught. That was when all the stuff about Peter taking over from Salvatore came out. "What will we do without you Marion?"

"You'll carry on" said Marion. "You've been doing fantastically, anyway. Reaching out on a new career path, getting over Michael...you don't need me around to stop Peter in his tracks. Sounds like Mi-Ling is a pretty sussed sort of girl." Bea didn't dare admit she actually found this "assignment" quite exciting, but the reality of it was starting to seep in. She didn't want to be accused of thinking she was Batman any more, after all.

It was a big deal, and Roberta's future was at stake as well. She had to do something. "Meet me for tea. One last time" Bea asked Marion, realising Marion was crying as she said it. It was all very well going off into the sunset, but really, just how easy was it to leave your past behind? Only a short while ago, Marion had been at Bea's place and Bea had hastily switched channels when a programme called "Wanted Down Under" came on the television.

Marion had commented that it looked quite interesting, but Bea hastily dismissed the show as boring. When Marion deliberately put the programme on her own television the next week, she could see why Bea had discouraged the viewing. The programme featured families who were in search of their dream lives in Australia.

With financial backing, they were given the opportunity for a trial run. There would be no chance of that with Salvatore. Then Marion saw the part she knew Bea didn't want her to see. There was one particular section when other family members and close friends of departing families sent video messages saying how much they would miss them, how empty and hopeless their lives would be without them, even though they "understood how much it meant to them."

Of course, when Marion watched this part of the programme, it tugged very closely at her heart strings. Girlfriend banter had become an inextricable part of her life and there was so much she was giving up. Yet, Marion was also adamant this was the final coffee. Cafes were synonymous of a life with the girls and never being a lover of nightclubs or bars, Marion had actually looked forward to the day when she could make dinner parties without being laughed at for being middle-aged.

There was no time to cook or shop these days though, and so cafes had become the venues for social gatherings. Felice's was one of the few remaining originals – all other cafes had been taken over by large corporations who were the only ones who could afford the rent. Felice had managed to survive by way of his very loyal client base and the best spaghetti Neapolitan in town.

The cafe was always heaving, full of locals and not so locals who had heard the word. Mrs Felice, Maria, seemed to have been born to make the most delicious pasta sauces known to man – Felice had got lucky marrying her, Marion thought. Strangely enough, when she'd taken Salvatore there he never seemed that keen to have a pasta dish, usually going for a simple panini or just a slice of cake. He did drink a lot of coffee, though.

Marion took a long, deep sigh. Bea muttered something down the phone about Peter and Mi-Ling but Marion was lost in her own thoughts. Suddenly she felt a little twinge right in the middle of her solar plexus, although it was really her heart that was hurting. She wished she knew where she was going. Would there really be sea? Cafes like Felice's? Interesting places to work? Would she fit in – be accepted?

Suddenly the thought of what she was leaving behind overwhelmed her and she felt an indescribable wrench. All she heard Bea say was "....so, two o'clock in Felice's, ok?" and that was actually all she needed to hear. For now this was enough – something to ground her before she well and truly had to fasten her seat belt and cling on for dear life. At least, it felt like that.

****

Helen had circulated an email. At the Royal Academy of Art, art critic Theolonius Poole was hosting a private viewing by a contemporary 'conceptual' artist who had been causing quite a storm in the tabloids with his oil paintings of spaceships he claimed he had actually seen. Quite why there should have been anything extraordinary in this when millions of people in Middle America had been doing the same for years was a mystery, but for the fact that the painter had already made a name for himself with his paintings of...squares.

This was going to be a well-attended celebrity event and Theolonius Poole had already courted controversy and hence got some publicity for the event, claiming that aliens only ever seemed to have been painted by "white trash" and not anyone with talent. There began an amazing argument in magazines and documentary programmes with the hypothesis that if these were the type of people that aliens visited, then they must have been of a similar level of intelligence.

If this was the case, what did the art world want to do with aliens? What could they possibly show us but another planet full of Starbucks and self-destruction? Maybe there was no "higher intelligence", as no one had ever painted it. This was why this particular exhibition had quite a build-up to it.

The paintings were almost photographic style and looked very convincing. There were no green men or Little Greys – just lots of beings that looked quite human. There was a huge amount of talk about whether these beings were people observing the landings, or were the actual aliens themselves... whatever it was, it was certainly different.

Bea was extremely keen to beg, steal or borrow an invite and Roberta wanted to go as well. She wanted to ask Gabriel, but Bea pointed out that two tickets would be hard enough to get. Both of them replied to Helen. Anything where aliens were, was where Bea wanted to be. Besides, she had to be on the ball and with the trends if she was seriously going to embark upon this study as a career. Then she remembered she also had to meet Mi-Ling, and Marion and Bea's own past and future and current priorities suddenly became inextricably intertwined.

****

It was the 'last coffee'. Felice came and joined Bea and Marion at their table and Marion would see Carolyn later and bid her last farewells to all, even though everyone would probably be in Glastonbury for the Cosmic Conference a few weeks hence. Felice kissed the back of Marion's hand and smiled sadly.

"So – Missa Marion....wassa wrong, huh? You no longer like my coffee?"

Marion laughed. "I adore your coffee Felice, you know that. But I have the opportunity now to go and spend the rest of my life with someone I really love and I can't spend that in Crouch End. Maybe I can import you, somehow?"

"You will email us, Missa Marion? Tell us how you're getting on?"

"Of course I will" said Marion "I'll tell everyone. I have absolutely no intention of losing touch or not visiting, for that matter. I don't care how expensive flights are –we'll find a way." Suddenly Bea looked incredibly sad. It was only being physically next to Marion that she realised the true extent of how much she would miss her. Yet she knew she also had to let her go, as well.

No real friend would try and hang on to someone when they knew they had the real deal. Marion and Salvatore. This was about as close to the 'real deal' as surely anyone could get. Bea allowed a few drops of tears to shed and Felice brought over some cappuccinos and watched the heartache and joy and laughter and anguish that he had seen in so many others, whilst they drank coffee over the years.

His place, he knew, was a safe haven where people could come and bare their souls on his coffee tables and judging by the queues on a daily basis, there was a real need for that venue. Felice was actually a modern-day healer of the highest order. Suddenly Marion noticed that he seemed to be sniffing a lot into a greying handkerchief.

"Felice! You're crying!"

"Ah – no my dear....bit of a cold...." But Felice *was* crying.

"Don't deny it" sniffed Bea, "You'll miss her too."

"I miss all my customers" Felice retaliated, "But with Missa Marion, I think I be at least twenty cappuccinos a week down – my business will be ruined!" The three of them laughed. In a rare moment of quiet, Maria came and joined them.

"You know, he won't say this" she said, "But secretly, I think you and your friends are his favourite ladies. He thinks you have, how can I say – Italian humour? You fill the place with laughter. It won't be the same without you. You know, if he wasn't married to me, well then...."

Felice blushed and sensed it was time to head back towards the kitchen. Maria took hold of both Marion and Bea's hands. Marion wondered if Maria or Felice could sense anything of the Italian in Salvatore – they had never spoken to each other in the language. Being her last opportunity to find out, she thought she'd ask Maria.

"I don't think so, no" Maria said. " He is a cultured and sophisticated gentleman, no doubt. But...Miss Marion.. do you mean *you* don't know where he's from....?" Marion shook her head. Maria looked shocked. "Well then. This will be a *real* adventure!"

Marion and Bea looked at each other, then the other people in the cafe, then out the window and finally at their menus. There was always something unspoken between very close friends, always something that words just couldn't say. Bea knew exactly why Marion couldn't just have asked Salvatore where she was going to live, much less his true origins and even less than that, neither of them could explain this to Felice or Maria.

Eventually, Bea spoke. "Oh Marion...I know you said you'd come back and see everyone and that you'll always be in touch, but....that could be a very long time. I know we're important to you, but I have this very strong feeling about your new life...you're not going to want to leave it, once you're there. It's going to be so different. So different to anything you have ever known." Marion started crying and it was hard for Bea to say anymore.

Maria walked back towards the counter and put her arm around her husband's waist. "We won't see Miss Marion here again, will we Felice?" Felice shook his head, then gently stroked his wife's face as he untucked a silver chain necklace from her roll neck jumper and gently held the little silver fleur de lis pendant in his hand.....

****

CHAPTER 11

ALL PLACES

Roberta gazed wistfully at the froth on the top of her cappuccino as Bea waved her hand in front of her face. She'd never seen her look so far away and that look could only mean one thing - Roberta was in love. Ostensibly, Roberta had met Bea in Felice's to discuss how they would proceed with Mi-Ling, but Roberta seemed nonchalant and unattached to the hard core fact that that the man who'd tried to rape her was just about to become her tutor.

Bea knew a little about Gabriel and was trying to come to terms with it herself; she'd always known about him but the irony of him showing up after all these years – just as Marion was about to go away. Bea conceded that sometimes it took just one thing, one person to be the catalyst for the most incredible change in a persons' life.

Marion and Salvatore had given Bea cause to hope; that there was hope for progress, for love in this world. Here, in front of her now was another friend in love, although she couldn't tell if this particular relationship was destined to head down the same path. Roberta stirred her coffee and didn't drink it.

"I think I love him" she said, trying not to choke up. Maybe Bea could help her friend. Roberta may be new to unrequited love, but Bea considered herself mistress of such matters. She knew all about how it felt, how to deal with it and that eventually you got over it. How you finally learnt not to love someone who didn't love you back.

But Bea also knew there were some people who never did move on. They clung tight to some fantasy, never wanting to face up to reality, lest the pain would kill them. Roberta was young, she would recover and besides – it wasn't such a bad thing. The experience necessitated that she left her ego and vanity somewhere far behind, and that actually made her a much nicer person to be with.

Still, Roberta had been through a lot of late – it was going to be hard enough coping with the tutoring situation and losing Salvatore. Bea looked at

Roberta and realised how the whole situation had kick-started the process of her own emotional detachment from Michael. Only when a close friend became involved in extraordinary and unexpected circumstances, could she face her fears and look at what was truly occurring. Michael had attempted rape. He and Peter, with Priyanka as an accomplice. Michael, the man who had thoughtlessly and selfishly left Bea's heart in muddy puddles, on kerbsides and in ditches.

"I think I know some of what you're feeling" Bea told Roberta, "It's like having an operation without an anaesthetic." Roberta's eyes widened. "The thing is" Bea continued, "If you look down, you'll find none of your major organs have actually been removed. It's painful as hell, but everything is still there. Take the bits out, hold them a bit – see how they feel. It's an opportunity to check if everything is still working ok."

Suddenly Roberta felt like a weight had been lifted off her. *She* was all still there. Seeing Gabriel every day, that was going to be hard, but seeing as she still had all of herself, then it would be alright. It was the first time that Roberta had felt insecure when it came to a man – the first time she'd really opened up about feeling awkward and anxious.

Roberta had been used to walking into any bar or cafe and all male heads turning. She was used to wives angrily watching their husbands as Roberta felt men's eyes check her out from head to toe. This power over seemingly helpless men, was one Roberta thought applied to every single man. So to meet her match, someone like Gabriel was a real shock.

He was not yet in his thirties, yet he had an incredible maturity, a yearning spirit, determination and steadfastness. He wasn't going to rush into a relationship or even bed with someone he wasn't sure of. Roberta had never known a man like him, and that may have been what had made her fall for him so badly. The voice of wisdom and experience, not to mention suffering, spoke.

"You know, this might just be a slow burn situation" said Bea. Roberta relaxed. Her eyes, which seemed to be welling up on a fairly regular basis these days became bright and alert like they used to. Bea had planted a germ of a thought, a notion that hadn't even applied to her as she rushed through each day and the fast-paced society in which she lived. The thought was - wait.

Bea's phone rang. It was Mi-Ling. "I'm going to meet Peter" she said. "I'm doing it under the auspices of him persuading me to return to Michael. I'm not going to mention the lecturer's position – I'm just going to see if he volunteers information." Bea asked Mi-Ling what she wanted the girls to do. "Nothing for now. Let me tweak some information out of him and we can work it from there. I know we don't have much time – I found out from the University that a new Esoteric studies lecturer will be starting in a few weeks. I'm thinking about paperwork....."

****

A round robin email arrived courtesy of Stephen the Wizard. Again, it was all very factual, like it was a given that a UFO would actually land. For every shred of "evidence" Bea would present, Marion always had a counter reaction. There were times when Bea hadn't even finished a full sentence before Marion cut in, saying what utter nonsense it was. It was hurtful to Bea, and at one time their close friendship became tenuous and a bit edgy.

Bea had confronted Marion – told her that her aggression just meant she was scared of thinking about it. During a time when they put their differences aside, Bea suggested that Marion had watched too many disaster movies. Hollywood rarely made alien movies about ones that were out to help the world, rather than destroy it.

Marion accepted that most of these depictions featured evil, terrifying, man-chomping aliens, whilst Bea was adamant that many were benevolent, protective and like guardian angels. These, Bea believed, had been on the planet since time immemorial. Marion put it to Bea that if the aliens were really so friendly, how come they always had to be in disguise?

Bea argued that if humans knew the truth, then it would blow their minds – they had to be *ready* for it. Bea spoke about highly spiritually evolved beings – things unseen by your average Earthling. Salvatore had sometimes spoken of such beings and seemed to have swayed Marion in the argument.

This had annoyed Bea. She'd been trumpeting the cause for years and yet this man, a scientist with his research could swing round her best friend in a matter of months. Now, Bea had let her anger go. Marion was going away, and it was better that she had opened up to possibilities, than never consider such things at all.

Bea blinked again at Stephen's emails. There was a time, place, date – how could anyone be so sure...? Bea emailed back to ask if the alien landing was going to be in Earth time or Alien time – had anybody thought of *that?* Never mind how many hours - how many light years ahead was Venus, for example....? When Bea re-read the information, she saw that there was actually a discrepancy between a few days.

She envisaged loads of people setting up camp on the top of the Tor, and waiting for the show of a lifetime. It was out there, everywhere. Facebook, Twitter, every personal email link, every group she belonged to – everyone, but everyone was talking about this. Bea scrolled down to see Stephen's phone number at the bottom of the email. Marion and Carolyn would have received the same information, but Marion was too pre-occupied with her own departure.

Bea decided to call Stephen. A woman who sounded very young answered the phone, giggled and said Stephen was in the bath, at which conjecture Bea heard in the background, noises of splashing and laughing. The woman started telling Bea to call back later, but Bea had already put down the phone. She was annoyed – both with Stephen and herself. On the one hand, why shouldn't he have a private life and on the other, why couldn't she just *speak* to people anymore? Why did everything have to be done online?

Carolyn had taken to Facebook with relish. Marion mostly ignored it, saying she had too much University work to do. Bea said she had "dabbled" in it, but these days it was almost impossible not to be completely isolated from the rest of society unless you signed up.

Being of the older generation, Marion only used technology minimally; it never felt natural to her – wasn't something she had grown up with. She found she needed it for work more and more, despite spending years working from library books alone. Downloadable art never had quite the same quality as the photos in picture books, or better still – live trips to galleries.

Carolyn argued that you could communicate with a whole community of artists online. Bea thought both mediums were necessary. Bring in the new by all means, but don't entirely get rid of the old. If you totally eradicated History, then nobody could ever see where you had come from. It was a rather profound thought Bea had had, early in the morning.

Immediately, she began rattling off a longer email to Stephen. Something was really niggling her about the Cosmic Conference – something she couldn't put her finger on. Maybe that it was becoming like a celebrity event – that only TV presenters could get to a VIP tent; maybe even reality show winners would come and greet the aliens....

Expressing all her doubts and uncertainties at the great P.R. exercise, she hit the "send" button. A second later, she wondered if this had been the right thing to do. That was the problem with email – at least on the phone you could hesitate if someone asked you something. Once you'd hit Send, there was no going back.

Much to Bea's surprise, she received a lovely return email in no time at all. Stephen must have got out of the tub... It stated that with Bea's passion and interest, Stephen himself would ensure that she got to Glastonbury and that he'd help her stay. He went on to say that he'd spent a long time involved in all kinds of rituals, ceremonies and workshops with people all over the world, but nothing like this time had ever happened before – the time was now.

In a short while, the people of Earth would witness something remarkable. Preparation was being made in Glastonbury as best they could – townsfolk were offering up other accommodation, as were the surrounding areas, and Stephen and some friends from his Druid group were volunteering to run some form of catering. He could also offer Bea a place in one of his tents, at the top of the Tor.

He said that she and her other friends were most welcome to pitch up on his allocated patch and spend some time with his folk, discussing what might be expected. It was an offer Bea couldn't refuse. She didn't know what plans Marion and Salvatore had already made, but Carolyn might come...that was, if she'd actually like to meet in real life, all these people she now spent her time emailing....

And Roberta...and probably Gabriel...Then Bea nearly kicked herself as she remembered about Mi-Ling. She was sort of hoping she'd be able to forget about what was happening on Earth – at least for a while. Problem was, thought Bea – we all still live *here*. Whatever encounters we may have, we need to keep a sort of maintenance going on, so that we can *still* carry on living here. The Aliens might be coming, but no one had said anything about what they might take away with them...

Bea clicked open another email. Tickets to the Alien Artwork exhibition at the Royal Academy. Helen had managed to secure three for Bea's personal use. This meant she could take Roberta and...Mi-Ling. She could see her before she set off for Glastonbury – sort out a quick run to Brighton, if necessary as well. This was the sort of "earth stuff" that needed to be taken care of.

****

Salvatore didn't have, had never owned or ever needed a car. He intended to catch the Brighton train back into London and then take the coach direct to Glastonbury. He'd lived out of a suitcase for such a long time now, he'd hardly need a car boot to pack everything in – all his boxes had been sent ahead of him anyway, and could stay at the Cosmic Conference offices until he collected them.

With just a suitcase and rucksack, Salvatore sat and stared out of the coach window as it drove out of the built up urban surroundings of Central London and down the motorway. He felt strangely relaxed considering what he was going to attend, and let the shapes of blurred trees and hedges lull him to sleep, but not before he had taken a book by Salvatore Rosso out of his rucksack and bookmarked it with a small photograph of the front of Felice's...

****

Marion couldn't sit in Felice's and cry anymore. It was therefore ironic that the real last coffee was in Starbucks. Sat now with Bea and Carolyn and chocolate fudge cake in front of her, she felt like she had gone through a portal into an American situation comedy show, and all this was occurring for filming purposes only. She remembered doing a course somewhere, sometime ago, where the tutor spoke about pre-writing your life as a script.

Her story now, was not one she felt she could have written if she'd tried. Only a year ago, it was very different. It wasn't that she was closed down to the idea of having a new relationship; she just wasn't expecting one to manifest. Life was pretty busy, anyway. Marion remembered some workshop she'd done called "The Mysteries of Men and Women" – a seminar she couldn't quite grasp the meaning of to its full extent, at the time.

One thing she did remember was a man asleep in the corner of the room and thinking that was no mystery... However, she also remembered the man taking the seminar describing what really made a woman beautiful, whilst scattering magazine pictures of models across the floor. He said something about the essence that shone out of a woman's eyes when she was really engaged in the world was what made her beautiful and how Marion wanted, more than anything else in the world, to believe that was what a man *really* saw when he looked at her. Instead, she found herself thinking, "Yeah, right."

Now she wondered how tainted she had been by the culture, society – her upbringing at such a time in history, in such a country. OK, she didn't look bad for a woman her age – in fact, she looked pretty good for a woman of any age, but if it came down to youth or looks, then there was no way that Salvatore would have been attracted to her. Perhaps the fleur de lis was just an excuse...

What Salvatore *had* seen that day was a woman who was really living in the moment, happy to be outdoors, taking in a new environment and ultimately doing something to which every woman was entitled – buying a new pair of shoes. Maybe Salvatore had seen the "light shining from her eyes" before he had seen them. It was at this moment that Marion looked across at Bea.

She had a very pretty face, but for years her light had been hidden. It seemed she had deliberately switched it off, unable to shine again after the dreadful hurt she felt over Michael. Now, however, this funny, intelligent woman was beaming again and judging by the number of men who noticed her walk down the road, they could see it too. Maybe it was true, after all.

Carolyn arrived at Starbucks just after Marion, who had been snivelling a bit. "Stop this bollocks and go and get some cake" she said, handing Marion a twenty pound note. Marion went to the counter. No Lemon Drizzle...? She asked if there was more. They'd run out.

"B...but you can't" said Marion. The waitress looked at her red-rimmed eyes and runny nose. Surely this woman couldn't be that upset about a bit of cake? Marion looked anxiously across at Carolyn and shook her head.

"Bollocks, I'll have chocolate" she said. "Date slice, anything – don't care, as long as it has loads of carbs." The waitress served them quickly. They spent all of the money on cake, with no change to spare. "Let us eat cake" said Marion, "For I have no idea when the next time will be. I sure as hell hope they have it where I'm going."

Carolyn lifted a flapjack and toasted a bit of chocolate cake and Marion clinked the plates together. Then, the tears turned to laughter and the laughter went on, as a reminder why these women had laughed and cried through many years together, until only the laughter remained. "Do you really think Salvatore would make you live anywhere there was no cake?" asked Carolyn.

****

Mi-Ling got the email with the exhibition ticket. It was perfect. This way, she could arrange to meet Peter in Central London whilst he was there for work, then she could run over to the Royal Academy and put a plan into action with the girls. Peter seemed relieved that she'd eventually called him back – apparently, he'd never seen Michael in such a state.

There was no way Mi-Ling would go back to Michael, but she needed to stall Peter – he couldn't, shouldn't ever have that lecturing position. When she boarded a bus late in the afternoon, the blustery weather didn't seem fitting for late spring. She wondered about the British weather and if the aliens could actually land in it – why they had chosen this particular country. Thailand had far more pleasant conditions....

Piccadilly was crowded at 3pm as people dove in and out of shops and cafes and tourists made their way down Shaftesbury Avenue and into the arcades at the Trocadero centre. Meeting by the statue of Eros seemed such a dreadful cliché, but Mi-Ling didn't know London all that well. All she thought of was the irony – to meet a promiscuous, corrupt and unscrupulous man by an emblem of love.

Peter's girlfriend Priyanka seemed cold-hearted and ruthless, but that was just the uncomfortable thing about Peter – he didn't come across like this at all. She'd seen him teach and he genuinely appeared to be warm and supportive; he was well-studied with a wealth of information. He was also well respected in New Age circles and people flocked to his not particularly cheap workshops and training weekends.

It was curious how this group of women Mi-Ling had only recently met and who lived in North London had seen right through him. It wasn't just about what had happened to Roberta – it was mostly Marion who had a good instinct about the other side to Peter. It happened during the final stages of the Internal Feng Shui workshop when Peter had gotten everyone to share and talk about their lives in a very personal way. However, neither he nor Priyanka revealed anything intimate about themselves.

This sort of distance and coldness right as the course was ending, left many participants feeling vulnerable and alone. Not only did Peter and Priyanka not join in the sharing, they also seemed shut down when it came to listening. It left people feeling confused. They felt a bit like Mi-Ling did now; that maybe they judged people too quickly – maybe they expected too much or shouldn't question things. They even felt a bit guilty. Of course, Peter's behaviour was deliberate.

This was exactly the time when feeling lost in the wilderness, participants would come and ask Peter what they could do to counteract the difficult feelings they were experiencing, at which point he would offer them his latest workshop, at a discount price. This ensured that they did feel heard and cared for and they would always sign up.

Something had cracked in Mi-Ling that day when Roberta was round at her place. She didn't know why Roberta in particular – she'd watched loads of young girls participate in group sex, often reluctantly joining in herself. Once, she'd had sex with Peter and the experience was anything but spiritual. How he could disguise and transform himself so well was a complete mystery to her.

To those who took his courses, Peter was an enlightened and benevolent man. To anyone who was sober when they slept with him, he was rough, clumsy and manipulative. He'd continued this way for years and how prestigious it would be to his career to gain a much coveted lecturer's position.

Mi-Ling had sadly discovered that Michael was not dissimilar to his best friend. How could the perceptive and clever Bea have fallen for someone like this big time? British women were peculiar, she thought. They had no idea what it was like for women in her country. Most of them had no choice – there were many reasons why they had to stay with their husbands....

All Mi-Ling knew was that she needed to stay in London, keep working, waitressing – whatever she could do to survive and eventually move on and then send some money back to her family as she had promised. Peter looked dusty and tired as she spotted him wearing a suit and grasping a briefcase. He had other appointments and was then heading late to Brighton.

He'd already left Glastonbury at 5am, came and worked in London and was going to stay overnight in Brighton for a morning appointment with David and Mira. He'd better be brief with Mi-Ling and get from her what he came for...when he saw her, he ran up to her and tried to kiss her on both cheeks, but she recoiled. "I'm so glad you agreed to meet me" said Peter, as he led her to a little cafe along the quieter Jermyn Street.

Mi-Ling didn't want Peter to think she would agree to go back to Michael, but she needed to keep him there as long as possible – she didn't want him to go to Brighton in a hurry and she desperately hoped she and the girls could get there before he did. Roberta had eventually gone to the police and she would testify, with Mi-Ling presenting evidence as a witness. They needed to do something before Peter was officially employed.

Mi-Ling felt nervous and wanted to call Bea. She made an excuse to go to the loo and as she did so, accidentally kicked over her bag which she'd placed by her feet under the cafe table. Peter tried to help her retrieve whatever had fallen out, but she waved him off as she scrambled on the floor for lipstick, tampons and coins which were rolling their way towards the counter. "Mi-Ling...please... I know you don't want to come home, but you've agreed to meet with me, so that's at least a start isn't it?" Peter could charm for England. The nerve of the man. His arrogance convinced him he was an entirely innocent party.

"You tried to rape my friend" Mi-Ling retorted. She clicked on the little recording function on her phone, concealing it in her coat pocket as she did so. She hoped to God it would work.

"Mi-Ling...." Peter sounded tired, weary of being accused. "No one ever does anything against their will, you know that. It wasn't like that. Michael and I aren't like that. She came to the cottage of her own free will. She could have gone out with her friends and she chose to spend the evening with us."

Mi-Ling gave Peter a very serious, oriental Samurai scowl that actually sent shivers down his spine. Nonetheless, he continued. "We only seek to serve. We want people to realise the beauty of Tantric Sex, to have pure release, to experience the...." Mi-Ling stopped him.

"People? You mean beautiful young women under the age of thirty. Women who aren't quite old enough to be cynical and some of them rather gullible. I never noticed you invited any young men back to the cottage for me....You used me. Both of you. And I hate you for it. You get that, huh?" Mi-Ling let her pent up venom spill, forgetting for a moment that she was trying to keep Peter held up.

Much to her surprise, he didn't try to fight back. "I'm sorry you feel that way" he said. "I can understand. And I am sorry. Really. Maybe this will help." Peter took a cheque book from his pocket and started to write.

"You're paying me off?" said Mi-Ling. This was good for the recording. "You've got to be joking!"

"Whatever will help you" said Peter "Look – I really have to go. Please call me if you need me – I mean, if you need more money." This shocked Mi-Ling and as Peter left the cafe she followed him, but lost him in the crowds. Panicking, Mi-Ling called Bea, but her phone was switched off; she must have already got on the tube. Mi-Ling ran all the way to the Royal Academy. Her heart had never beaten so fast.

****

Peter sat in another cafe before his next meeting. It had been mission well accomplished with Mi-Ling, if he said so himself. He phoned Michael and told him what had happened. "Hiya mate, yeah.....too easy really. She got in a flap, kicked her handbag over....I seized the opportunity. Got her passport back....she can't go anywhere, you've got nothing to worry about....."

****

Mi-Ling dodged people on the busy high street and thought about why Michael and Peter were so invested in her coming back to Glastonbury. She'd been a chef, home-keeper and sex party organiser, unable to do anything independently without money or her passport. It was only when she sat down on a bench in the courtyard of the Royal Academy, that she realised her passport had gone.

At first she didn't panic too much – maybe she'd put it into the zip up part of her bag, but after thoroughly going through it twice, she realised this wasn't the case. Frantically, she started trying to re-trace her steps, eventually breaking down outside a newsagents. She sat on the pavement and wailed, much to the consternation of passers-by who ran by quickly, thinking she was about to commit some obscure form of Oriental suicide.

Eventually the police came and then more police came with a Chinese woman who had come to translate and then things got very confused when everyone realised Mi-Ling was from Thailand, and not only that but she spoke perfect English with no hint of a foreign accent.

****

Had she not been early and had she not an excellent knowledge of Central London side street cafes herself, then Bea would never have seen him. Upon seeing Peter sitting in the window of one of them, she emitted a little whoop of both pleasure and dismay. He was in a little pizzeria she'd sometimes sat in with Marion when they'd been on an "art outing". Bea wondered how she could sneak in and sit close enough to him and yet far enough away as well.

She glanced at her watch. Mi-Ling must have already met him, but she wasn't around – obviously she'd not been able to stop him heading off. To her horror, Bea saw Priyanka come into the cafe and she ducked down behind a menu. "It was too easy" she heard Peter say. "Her passport was sticking out the top of her bag when everything spilled out everywhere."

"So – she'll have to come back to Glastonbury then?" said Priyanka. Bea felt ill as she watched Priyaka finger the passport. "What do you think you'll do with it? Sell it?"

"I'm going to give it back to Michael" Peter replied "He needs her back home."

Priyanka gave the passport back. "So...in Brighton tomorrow...it's just a case of you dotting the i's and crossing the t's? Just need to sign?" Peter nodded. They laughed and ordered pizzas – Pepperoni for Peter and Mixed Meat for Priyanka. On the Internal Feng Shui course, Bea remembered Peter extolling the virtues of vegetarianism, as a way to purify the body. Bea quietly slid over to the counter, pulling up her coat collar, and paid for her cafe latte. Then she slipped out the door of the pizzeria and called Mi-Ling, hoping she was somewhere near the Royal Academy.

Two calls to Mi-Ling's phone frustratingly went to voice mail, but when Bea eventually got through, it wasn't Mi-Ling who answered but the Chinese interpreter. Confused, Bea thought she must have misdialled and hung up, but when she tried again the same woman answered and told Bea Mi-Ling was talking to the police.

"Where is she? Where are you?" asked Bea frantically, but the woman demanded to know who Bea was before she would give an answer. Bea swore in frustration – she knew who had Mi-Ling's passport and she needed the police there now, but instead they were taking Mi-Ling in for questioning, thinking she was an illegal immigrant, without a proper passport.

There was nothing else for it. Bea would have to follow Peter and call the police and then maybe if he could be found with the passport on him, there would be some hope.

****

"What do you mean you're not coming to the Royal Academy?" said Carolyn when Bea hurriedly tried to explain she had more urgent matters to attend. "Don't you know people are killing each other to get tickets?" Bea sighed, said she knew that but that the emergency couldn't be helped. "Well, Roberta will be extremely pissed off with you" said Carolyn "She would have loved to have been able to bring Gabriel if she'd known there was a spare."

Didn't Carolyn think Bea was making a huge sacrifice not being there? There'd be all kinds of people to network with and the exhibition itself would be pretty fascinating. Bea was missing a huge alien event to help a woman who had been badly wronged and to try and prevent more women from suffering further. When Bea explained what had happened, Carolyn changed her tune.

"Christ, well good luck. The police are heading towards you now, did you say?" Bea said she felt like a female detective in some drama series only far more scared, but she was nothing if not determined. "Go for it, Batman" said Carolyn.

****

Really, he knew he shouldn't interfere as he was leaving, but Salvatore felt obliged to do one last thing for his friends in England. Once he was settled into his digs in Glastonbury, he called Professor David Pepper. David was delighted to hear from Salvatore – he kind of hoped he was ringing because he'd changed his mind and half joked that the contract would always be open to him.

Salvatore, however, asked David how thoroughly he had checked Peter's references. David said he'd looked into Peter's background as far as he could and everything came back glowing, but now that Salvatore mentioned it, there was a student – a young lady on the Esoteric studies course called Roberta who had gone a bit green at the gills when Peter's name was mentioned.

"I'm not suggesting anything untoward" explained Salvatore "It's just that – I get this feeling. How do you English say it? In my bones. I've never met the man, but something tells me he just isn't the one for you. Not the right person to take over where I left off. Just thought I should tell you...."

David grumbled and muttered something about having more than enough to worry about what with his wife leaving him and his mistress confessing that the sex had always been lousy, and that now he'd have to find a new lecturer as well, but there was something about Salvatore which made people have the utmost respect for him. Even Professor David Pepper.

Salvatore was one of those rare beings who always strived to be truthful. He never said anything just to be popular or go with the general trend, but whatever he said came truly from his heart and it was for this which Marion loved him so. It was certainly true that he'd struggled with honesty when it came to his relationship with Marion.

This wasn't because he didn't absolutely adore her down to the depths of his very soul, not because he would even consider being unfaithful, but because there were certain things he just couldn't tell her. Still, he had earned her trust and if she did actually come with him, well then... she would know. Everything.

He'd tied up all the loose ends as best he could and now the rest was up to everyone else.

****

David Pepper certainly didn't expect Marion's best friend to be banging on his office door, demanding to see him that early in the morning, just before Peter's appointment. He would have told her to go away, but for Salvatore's call the previous evening.

Begrudgingly he let Bea in and she sat down and told him as much as she possibly could. Much to her surprise, he listened. He admitted that he couldn't really take in what she was saying, but attempted rape, an issue with a passport; this did all sound rather serious.

"Please find a way to check his bag" urged Bea, hoping he'd not taken the passport out for any reason. "Just get your secretary to do it – say it's a security measure, or something. If it's in there, that should prove I'm telling the truth. I have no other reason to come all the way to Brighton, than to tell you this. I've alerted the police for theft of the passport as well, so they might find him before he gets here, although I doubt it. A tall man with a briefcase, somewhere in Central London. I couldn't exactly give them much to go on..."

David was incredulous, but agreed to Bea's suggestion. It was ridiculous, but he'd just lost Marion, Salvatore, his wife and his mistress so what harm the loss of someone he didn't even know yet....?

****

Carolyn wondered how Bea had got on. At the exhibition, she had found Roberta to be withdrawn and pensive. She was pensive because she was as ever, thinking about Gabriel and withdrawn because she wondered what would happen with Mi-Ling and Peter beginning his lecturing post. Carolyn couldn't imagine that everything would play out smoothly, but she hoped it would.

It was a shame Bea had missed the exhibition. It was right up her street. Carolyn had put her glasses on to survey the paintings more closely, when she could finally get a look in amidst all the crowds. One thing she had noticed about the human - featured aliens when she could get close enough was that they seemed to have a strangely Italian features...

****

He decided to play it extremely cool. Perhaps he needed to take a long hard look at his love-making skills, but if there was anything that Professor David Pepper could do well, then it was being Head of a University Department. God only knows why he had decided to listen to a somewhat flaky friend of Marion's, but for now he would just go with the flow. Go with the flow... David found these words popping into his head without any idea how they had got there.

It wasn't something he ever said – it sounded much more like something Salvatore or Marion would say. If only he could go with the flow as easily as they could. He was on the verge of an expensive and messy divorce and had to continue working with Mira who either just ignored him or sneered at him all day. He wondered about keeping the Esoteric studies course running.

The thing was, it had gained an excellent reputation and was a financial godsend. He would be cool. Very cool. Nothing else would do. David's secretary buzzed the office to tell him Peter had arrived. He told her to send him in, but also that she needed to come in as well and stay. If this apparently bizarre account of events that Bea had told him, as well as Salvatore making hint of it were true, then he was going to need a witness.

Coldly, he shook Peter's hand and walked over to his filing cabinet to get a copy of Peter's contract. Then he sat down at his desk with his hands clasped in front of him, in that particular way that only a University Professor or a James Bond villain can do....

"Just before we both sign this, there's something I need to put to you" said David. Peter looked irritated. It was obvious he just wanted to sign and go. "Should really have done it before you came in, but as you can see, my secretary is so busy with the new term stuff at the moment, that I'll have to do it." Then he sort of smiled which made Peter feel very uncomfortable.

"Just a formality" said David, continuing to smile, "It'll only take a moment...I wondered if I might just take a look in your bag..." Peter stiffened and all the colour drained from his face. For a minute he considered making a run for it, but then that would be worse – he'd definitely be found guilty if he did that. How could anyone possibly know? It was silly. This was just a formality, as David had said. Besides, the passport was tucked in a plastic zip up holder and between a pile of papers for safe-keeping and there was a good chance David wasn't actually looking for it anyway.

"Of course – of course you can check my bag, if you really need to" Peter coughed. Much to his horror, David proceeded to check thoroughly every single bit, even pulling out a diary and some personal papers. He put these back in the bag. Peter wanted to tell David to be careful with his belongings, but he had to remain silent for his own sake. Finally, after what seemed like an age, David handed back the bag.

Peter heaved a sigh of relief, but this was short lived when David lifted his hand from beneath his desk to show that he was clearly holding Mi-Ling's passport. "Just as I had feared. I'm sorry Peter, but I have to follow this up." Then David turned to his secretary and told her to call the police.

****

Bea should have been in Glastonbury. But then she should have been at the art exhibition as well. She'd received a call from the police; Peter had been arrested – her work on the South Coast was done, and now she was satisfied that she could leave Brighton. At Victoria station, Mi-Ling came running towards her. "Thank you Bea, thank you so much. You didn't have to help me, but you've literally saved my life. I'm free now – free of all those awful people. I'm sure there'll be a more thorough investigation and trial. I'm so glad Roberta testified. Maybe this will encourage the other young women they manipulated to do the same. Please Bea – you will stay in touch, won't you?" Bea smiled. Of course she would. She had found an unlikely new friend, now that her old one was going.

"I like you" said Mi-Ling, "You're...sassy." Bea raised an eyebrow. As far as she could remember she had never been called that before, but she kind of liked it. Sassy. Bring it on.

****

In the half light of the summery evening, Salvatore strolled out across the moor land surrounding Glastonbury Tor. Looking down from high up, he could see the throngs of camps and people gathering by the minute, but amongst the thousands he only wondered about one – he wondered if Marion had arrived. If she had, she knew where to go.

Salvatore had obtained for her a special V.I.P. pass, so that she could get as close to the alien landing as he could, what with his scientist's credentials. He sighed deeply and began his descent. There wasn't much left now to organise.

****

How on earth was Bea going to find Stephen the Wizard in amongst all those people? And all those people with long hair and beards, especially... She had his phone number, but it would be a miracle if he heard his phone ring. She texted him to say she was near the ashram at the bottom of the Tor and was surprised upon receiving a text with instructions to walk due North, whereupon she would find him just a few yards away.

Sure enough, there was Stephen, surrounded by skin drums, wooden flutes and several friends. He greeted Bea with a big hug. "Welcome! Isn't it magnificent? I have to say, I don't think I've ever been so excited in my whole life!" Bea had to admit she was feeling that way, too. A friend of Stephen's who had long hair but no beard, beckoned Bea inside a tent and started to show her star charts that he and Stephen had drawn up, as well as giving her loads of information sheets. She found him strangely attractive....

So. It was really going to happen. Planet earth was going to witness alien spacecraft not only landing, but if the predictions, scientists and diagrams were also correct, then at least one alien, as well. Bea felt her heart thump in her chest and a kind of euphoria that she would normally only have associated with falling in love.

Yet, she was in love. With all the wondrous and amazing things going in and around her and the letting go of her other, more miserable life. There was more to come. She saw her phone was registering a voice message and listened to it, hoping it might be Marion, but it was from David Pepper. Surprisingly he said nothing of the scenario regarding Peter, but it sounded like he might be offering her a job...She tried to listen to the message again, but it was too noisy, so she sat down on the grass near Stephen's tent. His friend had even more charts spread out across the ground now and was becoming very animated, waving his arms around and shouting, "Oh my God!"

Bea really needed to hear David's message, but got caught up in the phenomenon of an incredible happening. Had she heard her message, then she would have heard David telling her that Salvatore had recommended her for the job. Apparently, he'd left many notes for whoever the new lecturer would be, with his recommendations for seminars on life from other planets and astronomy.

He knew Bea already had a top qualification in this area of work, had lectured in other subjects and being so close to Marion, would fit in well with the ethos of the course. She was passionate about her studies and as far as he was concerned, would be the perfect replacement. It was perfect timing for Bea. If only she had known then that she was about to fall in love with a Glastonbury-based astrologer, as well....

****

Carolyn and Roberta lugged sleeping bags and provisions on their backs as they wended their way in and out of people climbing the Tor. Roberta hoped she could find her University friends and hoped Gabriel would be amongst them. Every bed and breakfast in the town was packed to the rafters and they could see that for miles around there wasn't even any camping space. No one was going to sleep that night anyway.

****

Salvatore took one last look at the Glastonbury night sky. It really was one of the most beautiful skies he had ever seen. The moon was small, but perfectly formed and several planets were in perfect alignment. It was time. Astronomers, astrologers, scientists and seers all around the world must have been having a field day.

A sense of calm descended upon Salvatore as he made one final check through his belongings and walked away from the whole conundrum in the direction of Bristol, away from the Tor, away from Glastonbury. With just a rucksack on his back, he started out on his journey home...

****

Bea suddenly felt an overwhelming sense of urgency that she should get as close to the action as possible. Stephen tried telling her that she'd probably have a much better view staying where they were and in true tradition of anything like this, giant film screens were probably being erected anyway, but Bea didn't want to observe the first mass witnessing of aliens on earth in the same way you would a rock concert.

Thanking Stephen, she said she was going to "make a bid for freedom" anyway, and with sheer guts and determination, managed to shove her way through the crowds and stand very close to the scientists' and V.I.P quarters where Marion was waiting in anticipation for Salvatore to arrive. Bea knew she just *had* to be somewhere close – there was a complete conviction that she needed to watch this live, with her own eyes, on the same spot.

Suddenly, a collective gasp and people oohing and ahhing went up as everyone pointed towards a spot in the direction of South West. Then, there was complete silence. It was there – clear as day. A small, saucer shaped ship could be seen rising up from beneath the hills and making a descent over the Tor.

It was hard to make out the colour of the ship in the evening sky, but as it got closer, the floodlights set up by humans caught flashes of a very pale blue colour. There appeared to be stencilled symbols on the top and sides of the ship in black. There was most certainly what could only be described as a deafening silence as the space ship gently landed and open-mouthed awe as a hatch opened up, not dissimilar to any science fiction film anyone had ever seen.

Looking up at a screen, Stephen could see what the spaceship symbols were, close up. "That's it!" he told his friends, "The fleur de lis, as predicted! The petals of perfect union. Perfect union..." his voice trailed off. It looked like the alien might be coming out the ship.

First of all, there seemed to be some commotion around the media and V.I.P. area. Finally, a man was let through the cordoned off area and walked on his own carrying what appeared to be a cup of coffee towards the spaceship. Felice carefully put the coffee down by the hatch and then walked back towards the crowds.

Then, the 'alien' came out. He hovered in the frame of the hatch, so couldn't be seen clearly, but he appeared to take the coffee, pick it up and drink some. And then he came. He showed himself. As he came closer to the cameras and screens, just like the Royal Academy paintings, he appeared to be quite human. He wore what looked like a simple protective suit that people who worked in nuclear power plants or other charged environmental work might wear, but like his ship it was pale blue and not silver.

The alien walked towards the V.I.P. area. "He looks a bit Italian" a woman whispered to Bea. Bea shoved her way further forwards, but was pushed back by the crowds. Yet, they automatically moved aside when they could see the alien making his way towards one person in particular; a pretty, petite older woman with short red hair and a V.I.P. pass around her neck. She was at the front of the scientists group. She must have been a terribly important scientist.

Salvatore took his space suit helmet off. Then, he touched the fleur de lis on his sleeve. It glowed. He placed his helmet carefully on the ground and stretched his arm out towards Marion, offering her his hand. To the amazement of everyone, he then spoke in perfect English, with a slight Italian-sounding accent...

"Well, Marion – are you coming...?"

****

Lightning Source UK Ltd.
Milton Keynes UK
UKHW012249260821
389545UK00001B/6